THE
LAKE
HOUSE

A totally gripping crime thriller full of twists

KATE WATTERSON

Detective Chris Bailey Book 1

Joffe Books, London
www.joffebooks.com

First published in Great Britain in 2022

Cover art by Nick Castle

ISBN: 978-1-80405-092-7

CHAPTER ONE

The roses were blooming.

He knelt there in the grass by the flower bed in the only unshaded place near the house, the almost ghostly fragrance of the blooms intoxicating.

Blood red and pale yellow and snow white. A well-tended garden was important, like a well-tended life. As soon as a bloom started to fade, he clipped it. Once something lost its beauty, there was no use for it.

An apt analogy.

He was going to kill his wife.

It wasn't so much that he'd finally made up his mind, it was more that he'd known it for a long time, and was just now acknowledging it. It had been there, like a fly at a dirty window, buzzing around, pestering him.

The sun was warm on his shoulders and the sky above, a perfect azure blue.

It wouldn't be hard.

Maybe he'd even do it tonight. Quiet all around.

The time was right.

* * *

The only thing to mark the drive was a discreet lip of asphalt off the winding road and Drew missed it the first time. It wasn't until they wound up on a loop back to the small county highway that they noticed it.

It was fine with her, Lauren Mathews decided, as she looked out the window at the late-afternoon sun dappling the crowding trees and sending shadows across the hood of the car. The later they were, the less time they would spend on this vacation. Every lost minute was a reprieve. She'd actually been grateful for gridlocked traffic on the interstate for the first time in her life.

With a muttered expletive, Drew turned the car around on the narrow road and they headed back.

"Rob has always said it was hard to see and even he still misses it. I agree. Even though I've been here before, he's right."

She glanced over. They had been dating about six months now and she knew he was tense just by the set of his wide shoulders, probably from the long drive. In profile, his familiar features were clean-cut, with a slight frown gathered between his fine brows, the sifted light through the forest coming in the window accenting the nice line of his lean jaw. Thick, dark-blond hair, always a little unruly, gave him a surfer boy look, as did the honed athletic body beneath the Ohio State University T-shirt and tan shorts. Blue eyes the same color as the summer sky above the canopy of trees narrowed in concentration as they drove much slower back the way they had just come.

It was popular opinion Andrew Fletcher was very hot and she was a lucky girl.

She *was* a lucky girl. That was part of the problem. He wasn't just attractive but also intelligent and considerate.

But . . .

Shake it off. Stop thinking about it and maybe it will go away.

"Is that it?" She pointed at a gap in the trees. "There's a mailbox."

"I think so. When he says private, he means it." Drew carefully pulled his expensive sports car into the narrow lane, which immediately curved to the right through the woods. "Yeah, this is it."

2

She had her first glimpse of the water, a sparkling peek as they slid around a corner. It was a half a mile at least before they spotted the cabin and a few minutes later berthed the car next to a silver pickup truck also sporting Ohio plates.

Some cabin, Lauren thought with amused assessment, trying to ignore the knot in her stomach. The place was stunning with a pitched brow front three stories high overlooking the lake, all glass windows and huge decks on the lower and second level. The area around the structure had been carefully landscaped to look natural but was free of the tangled shrubs and wild vines and instead planted with a variety of ferns hanging delicate lacy leaves over the pine needles. The effect was expensive rustic at its finest, but then again Rob had mentioned his uncle was filthy rich.

Actually, he'd said in his reserved way his uncle was quite well-to-do.

Drew switched off the engine, took a look at his watch, and gave her one of his hundred-watt smiles. "Quite a place, isn't it?"

"That's an understatement." She stared at the house, amazed. "Gorgeous."

"We're only an hour and a half late. I guess that's not bad considering the traffic and construction zones, but I'll be glad to get out of this car. I'll get the bags and you go on in."

"No, I'll help you."

"It's okay, I've got it." He pushed a button and got out to go around to the trunk.

Since there really wasn't much choice, she got out too, and had to admit even though the very idea of this vacation made her uncomfortable, the air did smell fresh and clean and the view to the lake was spectacular. Down a narrow path, she could see a boat slip and the jut of the dock, and then a vista of deep blue water all framed in thick trees and not a soul in sight.

"The lake is very pretty." The remark was a little inane but she wasn't at her finest, the hours in the car aside.

Not staring the week from hell in the face.

"I told you. Quite the place. I'm looking forward to a great time." Drew hefted both their bags and nodded at the steps up to the first level of the house. "But I'm going to have to admire the view later. After you, babe. I'm dying for a cold beer."

Even as she turned to comply and started to go up, a tall man came out of one of the sets of French doors on the front lower deck. Like Drew, he was dressed in an old comfortable T-shirt and shorts, and a welcoming smile lit his face. "It's about time. I was just about to call your cell and ask what the hell was going on. Come on in."

The only thing she carried was her purse and cosmetic bag, and Rob Hanson came forward politely and took them from her despite her protest. He was the antithesis of Drew in every way except he was just as good-looking. There was nothing boyish in his dramatic dark coloring — wavy black hair, ebony brows, and skin bronzed by a light summer tan. Even his lashes were thick and dark, framing eyes that were a startling gold-green hazel. His gaze flicked over her skirt and silk blouse, inappropriate for the wilderness surroundings, and she said defensively, "Drew picked me up from the office."

"You look great but you might want to change and just be comfortable. After all, we're all on vacation. Let me show you to your room." He didn't bat an eye but turned to lead them into the house, the interior proving to be just as stunning as the outside. Vaulted ceilings went up two stories in the great room, and there were lofts above on both levels. A huge stone fireplace, scattered leather furniture in comfortable groupings and an open state-of-the-art kitchen did not really represent the fishing lodge he'd offered for their proposed and much-discussed mutual getaway. Somehow she'd pictured pine walls and sleeping bags, not this luxury.

"Nice to be here," Drew commented as he followed with their luggage. "I'm impressed every time."

"Yeah, Uncle Jim spends most of his time in Italy now, and it just sits empty, so we might as well use it. He wants us to use it." Rob pointed. "You have the master suite."

He climbed up the first set of stairs. As she followed, Lauren felt a frisson of discomfort. Again. She objected, "We can take a guest room."

"Karen isn't coming. I don't need a room this size just for me. You two can have it. Wait until you see it."

"*What*? Your girlfriend *isn't* coming?"

He turned around and she realized she had said it out loud. Rob lifted his brows a fraction. "She had to cancel. I thought Drew told you. It's just the three of us."

* * *

No, Drew hadn't told her a damn thing and the expression on her face spoke volumes, so maybe he should have in retrospect. Lauren looked even unhappier than she had the whole drive down through Kentucky and Tennessee, and though most people of his acquaintance would love a free vacation courtesy of a friend's uncle with way too much money, she wasn't exactly jumping for joy.

As long as she didn't jump overboard on their relationship, since that was Drew's real worry.

"You don't like her much anyway," he said casually as he walked past her into the room. "I figured you'd be more relieved than anything." It was true, and actually neither of them was very crazy about Rob's latest romantic interest. She was shallow, something Lauren definitely was not.

"Drew!" she protested, color flooding into her smooth cheeks. Looking mortified, she gave Rob an apologetic smile. "I've never said that, by the way. You are getting his opinion only."

Rob didn't look offended, his face impassive. "That's all right. To tell you the truth, my heart didn't exactly break when she told me she had to work on some emergency legal case that came up. We're more off than we are on these days and we were never that serious anyway. This way, you can relax, read, and do whatever you want instead of hanging around with her. Fletcher and I plan to fish the day away and drink copious amounts of beer. No rules this week, just whatever anyone wants to do. Swim, take a nap, watch a movie, sit on the deck with a glass of wine."

Lauren murmured in a halting voice, "That sounds nice."

The bedroom *was* enormous, with a fireplace, huge windows facing the back of the house and the expanse of forest around them, and a bed the size of a football stadium. The carpet was lush, and the private bathroom had a jetted tub, marble floors, and a separate walk-in shower built for two. There was even a small bar with a refrigerator and a flat-screen television on the wall.

Lauren seemed unmoved by all the opulence, still just inside the door, her slender body betraying a language Drew didn't have to be a psychologist to read. He'd been interpreting the signals without any problem for some time now and just wasn't sure what to do about it. Maybe he should be angry, since it was the logical reaction. But logic didn't seem to apply to this situation, not if he wanted to keep her.

And he did. The moment he'd met her he'd been drawn in.

Rob eased away from the doorframe in a smooth athletic movement. "I'll go downstairs while you all unpack. There's a deck chair with my name on it and a cold one on the table next to it. Come and join me after you are settled in. The view is pretty amazing."

"We'll be right down." Drew made the promise as he deposited their suitcases on the floor. As soon as Rob was gone, he asked, "Are you upset?"

She gave him a look he couldn't quite interpret. "Because Karen ditched out? I won't miss her I admit it, though you weren't supposed to announce it to Rob. What if they stay together and eventually get married or something, Drew? Now he'll always know I don't really care for her."

"They won't." He spoke with complete confidence because he'd known Rob Hanson since they were both in grade school. Rob was not into his latest girlfriend except in the most casual of ways. Drew was pretty sure they weren't even sleeping together before this trip and apparently that wasn't going to happen now either. "They haven't dated very long. He seemed relieved to me she didn't come and I'm personally happy as hell because I couldn't quite picture her enjoying the 'vacation in the woods' theme. You said you wanted to sleep in, read, lie in the sun, and swim a little. She'd be texting the entire time and checking email. Think of it this way, you'll be able to do whatever you want and not feel obligated to entertain her. It isn't like you don't know Rob pretty well, babe. We're all friends. It'll be fun."

She moved toward the suitcase he'd set down, unbuttoning her blouse. "A week with the guys for me? Hmm, I guess as long as I don't have to go fishing with you two or do all the cooking, it'll be fine."

"You have my word on it." He watched her slide the silk material from her shoulders, a familiar hunger shooting from brain to groin. Lauren was beautiful in an understated way, slender but feminine. She had perfect firm, high breasts, not too big but still shapely and sexy as hell, a slim waist, and nice long legs. Her hair was a rich chestnut brown that glimmered with golden highlights, worn down past her shoulders in a simple elegant straight swing, and her skin in contrast was fair and flawless. The almost fragile beauty of her face was accented by enormous dark-blue eyes under arched brows, high cheekbones, a straight nose, and a very soft, pink mouth she rarely accented with anything but clear gloss. Other than a little mascara, he knew she wore hardly any makeup, but she didn't need cosmetics anyway. Mother Nature had done it all for her. She was a knockout and the physical part of their relationship was more than satisfying. All he had to do was look at her and he wanted her.

It was happening at the moment, he thought in amused self-reproof as he watched her step out of her skirt. In just her bra and skimpy bikini panties — both a delicate pink that turned him on even more — she went over to rummage in her case. He got a world-class view of her tempting, world-class ass and his body went on full alert.

Later, he promised. When they went to bed for the evening, he'd start the vacation out in a way she wouldn't forget. It had taken him months to finally get her to sleep with him, but the wait had been more than worth it. With her looks, he'd been astounded to discover that at twenty-four, she'd been practically a virgin.

He was edging past infatuation into something more serious. But they had one big issue he had a feeling wasn't going to go away.

Well, make that two.

Lauren found a pair of white shorts, slipped them on, and then pulled a pale blue tank top over her head. She shook back her shining hair, so it fell gracefully over her slim shoulders again. "You go on down if you want. I'm going to brush my teeth and put a few things away."

"The minute you join us, I'll pour you a glass of wine."

She smiled in a tempting curve of her mouth that lit her face with the familiar warmth. "That sounds pretty fabulous. You know how to win a girl over."

"*You're* fabulous." He walked over, pulled her into his arms, kissed her lightly, and looked into her eyes. "I'm really looking forward to spending this week with you."

Her hand lifted to touch his cheek and lush dark lashes lowered a fraction over the deep blue of her eyes. "I feel the same way."

He believed her. That was part of the problem. He wanted to believe it.

"I'm glad." Drew let her go before she figured out he was aroused just from watching her change her clothes. "Take your time. It sounds like we'll be out on the deck."

"It'll just be a few minutes."

The house really was spectacular, he thought as he went down the stairs and through the open great room. Rob was on the deck as promised, sprawled carelessly in an Adirondack chair, the light breeze ruffling his dark hair. Without a word he reached into a nearby cooler, pulled out a dripping cold bottle, and handed it over.

8

"Thanks." Drew twisted off the cap and dropped into the chair next to him. "This is so sweet. How big is the lake? I've been here before but I don't think that I've ever asked." He meant it. The view could not be beat.

"A couple hundred acres. Not huge, but all private, and from what I've seen each time when I've been up here, pretty much all ours. The houses are like this one. Big expensive places built by people too busy to use them much. On the weekends there are some boats out, but during the week it is dead quiet."

"Thanks for inviting us. Heaven on earth. I was going to take Lauren someplace in the Caribbean but the thought of a crowded beach doesn't do much for me, honestly. When we went in college for spring break that infamous year it was a little different."

Rob took a drink from his beer bottle and laughed. "Yeah, that whole trip is a bit of a blur. Who knew we'd someday turn into responsible adults and prefer peace and quiet? Hell, before you got here, I even made a salad, put the steaks in the marinade, and got the baked potatoes ready."

"You're a regular chef." Drew grinned.

"Well, I wouldn't go that far. That's a pretty elaborate meal for me. I can make a decent spaghetti sauce but brace yourself for burgers and brats the rest of the week. I don't have time to cook. You aren't a culinary genius with your schedule either, Fletcher."

It was true, Drew acknowledged. Six years before they had both graduated from Ohio State, and Rob was now a computer engineer for a software company, while Drew had managed to capitalize on a love of flying and ended up a corporate pilot. A lot of hard work and some luck and they'd done fairly well. They were busy as hell, both of them, and Drew was out of the country half the time, so this week was even more special because they'd get to spend some time together. Of course, he would also get to be with Lauren.

His private life hadn't gone as according to plan as his career.

"Simple is fine with me. Besides, Lauren is a great cook, and though she said she doesn't want to get stuck with all the cooking, I'm going to guess she'll be more than happy to pitch in if it comes down to the bologna sandwiches I can make. I can spread mayo on the bread, that's about it."

"Is she unhappy about Karen not coming or is what you said true?" Rob sounded casual — almost too carefully casual.

"She's fine. More than happy to do her own thing."

"That's good since there isn't a lot of excitement around here."

The ensuing silence was just a little strained and Drew uttered a silent curse at the situation that was fast becoming the norm between two friends who were as close as brothers.

Just one word summed up his feelings.

Fuck.

CHAPTER TWO

It was prudent to wait until after dinner. Because, of course, one must eat, and a few glasses of wine wouldn't hurt the cause.

Diabolical *was the title of his latest work in progress. He'd looked it up just to make sure he understood the true definition and he had this old tome of a dictionary that had proved invaluable. Webster's. He used it all the time. It was more reliable than using the internet.*

It said: Outrageously wicked.

Maybe he'd always wanted to be that way. It was possible and he'd just missed the warning signs.

Those signs? What were they? He didn't know.

As a student of human nature, he found it fascinating.

In a diabolical way.

* * *

Lighting the candles was too much in retrospect. Candlelit dinner for three. *That's romance for you, Hanson.* They were just there and he'd lit them before thinking it over.

Rob took another bite of his steak. It was actually really good, the spice rub the butcher had recommended doing the trick, and he managed to get it just medium rare with a nice char on the outside. Even the baked potatoes weren't underdone, which he had a habit of doing since he seemed perpetually in a hurry.

Maybe that was why he couldn't completely relax.

Yeah, right, who was he fooling?

The real reason sat across the table, the theatrical light playing over her shimmering hair as she sipped wine and picked at her food. Since the steaks were delicious and it was hard to go wrong with potatoes and salad, he knew it wasn't the meal. Just what it was affecting her appetite he wasn't sure, but he hoped the only vibe he was sending was platonic brotherly affection.

He was doing his best anyway.

". . . back to Japan again," Drew was saying with a small grimace. "It'll be the third time in two months."

Rob jerked his attention back to the conversation. "I've always wanted to see it and now that we acquired that new company, I might have to go someday, or so they've mentioned in a couple of memos."

"Believe me, *I've* seen it." Drew lounged in his chair, toying with the stem of his wine glass. "Once we get there, I have nothing to do until they're ready to leave. I just walk around and take in the culture. Last time we were there ten days. It's an interesting place, but you can only play tourist for so long. I think Indonesia is after that."

"You could fly for a commercial airline." It was an old debate, and Rob grinned, knowing the answer.

"No thanks." Drew shook his head.

Lauren, who had been quiet through the meal — the whole evening, actually — spoke up. "Heaven forbid he be boring and conventional and have a regular schedule."

"Like I said, no thanks." Drew smiled at her, the expression on his face teasing with the intimacy of a lover. "I thought you liked the fact I'm not another executive in an Armani suit."

"It'd be nice if you were around a little more, that's all." She smiled back, but it was fleeting, and she got to her feet to gather her still mostly full plate. "That was delicious, Rob. Thank you."

"You didn't eat much," he pointed out in a neutral tone.

"I'll save the rest for lunch tomorrow. I don't know why, but I'm really tired tonight. I went in early to try to get as much done before noon when Drew picked me up, so maybe that's it." She moved gracefully toward the kitchen, a slender shape in the inadequate lighting, though a spectacular moon had risen and was visible through the glass wall facing the lake, helping light the cabin with the illumination. "If you'll excuse me, I'm going to go up to bed after I help clean this up."

"There isn't much to do." He got to his feet with alacrity and switched on the light in the kitchen. "I'll take care of it. I know where everything goes. You can have clean-up duty tomorrow if you want."

"Okay . . . fair enough." She relinquished her plate as he reached for it.

Unfortunately, their fingers brushed. Just a touch, but enough to make his entire hand tingle in some ridiculous adolescent way that — if it was physically possible to do so — made him want to kick himself.

She's off limits.

For a second, her eyes, so lovely and luminous with that indigo color, widened almost as if she could read his mind, and then she turned to leave, going past Drew with little more than a murmured good night and hurrying up the stairs.

"Not exactly how I'd thought the evening would go." Drew's tone was joking, but there was an underlying edge to it. He still sat and stared at where Lauren had disappeared into the small hallway to the master bedroom. "She's been pretty tense lately and I've been trying to figure it out."

Well, shit.

"Maybe she *is* just tired." Rob hoped he sounded casual as he moved to find some plastic wrap and put it over her plate. "We all work hard. That's why we're here. Tomorrow, when she gets to sleep late, hang around catching some sun, and maybe go for an afternoon boat ride, she'll relax."

"Our relationship has always felt solid, right from the beginning."

Why did they have to talk about this *now*? "It's seemed that way to me all along." Rob slid the plate into the refrigerator. It was true.

"I'm in love with her, or that's what it seems like . . . whoa, what the hell was that?"

The doors to the deck were open to the sound of the creaking insects and the gentle lap of the water on the shore. The faint sound came again, an eerie high-pitched keen that seemed to echo in macabre desolation until it died away.

It sounded like a woman screaming.

Both of them went still — he in the act of walking back to the table and Drew as he lifted his wine to his mouth. After a second, Rob said, "Could be a bird or maybe a bobcat. They have them down here."

"You think so?" Drew frowned, turning to stare at the open doors. "I've heard screech owls before. I suppose that could be it. Maybe we should take a look outside. It's hard to tell how close it was."

"If we hear it again, maybe we can tell."

They waited but from outside all there came was the constant sound of the cicadas in the trees and the chirping of what seemed like a million tree frogs.

"I'm going with the owl/bobcat theory." Rob sat back down and reached for the almost empty bottle of Merlot to pour the last into his glass. "Are we going to get up early tomorrow and try for some largemouth? The last time I came I caught one that was probably close to seven pounds."

"Huh, you say, Hanson. What's your idea of early?"

"Uhm . . . six maybe." Fishing was a safe comfortable topic. Much better than discussing how his best friend was in love with the woman he couldn't seem to get off his mind.

"Six?" Drew's brows shot up. "Well, yeah, I suppose that's fine since Lauren will probably sleep in anyway. I just don't want her to feel like a fifth wheel because Karen bailed out."

"I think I'm the fifth wheel." Rob took a deliberate sip of the red wine and looked out over the moonlit lake.

What an understatement.

* * *

She was restless, even though she was exhausted and the night had cooled off nicely, the breeze coming off the balcony brushing across her skin. The shorts and T-shirt she'd put on seemed to cling to her body and she slid out of bed and slipped both off.

The look on Drew's face as she'd passed him and rushed upstairs had obliterated any possibility of sleep. It wasn't guilt precisely that kept her tossing and turning, it was just plain confusion. She was involved with Andrew Fletcher. It was unsettling, because she'd never felt this way about anyone, not with the same intensity. The flash of his mesmerizing smile, the way he moved with such easy masculine grace, the skillful way he touched her . . .

Before him, she'd thought sex overrated, a Hollywood commodity peddled like plastic surgery and breast implants. An illusion, when the reality was more about messy, less than satisfying intercourse with absolutely no rockets exploding in the heavens. Disappointed was her overall rating, but then again, she didn't have a whole lot of experience.

Drew had changed that the first time they'd slept together.

Maybe this current state of turmoil was all his fault, she mused in disgruntled discontent as she punched the pillow under her head, kicked off the covers, and closed her eyes for the hundredth time. He'd made her aware of her body, of how a woman could respond to a man, and as a result, she was having some very disloyal and entirely erotic fantasies about Rob Hanson.

She was seriously involved with Drew. Why was she so aware of Rob? The problem had been growing for the past few months and she had a feeling Drew might have started to notice. For that matter, Rob seemed just as uncomfortable around her as she was around him, and she had begun to have a love–hate reaction to the idea of double dates. A traitorous part of her wanted to see Rob. A more practical part of her brain told her it was better to just stay away.

She finally had found a great guy who was everything any woman could want, they got along, laughed together, enjoyed a very healthy satisfying sex life, and there she was, having impure thoughts about his best friend.

You're an idiot, Lauren.

Maybe it was because the two men shared a lot of the same characteristics. They were both self-confident, intelligent, and had a good sense of humor, but while Drew tended to be straightforward and dealt with life in a very direct way, Rob seemed more sensitive and actually a bit old-fashioned if Karen's complaints held any truth. She had never gotten him into bed, his girlfriend had confided with bitterness the last time the four of them had gone out together for dinner and she and Lauren had gone to the restroom at the same time. A successful attorney, statuesque and blonde, Karen seemed more than a little irritated with his reluctance over sex, so maybe the cancellation wasn't that much of a surprise after all.

Rob's girlfriend had speculated he might be interested in someone else.

Is it me? Lauren wondered.

It wasn't like he'd ever done or said anything that could even be remotely construed as flirtation. He wouldn't do that to Drew. Lauren just got this feeling his unease around her might be a reflection of a similar problem to the one she had with him.

She rolled over and was suddenly aware that the figure of a man lounged in the doorway, one broad shoulder against the frame. With the moonlight, it was easy enough to see Drew's face in angles and planes, his gaze riveted on her exposed body.

16

"Hmm, nice view. Gorgeous naked woman in my bed, it doesn't get better than that. Waiting for me? I'd kind of given up hope since you said you were so tired."

"I guess not as tired as I thought. I can't fall asleep." Her voice sounded husky, even to her own ears.

"Can I help?" He moved toward the bed and jerked his shirt off over his head. His bare chest was ridged with muscle and his abdomen flat and taut.

"Maybe." She needed him touching her, kissing her, anything to take her mind off her chaotic emotions. "What do you have in mind?"

"How about a little mind-blowing sex?" He unfastened his shorts and pushed them down his lean hips.

"That sounds promising," Lauren murmured as he climbed onto the huge bed and settled on top of her.

"Doesn't it?" he asked in a husky voice, and for a moment their gazes locked before he slowly lowered his head and captured her mouth. They kissed with mutual open hunger, his tongue tangling with hers, the weight of his body pinning her to the bed. Lauren ran her hands down the muscled contours of his back.

Drew licked a trail along her jaw to the sensitive spot below her ear as he cupped a breast. "Damn, you feel so good."

So did he. Lauren lifted her mouth for another kiss. Belatedly, she realized he hadn't even closed the door.

"The door is open." Her whisper sounded thick and off-key.

"So what?" Drew licked her collarbone.

"I don't want anyone to hear us." Lauren fought back an inarticulate sound of dismay.

"The only other person here is Rob and I hate to break it to you, babe, he knows we sleep together."

"Still, I . . . he doesn't have to hear it."

"Relax. His bedroom is on a different level anyway so feel free to make those sexy little sounds that turn me on so much."

"Please close the door."

"Okay, fine."

"Thank you," she whispered when he came back to the bed. "I do want you."

"I'm damned glad of that because the feeling is entirely mutual. I'll be happy to demonstrate."

He did.

Gradually she became aware again of the pulse of the insects outside through the open windows, the soft feel of the huge bed, and the uneven breathing of the man sprawled on top of her, his weight supported just enough by his elbows.

"Hmm." Lauren smiled and touched his face with a brush of her fingertips. "I somehow think I'll be able to drift off now." It was true, she felt sated and physically content.

"Call on me anytime." His breath tickled her throat. He kissed her bare shoulder. "We okay?"

A flicker of warning shot through her. "After what just happened you have to ask?"

"You've been a little tense lately."

"I have?"

"I notice everything about you." Drew stroked her arm with a light touch. "You can always talk to me, you know."

Not about this. She tried to picture the conversation in which she mentioned her romantic fantasies involving his best friend. How on earth would he understand if she didn't understand it herself?

Yeah, that would go over well.

"Nothing is wrong, Drew." Her voice softened. "I love you."

His arm tightened a fraction. "That works out, since I love you, babe."

Lauren gave a theatrical yawn. It was not the time to start thinking about her idiotic problem again. She was a grown woman, not an infatuated teenager, and this would pass.

Or she certainly hoped it would.

CHAPTER THREE

He listened to Mozart as he drank his coffee and felt no remorse for his decision.

None.

Requiem in D-minor. *It seemed fitting and suited his mood.*

But as he wandered out onto the huge deck, he noticed a boat on the lake and recognized it. He froze, cup in hand, and realized someone was at the cabin next door — if you called acres away next door, and if you could call it a cabin. Everyone with property on this lake paid dearly for their privacy, but acoustics were tricky.

Neighbors were unexpected. It was a vacation home and usually sat empty.

It took some of the joy out of the sunny morning.

* * *

At mid-morning the brilliance of the sun reflected off the water in a dazzling sapphire blaze and he'd decided sunscreen might not be a bad idea. Drew reeled in his line and opened the cooler to retrieve a bottle of water. Rob was right, the lake was very quiet and they were in the only boat in sight.

He took a drink and adjusted his sunglasses. "Who owns that place? Jesus."

Rob glanced in the direction of his pointing finger. A rooftop stuck up from the trees, the expansive length of the visible structure giving an idea of the size of the house below. It had to be enormous. "Uncle Jim said the place next door to his is owned by a professor who wrote a few books that made it big, but his real source of wealth was that he married money. How he knows all that I'm not sure, but my aunt is pretty social. I can see her taking over a bottle of wine and getting the scoop."

"Yeah, well, he didn't buy that place on a university salary." Drew capped the water bottle and set it aside.

"True enough. I want to say the guy is some sort of an expert on something offbeat like criminal history but writes bestselling fiction novels. I can't remember his name off the top of my head. Glenn something . . . like everyone else, they don't live there full-time."

"The boathouse is larger than my condo."

"I'm sure it cost some real bucks."

It was true. The structure by the elaborate dock was two stories, with three bay doors for the boats undoubtedly inside and the exterior was impressive with even a rooftop deck that looked like it might be connected to the house because there was a walkway off the back of it but obscured by trees. The place looked as deserted as the rest of the lake.

"I wonder if Lauren is awake." It was a neutral comment. Drew was just thinking out loud. "She's an early riser usually but she was sound asleep when I got up."

Rob said nothing, piloting the boat back toward their dock. The wind ruffled his dark hair and his face held no expression at all.

On purpose at a guess — an educated one.

It spoke volumes.

That was a big part of the problem, of course. He and Lauren were both being careful about it, so deliberately indifferent to each other, and if he hadn't seen that moment the night before, Drew might even buy into that he just had an overactive imagination.

He didn't.

The act of handing a plate to another human being wasn't significant usually. People had more physical contact on the subway each day and it meant nothing, but the look they'd exchanged over a barely touched plate of steak and potatoes had been telling.

He wasn't even sure when he'd first noticed something was up. Yes, they double dated often enough with Rob and whoever was his latest girlfriend because he and Rob had always done that, since before college. There had never been a conflict of interest before, but Drew had the feeling there sure as hell was one now.

He didn't need this, and he doubted Rob did either.

Lauren was clearly uncomfortable over the attraction, and since he knew Rob almost as well as he knew himself, it was also clear there was an ethical dilemma there as well. Neither one of them would ever do anything about it. Drew was as sure of it as he was the sun would come up the next morning.

But sometimes it was a cloudy day and all that sunshine was obscured.

The good news was he knew Lauren meant it when she said she loved him.

Desire wasn't an unhealthy emotion. It just depended on how the parties involved dealt with it. He still noticed other pretty young women besides her, of course. The key word was *noticed*. Noticing was fine, acting on it wasn't.

Lauren *was* awake, he saw, and must have heard them approach because she walked out onto the long dock just as they berthed the boat. Drew took in the scenery with pure male appreciation, her dark-blue bikini revealing a great deal of smooth flawless skin, her hair loose and shining down her back. The rich color was accented by the sunlight and the light breeze tugged a silky strand across her cheek. She pushed it away and smiled. "Any luck?"

He felt pretty damned lucky at the moment. As she bent to set down a beach towel, bottle of sunblock, and a paperback novel, her breasts swayed provocatively under the thin, barely-there material and he got a bird's-eye view of a great deal of enticing flesh.

"We caught a few small ones." Rob turned to start carefully tying up the boat with a line around a post.

Yeah, right, like he hadn't seen her bend over too.

"It's a beautiful morning though." Drew vaulted out to secure the other line. "Perfect for getting a little sun and maybe a swim."

"My thoughts exactly." She sank down and picked up her book, folding those long, slender legs underneath her.

"After we take our gear back up to the house, I may change into my trunks and come down to join you."

"I'll be here." She flashed them both another smile and then flipped open her book.

They gathered their poles and took the path up toward the house, the sun warm on Drew's back. Rob seemed in one hell of a hurry for someone on vacation, a good two yards in the lead right off the bat. It was an easy enough assumption his friend's goal wasn't so much where he was going as it was getting away from Lauren with all due speed and Drew stifled an expletive.

He really didn't know exactly how to handle this, but he wasn't going to pretend all week long he didn't notice the tension. It wasn't his style, and besides, this problem wasn't limited to just the next six days either.

Drew stowed his fishing pole on the porch and followed Rob into the cabin. He leaned against the counter in the kitchen and declined a glass of iced tea as his friend rummaged in the refrigerator. Finally, he simply said, "We need to talk. Now seems as good a time as any with Lauren down by the lake."

Rob glanced up from dropping ice cubes in a tall glass. "Talk about what?"

"I bet you could give it a good guess." Drew lifted a brow. "You know how I hate bullshit and as far as I know you aren't into it either, so let's cut through it, okay?"

22

"What particular bullshit are we referring to?" Rob gave him a level look but there was a tight set to his mouth and his eyes held a wary look.

He just laid it out there. "This isn't easy to say, but I get the distinct impression you have a less than platonic interest in my girlfriend. That's about as blunt as I can be. Correct me if I'm wrong."

There was an antique clock hanging above the fireplace in the great room. In the ensuing silence Drew could hear it tick with startling clarity.

Rob said nothing at first until he finally exhaled and ran his hand down his face. "There are times I wish we didn't know each other so well. I certainly wish you'd never noticed anything, because I swear I've tried to just ignore it."

It was a relief he didn't, in the end, deny it. Maybe for them both.

"Yeah, well, Lauren isn't doing too great a job in keeping it under wraps either. She's noticed because I've noticed *that* too."

"Lauren has?" Rob's hazel eyes took on a tell-tale glitter.

"She seems uptight around you." Drew groped for the right words. This was a lifelong friendship. "Look, I am not interested in losing her *because* of you anymore than I am interested in losing her *to* you because I'm a jealous asshole. She isn't the kind of person who would easily live with the idea she put a strain on our friendship. Already I sense she feels guilty as hell for being attracted to you and it's a problem. Or maybe she feels guilty because you're attracted to her. I'm not a psychologist, I'm just not blind."

He was also out of the country for good chunks of time. It had never bothered him before, but it certainly did now. It was hard to tell which one of them was in the most hellish position.

"She hasn't cornered the market on guilt." Rob seemed to remember the pitcher on the counter and lifted it to pour tea into his glass with a hand that wasn't quite steady. "I feel like a jerk. I wish I could tell you why I can't go for Karen, who's gorgeous and smart even if I don't disagree now that I've thought it over about the shallow part. Or go for any of the other women I've met lately instead of thinking about—"

"—Lauren all the time." Drew finished the sentence tersely. "Our real problem — for all three of us in my estimation — is we need to work this out somehow or more than one relationship is going to be destroyed. You and I have been friends a long time. I'd like it to stay that way. We've never had this kind of problem before."

Rob got it. That was part of the issue.

"I haven't done a single thing out of line. I'm not going to either, so let's just relax, okay? I admire your taste and good judgment. You have her. I don't. I know it, don't get me wrong. I'm even happy for you, because she's not only beautiful, but terrific in every other way — intelligent, has a sense of humor, is artistic . . . any man with half a brain would notice her. This whole situation isn't something I wanted to happen, believe me. If you're pissed, I understand, but it wasn't intentional. I'm the miserable one."

Since the misery wasn't all one-sided, Drew could not agree. He was apprehensive over the future. Lauren felt uncomfortable for thinking about another man. Rob was frustrated and guilty. Drew was afraid Lauren might just decide to walk away from the whole situation. Including him. She had good reason.

She had more reasons than she realized. That was his real problem. Rob wasn't the only one with a secret.

Dammit.

Surely there was some way to work this out. He was just having a hard time coming up with it.

"She and I could leave. This place is great and I've been looking forward to it, but not if we aren't going to enjoy it. I'm not sure how I'd explain my sudden reversal, but—"

Rob interrupted. "Drew, please don't. It won't just be the three of us. Karen sent a text. She's coming after all."

* * *

That text had been good news and bad news.

At least it was true, it wouldn't just be the three of them, but Rob had to admit he wasn't looking forward to navigating these turbulent waters. He hadn't particularly invited Karen in the first place. Over dinner one night on a casual date, because that was all it was in his mind anyway, he'd merely mentioned his uncle's cabin was free and he was thinking of inviting Drew down for a week of fishing and recreation. She was the one that suggested if Drew brought Lauren she'd like for them all to go together.

That was Karen. Not pushy exactly but determined for sure. She'd decided on the vacation, and that was that.

Being in her crosshairs made him uncomfortable because he really didn't feel the initial attraction any longer, and that was just how things went sometimes. The relationship was certainly superficial at this point.

He'd been too polite to point out he hadn't really included her. He hadn't invited Lauren then either, but if Karen was coming, he didn't have much choice because he knew Drew didn't really want to start a Karen Foxton fan club and he'd cancel if he knew she was going to be there unless Lauren was there too. So Rob *had* invited him to bring Lauren along even though he knew being around her for an entire week would be a form of emotional torture.

The relief he'd felt when Karen canceled was balanced by being the odd man out, but it continued to just get more complicated. She had just informed him a judge had moved an important court date and she could be there after all.

It was like he couldn't win. His connection with her was definitely not long term.

Rob ran his hand through his hair. "All I really pictured was you and me catching some fish and drinking beer in the sun. It's a little awkward being here alone with you and Lauren, but now there will be four of us. I think the least I can do is point out if you want to leave after this conversation I never wanted us to have, I understand, but I prefer some backup."

Drew smiled wryly though it obviously took some effort. "Actually, if the situation was different, I'd be giving *you* advice. Maybe I will anyway. Forget Karen, because it isn't going anywhere."

"I know." That was honest. He exhaled. "You're right. That has absolutely nothing to do with Lauren either. I'm being serious here. My interest in Karen has evaporated slowly the longer I've known her."

But it certainly didn't help the relationship that he had such conflicted interest in someone else.

Drew lifted a brow. "You do know Karen has told Lauren she thinks there might be another woman in your life."

At least Drew was being decent about this untenable situation, and no, Rob didn't know that. "There is no one else in a literal sense. Karen and I just haven't slept together and I know she's wondering why. I'm not — trust me — trying to get an award for moral man of the year, but our relationship is too superficial for that in my opinion. I do envy what you have with Lauren, no doubt about it, but that isn't a new story in the history of humankind. I want *us* to be fine."

'Thou shall not covet thy neighbor's wife' came to mind. Definitely not a new story or that biblical admonishment wouldn't exist, but in his defense, it certainly wasn't on purpose.

Drew was Drew. Straightforward as ever. "I don't love it, but I feel better we talked about it. If we relax over the situation, I think Lauren will too and that's important to me. Let's go change into trunks and head back down to the water. Today is simply gorgeous. I don't want to waste a second of it."

* * *

If the man hadn't glanced side to side, she never would have noticed it.

Lauren watched him walk to the end of a dock a hundred yards or so away, his gaze sweeping the perimeter of the

26

cove. What he was looking for was a mystery because the lake was deserted except for a pair of Canada geese floating by.

Maybe he was just enjoying the gorgeous weather. It was . . . idyllic might be the right word, with the verdant trees, the deep-blue hue of the rippling water, the warm summer breeze, and not to mention the solitude. Her last vacation in a bathing suit, book in hand, had been on a beautiful, but crowded, ocean beach. This was better.

It had been hot in the full sun and she wasn't too much for sunbathing anyway, so she'd taken her towel to where a weeping willow trailed branches into the water and the cobalt shadows were nice and cool, and settled on the grass bank. Propped on one elbow she'd watched the stranger turn and press a button on the device in his hand. One of the boathouse doors lifted and she realized it must be like a garage door opener. He went in through the door and a moment later an engine started and a sleek motorboat backed out of one of the bays. It was interesting he wore dark slacks, a light-blue dress shirt, and leather loafers. It was not exactly boating apparel in her opinion. His hair was fair and short, and he had a Roman nose, she could see even from a distance, that dominated his face.

The boat pulled up at the dock and the man clambered out, tied it to a metal cleat presumably bolted to the dock just for that purpose, and walked down the length of the pier. He dragged an oblong object down wrapped in a tarp and dropped it in the boat. It wasn't lightweight since the craft bobbed in the water and a second later he jumped in and went to unwrap the rope. He visibly froze as he caught sight of her on her towel on the bank, and then he just went about untying the boat, sat down, put it into throttle and sped away.

It was a little off-key, but then again Rob had said his uncle rarely used the house. Maybe his neighbor had just been surprised to realize it was occupied.

"Hey, babe."

Lauren glanced up. "Hey back at you."

Drew dropped on the towel beside her and smiled in his heart-stopping way. In only swim trunks, he was pretty noticeable from a female perspective all the way around. He picked up her novel, studying the cover. "*Seducing the Highlander*? Really?"

"I love it. Scottish historical romance. Who can beat that?" She snatched it back, laughing. "Men in kilts tossing logs around and wielding swords? When I'm done, I'll loan it to you."

"I suppose I could read it in a closet somewhere where no one will see me and doubt my masculinity. I'll have to watch sports twice as much in front of everyone to make up for it."

"I really don't see how that is possible. That's all you watch now anyway." He really did tune into ESPN or some similar channel the first opportunity he had in his free time, but he really didn't have a lot of it.

"Right now, I want to go swimming." He leaned forward and kissed her, his tongue doing a slow seductive glide along her lower lip. "With a beautiful woman in a very sexy bikini. Do you know one? I do."

Lauren eyed the lake. "It's hot out here but that water looks cold."

"Jump in and it is all over in a flash. Like ripping off a bandage." He got to his feet and reached for her hand.

She argued, as she evaded him. "When we vacationed in northern Wisconsin my grandfather always said it was better to be a warm chicken than a cold hero. I'll wade in and get used to it step by step."

"I'll help you be a hero." He flashed a wicked grin.

"Drew Fletcher! Don't you dare throw me in." She really didn't want to be tossed into the lake and scrambled up from her towel to flee.

Maybe two steps onto the dock and she slammed right into a hard, bare male chest. The man who caught her held her in the circle of his arm. He said, "Whoa, is this loser bothering you? I'll protect you, Lauren."

28

Rob. She just couldn't catch a break. They were skin to skin for a moment while she regained her balance, and she said almost inaudibly, "Sorry. I didn't realize you were back down here."

He let her go. "No problem. I like it when pretty girls throw themselves into my arms."

When she turned around Drew's expression was a little taut, or maybe she just imagined it. He shrugged and then grinned. "Okay, remind me to ambush you next time and skip declaring my evil intentions. I'm going in. Hanson, chicken or hero?"

Rob was already on the move. "I'll beat you in, loser boy."

"Like hell."

The competition was funny to watch, two grown men racing down the dock like young boys on a hot summer day. They both hit the water, Rob in a clean dive and Drew a cannonball, and they both came up at the same time, laughing and shaking the hair out of their eyes.

Drew shouted out. "And the winner is?"

"I declare a tie," Lauren said, the irony of it not escaping her once the words were out of her mouth.

CHAPTER FOUR

They were swimming, playing in the water, lots of friendly competition going on between the two young men as an impromptu race ensued toward the point that marked a channel to the rest of the lake. Glenn adjusted the telescope on the upper deck he used to see the night sky — which was often spectacular and astronomy was one of his hobbies — toward the water.

The young woman was floating on a raft and he couldn't help but admire the view. Those young, firm breasts . . . and she was slender but not so slender there wasn't a curve in sight, which he appreciated. His wife obsessed over her weight constantly and he'd grown weary of it.

Long chestnut hair with hints of gold . . . she was lovely. He liked that word. It implied both beauty and grace.

She'd seen him leave in the boat.

He really hoped that didn't prove unfortunate for her.

* * *

Great day.

Almost.

No argument could be made about the weather so far. Absolutely perfect. As it moved toward late evening white clouds began to build tiered castles in the sky, signaling a summer storm rolling in, as did the wind picking up and whistling through the trees. Drew was the designated cook for the evening since they'd promised to not pile it all on Lauren, but he'd cheated and gotten his Aunt Ida to make her famous lasagna and frozen it, so all he had to do was thaw it and put it in the oven. Purchased garlic bread and he was home free.

His cooking skills did not exist. He'd eaten exotic foods all over the world from Argentina to Bali to Morocco, but he couldn't prepare them.

Neither Lauren nor Rob was fooled. Rob said, "Please tell me what I smell is Ida's Italian."

Thunder rumbled in the background.

There were two open bottles of wine on the counter, one a Chianti to complement the meal, and one a crisp Sauvignon Blanc Lauren was sipping at the moment. She raised her brows. "Not that I object in any way to his devious plan, but do you think *he* made it? Drew might pull off heating up a can of soup if he had to do it."

"This doubt is shattering my self-confidence," Drew said in false affront. "Maybe I made it. Why couldn't she have given me her recipe? I can read. If you can read, you can cook."

They were sitting around the huge kitchen island comfortably after a day on the water, and Lauren had set the dining-room table. "You don't *want* to cook," she pointed out accurately. She'd changed into a filmy blue top over a camisole and shorts, pink toenails visible in her sandals. "And I don't know anyone with more self-confidence."

He took a piece of cheese and a cracker from a plate she'd set out. Those crackers were wafer thin and the cheese had some sort of spice to it. If he had to call it, horseradish. He was a fan. "On some levels I do okay."

He wished he wasn't joking. Normally yes, he took life as it came, but this situation was a little different. He wished they didn't get his meaning exactly but had a feeling both she and Rob did. The last thing he wanted was to ruin the evening, so he added lightly, "Lasagna just isn't one of them. If you think I baked the bread too, and whipped up the garlic butter, you are not living in the real world. That's not devious, that's just doing you a favor."

Rob laughed. "I was going to give you the garlic butter. I'm pretty sure either you or I could both manage that."

"Maybe."

"Hey, I'm not claiming I can do much better. I should have invited Aunt Ida to come with us instead of Karen."

"She's five foot tall, has gray hair, and her glasses are constantly falling off her nose, but if that turns you on, maybe you should have."

"I have a crush on her via her lasagna," Rob said with a small smile. "Does that count? It smells damn good in here."

"It counts." Lauren lightly twirled her glass. "When will Karen be here?"

"Not until ten or so."

"It is a long drive, so that makes sense. Luckily, she can warm up dinner if she's hungry. I hope she misses the storm." Lauren was obviously trying to be gracious, or else just resigned. It was hard to tell.

Drew would rather have Ida, but she'd never approve of him and Lauren sharing a room, so maybe not. Karen wouldn't care. If she sensed the truth, she'd prefer it so she could have a shot at persuading Rob into the same arrangement for the two of them. He suggested, "After-dinner drinks overlooking the lake while we wait for her? There's a full moon rising soon. According to my phone it should be beautiful out there with a starlit sky once the front rolls through."

"Sounds great." Rob backed him up.

"Hello?"

The rap on the screen door was almost tentative in nature, and Drew looked up, startled. They were all startled in fact. The man standing outside was tall and had sandy hair and an apologetic smile on his face. "I don't mean to intrude, but I live next door, and I noticed someone was here. I was out and about and thought I'd stop by."

Slight southern accent, maybe mid-fifties, a diffident air, and even on this warm summer evening, a nice golf shirt, tailored slacks, and expensive leather loafers. Rob was technically the host and slid off his stool to go over to slide open the screen. "We didn't hear you pull up. I'm Rob Hanson. Jim is my uncle." He put out his hand and the stranger shook it. "This is Drew Fletcher and Lauren Mathews."

"Glenn Heaston. You didn't hear me because I came by canoe. It's a perfect evening for a paddle, or so I thought."

"I would say it is going to storm in about two seconds." As if to validate that, lightning flashed in a vivid pattern across the sky, followed by a crack that rattled the expensive windows. Rob said nicely, "Come on in to have a glass of wine or cup of coffee? I don't think the canoe sounds like a good idea right now."

"Maybe you're correct. I'm afraid I've been working all day and didn't check the forecast. I'd love a glass of wine."

"Red or white?"

"Either would be nice."

That's how they ended up having a drink with a bestselling author on a stormy evening.

"My wife is out of town," Heaston said conversationally. "She likes to travel and I like to stay home. It makes for a more congenial relationship. Angela only likes the house here in small doses. I love solitude, and she likes to shop, which I loathe. So she joins me when she feels like it. Perfect. We have an understanding that when I am working on a new novel, she goes home to Lexington." He shrugged. "Or anywhere else she wants to go."

Drew had to laugh. "Rob and I like to fish, and Lauren likes to read. That works out for us as well."

"I think I saw her reading on the bank earlier today." Heaston gave Lauren a charming smile. "One of my books dare I hope?"

"Historical romance, I'm afraid." She smiled back. "I'm hopelessly hooked."

"It is a popular genre. Some of my books are historical but take a slant more toward a psychological view on the anatomy of how serial criminals behave. There are sexual situations certainly in there." He smiled. "There would be, of course. We are all human and that's perfectly natural, but they are based on true stories with a fictional set of characters. Not exactly romance — more people flexing their skills at intrigue and subterfuge, so sex included but never a happily ever after, I'm afraid."

"I know my uncle read at least one and enjoyed it because he mentioned it to me." Rob leaned against the counter, his expression thoughtful. "I think I saw it in the bookcase upstairs." Outside all hell had broken loose in the form of a furious downpour that pounded the roof and pelted the deck. "I hope you really tied up that canoe."

"I put it under Ms. Mathews' reading tree and turned it upside down once I heard the thunder. It shouldn't go anywhere."

The lasagna was ready and he needed to check the garlic bread, so what the hell. Drew offered, "Would you like to stay for dinner? If your wife is out of town, no need to eat alone. We have plenty." That wasn't an exaggeration. Ida had made enough for a small army instead of a pan for four people.

"I don't want to intrude."

Rob helped out. "You wouldn't be. Besides, once you taste this lasagna, you'll be happy this was a good night for a paddle even if it went south. Join us."

* * *

Nice dinner. Food was delicious because Drew's aunt was like a magician or something — just because he was blond didn't mean part of his family wasn't from Italy — and the storm rolled through and subsided as they ate, though the lights did flicker once or twice.

Lauren had to make the observation: "The lake is so beautiful, sun or storm."

"You can thank the TVA for its existence, though I think the dam has been rebuilt by the Army Corps of Engineers since it was created. They finally put in an overflow pipe so it wouldn't flood any longer. That pipe is about ten feet in diameter and allows the rising water to pour into the small river behind and eventually feeds into the Tennessee." He paused and quoted softly, "'Far off from these a slow and silent stream, Lethe the river of oblivion rolls'."

Automatically, she said, "Oh. *Paradise Lost.*"

His expression reflected surprise. "You know your Milton, I see."

"I love to read even the classics. I have a minor in English. So the lake has been here for a while. That's interesting."

Heaston's tone was reflective. "My wife's family was far-sighted and bought the property decades ago. They are the ones who sold off most of the lots for the houses to be built here once the flooding issue was solved. My wife is a part of the history of this place even if she finds it unexciting. So what do you do, Ms. Mathews?" Heaston asked between bites.

"I'm a graphic designer for an advertising firm."

"Artistic then. That always appeals to me, as I find imaginative people interesting especially when they are the prettiest one at the table, though your companions give you a run for your money. This, by the way, really is the best lasagna I have ever had."

She had no idea how to take that comment at all. It seemed odd.

Give you a run for your money?

His sexual preferences didn't matter to her, but maybe he was gay? He was a good-looking man, fit and certainly well dressed for a lake-house setting in the woods, but that would be to stereotype him, and she avoided doing that. She truly felt sexual preference was a personal choice and should be looked at that way and the right of every human being, but the remark was a little strange.

"Baked it myself," Drew said with a straight face, lounging comfortably in his chair.

"Note the way that is phrased," Rob said dryly. "And I believe a bakery on the way from Ohio to here is responsible for the bread, but I have to agree, use all available resources. In college we ate at this place called Ted's. The cheapest hamburgers ever . . . but for some reason I can't fathom, I miss them."

Drew agreed. "Ted's was the best. Ketchup and mustard, I think that was it."

"Oh, come on, there was that one pickle." Rob grinned.

"It *was* a treat when you found the pickle bite."

Heaston clearly found the conversation amusing. "You two are obviously old friends then."

"We are. Even survived being college roommates."

Lauren hoped they survived *her*. There was tension between her and Drew, there was tension between her and Rob, and there was certainly tension between the both of them. That moment on the dock, Rob had held her just a shade too long and she hadn't missed it.

And she couldn't believe it but Heaston apparently noticed on such short acquaintance there was an interesting dynamic. He said, "Ah, and our *femme fatale* here must also be a friend?"

"Not for nearly as long. They've known each other since grade school. I'm a newcomer to the mix."

That certainly came out awkwardly.

She stood up, suddenly glad the storm had passed, and picked up her plate. "Would anyone like dessert? Drew picked up some fantastic white chocolate and macadamia nut cookies when he bought the bread. I can make coffee, or there's more wine."

"I should probably take my leave and thank you for the refuge from the storm and lovely meal." Heaston stood as well. "Let me help you clear the table."

"We've got this." Rob and Drew were in accord and started gathering silverware, working in tandem. "This is the easy part," Drew said facetiously. "Whipping up that lasagna was the hard part. I will be eating cookies just for the record."

Heaston departed then on a gracious thank you, and none of them said a word about the femme fatale comment, which was telling because Drew would normally have cracked a joke of some kind.

It was Rob who said, "Nice man. A little interesting, but we aren't all cut from the same bolt of cloth, or so they say."

"Writers are supposed to be eccentric. It is part of the persona," Lauren commented as she rinsed a dish and handed it to Drew to put in the dishwasher. "Well, actually, that's what I've heard. I don't know that I've ever met one before tonight, or not a famous one like him anyway. I've certainly seen his books on the shelves when I haunt the bookstores now that I think about it."

"Eccentric certainly pairs with not bothering to look up at the sky before taking off in a canoe with a storm on the way," Rob commented. "I'm apparently not eccentric at all. I look at the weather forecast and take dark clouds on the horizon seriously."

"You're talking to a pilot," Drew pointed out. "I check it constantly out of habit. Did he imply you and I might be gay? Like . . . together?"

"I have no idea."

"Damn, I need a skull tattoo on my neck or something."

"Yeah, help yourself, and just so you know, you aren't my type." Rob took out some polish for the beautiful trestle table. "I think even with that downpour we can have our drinks outside because the covered portion of the deck should be dry."

Lauren carried what was left of her wine outside and chose a chair and naturally Rob chose one on her right and Drew on her left, so she was in the middle.

She was fairly sure Heaston had been trying to decide which way the romantic interest lay between the three of them. If she pointed that out to Drew and Rob, the three of them might have to talk about it and she just wasn't ready for it. Nor was she ready to ruin their vacation, especially right before Karen's arrival which was just going to add to the drama.

Actually, she didn't know *how* to talk about it.

The breeze smelled like rain — clean and cool after the hot day —and the eaves dripped in a steady rhythm. The lake view was enough to make anyone relax, and Drew was such a typical male he'd just brought out the bag of cookies instead of bothering with a plate, setting it down with a flourish. "Dessert is served."

Rob's phone rang at that moment and he answered it. "Hi Karen. Yes, rain here too. It's done and clearing. We're sitting outside. The stars are coming out."

They were, the clouds tearing apart like soft cotton candy, in long thin layers with small brilliant lights in the background.

"The driveway is hard to find, so follow your GPS. We'll have the place lit up, so you won't be able to miss it. Park out back, you'll see my truck and Drew's fancy car."

End of call.

Drew said conversationally, "Since we all three know the score, Lauren through Karen, and you talked to me about it, feel free to point out it's none of my business, but is Karen going to be pissed about separate bedrooms? If your answer is yes, I might go get another beer right now. I'm looking at the Rob Hanson weather report and seeing a dark cloud on *his* horizon."

Lauren wondered about that too, but leave it to Drew to state it out loud.

"Probably." Rob sighed and ran his fingers through his hair. "I am uninterested in giving her the wrong impression about our relationship. That's not fair to her or to me either. I half wonder if inviting herself on this vacation wasn't a test of some kind. Get me another beer too, if you don't mind."

Drew disappeared inside.

"I didn't realize she invited herself," Lauren said.

Rob looked out over the water, his expression hard to read. "It was my mistake to mention this trip. I believe I said key words that implied a masculine venue like 'fishing' and 'drinking beer' and her response was that if you were going to be here, she'd love to come. I could have lied and said you were going to hike up Everest this week, but that sort of thing never works in my experience since I'm not a great liar. When she canceled because of work I was relieved, but she seems bent on joining us, so brace for a lot of her company. I'm still fishing and swimming."

"I don't dislike Karen." Lauren tried to be as diplomatic as possible. "I'm still going to read and sit in the sun. I suspect she'll be on her phone and email the entire time, so it won't matter." She paused. "Without her being so pushy, would you have invited *me*?"

He looked at her directly then. "No. And I think maybe you know why."

CHAPTER FIVE

He recognized certain traits in himself for what they were. He'd ever been an observer, a perpetual player sitting on the bench, and his participation was minimal. His true skill was to discover what drove people, how to define motivation — in short, what were their demons.

Maybe it was a desire to discover his as well.

He wasn't sure he wanted to know, and that intrigued him.

So did the Beautiful Trio, as he'd dubbed them. It was interesting to spend an evening with two good-looking young men and a very pretty woman, and not get a sense of territory or power. Even in a pack of wolves there was a dominant male and he hadn't been able to put his finger on it between just two of them.

Mesmerizing.

He might set aside his current work for a bit and start a new book. He often did that when he was inspired.

* * *

The sound of a car made Rob set aside his drink and the next minute he saw the arcs of headlights hit the trees and water.

Here we go.

He got up and went down the steps just in time to hear the car door slam as he hit the bottom. That won him points and a kiss as Karen got out of the car. Her lips were warm against his. He could smell her perfume. "Um, thought I'd never get here. This really is remote."

Why he felt so guilty wasn't a mystery. She really was a knockout — blonde hair, intense dark eyes, tall and he wasn't sure if her breasts were real, but they certainly were worth a second glance. Smart was part of the package as well, but the chemistry just wasn't there, not like it should be anyway. He was twenty-eight and wanted a wife and to start a family at least sometime soon, but he just couldn't picture Karen in that role, so he was wasting his time, *and* her time.

Not necessarily his fault, but he still felt guilty all around.

That he could picture Lauren in that role was just plain unfortunate. It had occurred to him once again Karen would be much better suited to someone like Drew because she was so intensely career-focused his absences for weeks at a time wouldn't bother her.

Rob favored the sexy-girl-next-door type apparently.

"Other than the rain, was it a nice drive?" He took out her suitcase.

"I sat in stopped traffic here and there on the interstate, but all in all, yes." She gazed upward. "What a gorgeous place."

It did look impressive with all the tiers of lights up to the third story. "My uncle does okay."

"I'd say so. Tell me you're his favorite nephew."

"We haven't had that discussion." He gestured at the stairs with his free hand. "There's a glass of wine or anything else you'd like waiting for you. I'll take this upstairs while you join Drew and Lauren on the deck."

That was neutral enough.

Maybe there was a blow-up headed his way. He just wasn't looking forward to it. No one did, he knew that, but doing it in front of an audience was even worse. He climbed the stairs, took Karen's bags into the room across the landing from his, and set them down next to her bed.

More than once it had occurred to him he was overcomplicating the situation.

Deep breath in, and he went downstairs.

Karen was relaxed in lightweight jeans and a silk shirt, drinking a glass of wine, and he could hear her laughing before he even slid the glass door open. That was a good sign and probably due to Drew, who certainly could be a mood lightener if he sensed the wind needed to blow that direction.

It did.

They would share a bathroom, which was fine with him, but if they weren't sharing a bedroom, maybe not for her. He went and sat. "Everything is by the bed."

"A bathing suit and a pair of shorts and a sleeveless shirt are about all you'll need." Lauren indicated with a swirl of her hand at her own attire. "This is dressed up."

"Maybe we can ask Dr. Heaston if there's a decent restaurant nearby," Drew remarked. "It sounds like he spends a lot of time here."

"Closest neighbor," Rob clarified for Karen. "He stopped by earlier and is kind of an interesting guy. Professor of history, but also a writer."

"Not Glenn Heaston?" Karen looked impressed and that wasn't easy to do. "I haven't read him, but my sister has. She's into that sensational historical fiction. I recognize the name. If you know him, I wonder if I can get a signature for her. She'd love it. She's a real fan."

"I'm pretty sure he would," Rob said but without certainty. "Don't most authors want to do that, or at least that's my impression. It doesn't hurt to ask. He seems nice enough."

"*I* can ask," Karen replied with a small smile over the rim of her wine glass. "Don't sell me short. Shyness is not my problem."

A declaration he found to be true about an hour later. It was getting late when Lauren yawned and said she was going to bed. Karen had a long drive behind her, so she agreed she might turn in as well. To his surprise there was also no argument either over the separate rooms, she just asked for the bathroom first. He waited, brushed his teeth, stripped down to boxers and was half-asleep when he realized someone had come into the moonlit room.

Shit.

Karen was naked, the light slanting off her breasts, emphasizing the darkness between her thighs, and she shook back her hair right before she crawled on top of him. Bare breasts to bare chest. "I can wake you up."

He protested huskily, "Karen, I'm sure you can, but—"

"But what?"

Rob found she was right, because quite frankly she was stripping off the sheet, pulling down his shorts, and using her hands and mouth in a way his traitorous body responded to the physical stimulation, but . . .

It just wasn't a good idea.

He shut his eyes but didn't even for a moment let himself pretend it was someone else. "I don't have a condom." Last-minute thought, but a valid one. And the truth.

"I'm on birth control."

"I'm sorry to draw a line in the sand but no unprotected sex ever for me until I'm ready to have children and we aren't there yet, are we?"

He didn't add that taking her word for that birth control promise was a leap off a cliff into shark-infested waters. Not for a minute did he think she wanted to get pregnant because she was so career-oriented, but on the other hand they'd really only been dating a few months, so he didn't by any means know her that well.

She looked up at him. "Are you serious?"

"I really am."

"I didn't think guys like you existed." Her voice was curt.

But she left the room and he shut his eyes and swore softly under his breath, unsatisfied all the way around.

* * *

Lauren made omelets for breakfast. Cheese and green peppers and sausage, and she also knew the way to a man's heart with some cinnamon rolls, even if they were out of a can.

Drew's vote was she should take over all of the cooking but that really wasn't fair and he'd promised that wasn't going to be the arrangement.

They were all out on the deck and it was a beautiful morning. Rob had certainly been quiet when they'd gone fishing, game on, early that morning. Mist drifting across the water, no sound but the hum of the electric motor as they trolled . . . it had been perfect. Both of them had caught some respectable bass, and Rob had eased up a bit as time passed, because truthfully, fishing was a relaxing pastime.

It wasn't hard to guess at the source of the initial tension.

Lauren had fallen right to sleep the night before, making love not an option to his disappointment, but a long day of sun and water was why they were there, and she'd definitely drunk more wine than she usually did.

But he hadn't been quite so lucky. Lying there with his arms crossed behind his head he'd heard Rob and Karen talking on the next floor, and then maybe a little bit more.

He wasn't going to say anything. Rob wasn't happy in either direction and he couldn't really blame him. If Drew had to call it, whatever had happened wasn't on his initiative. In fact, he was certain of it.

For once he just left it alone. Usually if something was bothering him, he just said it, but for now the sun was shining, and things were complicated enough.

Karen on the other hand had been in a bad mood. Lauren certainly noticed. Drew could tell she mentally connected the dots and he wondered with a stab of jealousy he couldn't help, how she felt about it. From the unguarded look on her face the minute she realized why Karen's demeanor was so foul, she wasn't any happier than Rob.

Damn. That made four of them. He so wished he hadn't recognized that for what it was. He wished he didn't care about both of them, but he did, which made it all worse on his end.

"Back out in the boat?" Rob suggested once breakfast was cleared away. "I'm not willing to waste a minute of this weather."

"Sounds good to me," Drew agreed with alacrity.

Lauren said, "I'm going to get my book and you'll find me in my usual spot."

"No rest for the wicked, I have to prepare some briefs and make a few calls." Karen pointed to her laptop sitting on the kitchen counter. "Everyone, go and enjoy."

So much for the great out of doors, Drew thought sarcastically, but he'd never entertained the illusion that's why Karen had come in the first place. Rob had a target on his back and he'd won round one, but round two was coming.

"We'll give the fish your best regards."

At least Rob finally smiled as they walked out on the deck. "The 'fish your best regards'? Did you just really say that?"

Drew laughed ruefully, carrying a cooler down the steps. "It was a bit of a dig. Why is it I don't think Karen values the idea of R and R very much. We all work hard but at least you and I and Lauren can unwind a little bit. I think Lauren called it. Karen's attached to her phone with an umbilical cord or something. If you think I have mine on me, you'd be wrong. I might check my email the day before we leave just to see if there are any flight schedule changes."

"She's pissed at me."

"I know."

Rob followed him and went to unwind the mooring of the boat when they reached the dock. "Look on the bright side. I doubt she'll ask either of us to teach her how to fish."

It wasn't like Drew doubted it too. "That was never a worry for me."

"No, I can't see it myself."

"You okay?"

The question of the hour.

Rob straightened, dropping the rope into the boat, giving him a level look. "I'm fine."

Topic still off limits. Drew shrugged. "It isn't a mystery to me what happened last night and you don't seem too happy about it either."

"I'm not," Rob said shortly. "She sure forced a decision on me. A firm no thanks resulted in a midnight argument with a naked attorney. That argument was inevitable, but it definitely seemed like the wrong time for it." He got in the boat to hook up the trolling motor to the battery. "Sorry you had to hear it. Now I'm trying like hell to figure out how to avoid a repeat performance tonight. That wasn't a pun by the way."

"You do realize most guys *try* to get women into bed, right?" Drew said immediately after he uttered the words, "Sorry, poor joke. Karen isn't your type after all, and you think it is wrong to sleep with her all week and then break it off. Good summary of the situation?"

Unfortunately, Drew thought, Lauren *was* Rob's type. This triangle was unfair to all three of them if he looked at it dispassionately, which wasn't exactly easy. Loyalty was a fine emotion but torn loyalty was pretty hard to handle.

"Close enough," Rob said. "You and I both know there's more to it than that."

Drew settled into his seat. "It's a nice day and I vote we just talk about something else. Women's golf? I don't really know anything about it, but you can fill me in."

"I'd have to watch it first."

"Watch me catch more fish than you do, how's that?" Drew spun off a cast.

It was a nice one too, and the satisfying splash helped a little. He'd been raised by a wonderful mother who sometimes tried too hard, and a neglectful father who didn't try at all. Both made him determined to succeed, the first for how much effort she'd put in before she died way too young, and the second by him not giving a damn. His father had never taken him fishing — that had been his maternal grandfather. He'd loved that kind old man.

So he did know how to make a good cast, and he did appreciate the outdoors.

"You're dreaming about catching more fish," Rob informed him.

"We were tied earlier."

A gleam caught his eye, and Drew glanced up sharply. He had a clear view at that moment of Heaston's deck and realized the flash was from a telescope mounted on a rail facing the lake. It was a brief glimpse and he thought how he would definitely have one himself in this setting.

Except someone was there.

Looking at them.

It wasn't like a deep, dark secret, the man even waved. Drew waved back, and said, "Heaston's out on his deck above the boathouse. At least I think it's him. I'm not sure."

CHAPTER SIX

Well, he had to admit he was curious. The Beautiful Trio had added a fourth and it threw him off, because as the men went out in the boat, two women came out of the house. Not really comfortably chatting, but friendly enough with each other. He wondered where the blonde came in because he hadn't seen her before.

Nice bosom, tall for a woman, and she didn't go down toward the water, but settled in a chair on the deck and started playing with a tablet device. Lauren Mathews on the other hand headed right for her shady spot on the bank, book in hand. He admired the glossy fall of her hair, the gentle sway of her breasts as she settled into position, and wondered which of her companions she'd slept with the night before. It was an interesting sexual fantasy because there was a civilized — yet primal — battle going on over this young woman.

To couch it in academic terms, she was the prize both of those young men coveted on an emotional and physical level and Glenn had the sense she didn't want to choose. Throughout history men had fought over women. Brothers versus brothers, sworn enemies clashing weapons, friends against friends . . .

This was going to give him exactly what he needed for his book.

The blonde didn't really interest him at all. She was an annoyance really, disturbing his inspiration.

* * *

Lauren dipped a toe in the water, found it cool but it was a hot day so that was appealing, and she picked up one of the rafts Rob had brought down. Getting on it without falling into the lake involved some skill set she hadn't quite mastered yet and she managed only getting half-wet before she settled in.

She hoped no one was watching that graceless maneuver.

Blue skies and not one wisp of a cloud in the azure arc above her. The storm the night before might never have happened. She paddled with her arms backward until she was floating free and was happy she was wearing sunscreen.

Not so happy otherwise.

Rob was a grown man. He could make his own choices. But while she was pretty sure she knew what had happened last night from Karen's mood, she was positive he didn't like that the conflict had happened.

She just shouldn't care either way.

But, unfairly, she did.

The only redeeming thing was Karen hadn't directly confided in her, and Lauren was fine with that. Details she didn't need or want. It was between them.

This was only Sunday. She could get through this week, right?

The boat was quiet and Lauren was self-absorbed enough that she didn't realize Rob and Drew were back until she heard the splash. Drew surfaced next to her raft, grinning. He tickled her right calf with a wet hand. "What do you know, I found a beautiful sea nymph. Methinks she might be in danger of a good dunking. I was foiled yesterday, my pretty wench."

He could always make her laugh. "Is that your best pirate imitation? I think it might need some work. Sea nymphs and even wenches, just so you know, don't like to be dunked."

"Okay, okay," he said on a mock grumble. "Come on in the water and play. No dunking, I promise. The lake feels great."

She couldn't resist. It was just too tempting. She sat up on the raft — carefully — and dangled her legs in the water. "I'm a chicken, remember, so let me get used to it."

Then she abruptly pushed off and grabbed his shoulders and shoved him underwater. The element of surprise worked nicely, but she did a wise retreat. When he resurfaced, she was already a few feet away and reminded him, "You promised."

"Note to self, never trust sexy sea nymphs." He splashed her in retribution.

She splashed back. "Or call someone a wench."

There was no doubt she lost the ensuing war, and any fish in the vicinity had taken a vacation elsewhere due to the commotion. Trying to outdistance Drew in swimming was a futile effort, but she almost made it to the dock before he caught up with her. He whispered in her ear, "If we didn't have an audience, I'd kiss you and hopefully do a whole lot more, but for now I'll settle for a simple white flag of surrender."

"All right, you won."

"Oh, I intend to," he said softly.

She thought there might be an innuendo of a second meaning.

* * *

Rob retrieved the floating raft and tied up the boat.

He was pretty sure he didn't really want to go up and talk to Karen but felt he should at least join her. He ascended the steps and essayed what he hoped was a passable smile as he joined her at the glass table. "Enjoying the sun?"

"Nice to be able to work in my bathing suit." She shut off her device.

"I completely agree."

"I hope that's a compliment."

"It is." No doubt about it, she filled out that skimpy top nicely. He'd never denied her physical beauty. "Want a glass of iced tea? Wine? Bottle of water? I'm going to get a beer. It's past noon."

"Well, why not make it wine. I'm on vacation."

"Be right back," he promised and went in the French doors. The wall of windows showcased the cloudless skies but did not reflect his mood. He removed the cork from a bottle of Chardonnay from his uncle's seemingly vast collection — the wine cellar downstairs was very well-stocked — and grabbed a cold beer from the fridge.

He took the bottle and a glass both outside and set them on the table.

"Are you trying to get me intoxicated so you can take advantage of my virtue?" She leaned forward on purpose, so he'd get an eyeful. "No need. Last night could have been better."

This was treacherous ground. He said carefully, "I know I'm kind of on the conservative side and wonder if we shouldn't figure out our emotional relationship before we jump into a physical one. There's no agenda, just that."

Karen just looked at him with derision. "I hate to point this out, but physical is important."

There was the problem. She'd just blithely dismissed the importance of an emotional relationship. He raised his brows. "Shouldn't there be both?"

"Since we've only been dating a few months, last night would have helped a lot in the 'getting to know you' department."

"Sex is not the basis of a relationship in my opinion."

She poured a generous glass of wine. "Why is it I usually go for the conservative guys?"

He didn't have an easy response to that playful comment. "No idea," he responded dryly. "We're the boring ones."

"I don't find you boring at all." Hand on his knee suddenly, Karen looked at him meaningfully.

"I would think a hotshot pilot like Drew would be more your style."

"Seems to me he's taken. I'm going to guess you'll be best man at a wedding before long."

That was his fear too and the worst part would be that he'd want to be happy for both the bride and groom but might not be able to actually achieve that goal. There was going to be considerable personal conflict going on. "It's been put out there."

"I'd bet you make more money than he does. His job sounds sexy, but I have a fair idea what you IT guys can make. Sorry, but money is power, and power is sexy."

That was a superficial observation if he'd ever heard one.

"I actually have no idea," Rob said evenly. "He and I haven't exchanged that information." He glanced down at the lake. He'd never tire of the view of woods and water. "It looks like Lauren is back to her book and Drew is taking a siesta on the dock. I'm going to go jump in. Care to go for a swim?"

"Care to go upstairs? Like you said, they both seem occupied." Her smile was provocative despite their argument. "I've only had a little wine and here I am, thinking about sex."

Moment of truth. It was better, he told himself as he weighed his words, to get it over with.

"I'm pretty happy with a nice swim on this beautiful day." He might be conservative, but he was also a realist. He got to his feet.

"You're turning me down again?" She sounded incredulous.

"Remember that emotional thing I just mentioned? I meant it. For both our sakes."

"*Is* there someone else?"

That stopped him. Rob halted and turned around. "I wouldn't mind if you clarified that question."

"Are you seeing someone else?"

Rob squared his shoulders. He wanted this conversation, but yet he didn't. "I'm not seeing anyone else, but I am trying to get over an attraction to someone that just isn't going to work out."

"Is it Lauren?" She said it loudly too, probably on purpose because the woman in question looked up from her book.

He had to admit that took him off guard, but Drew had guessed it too. He settled on: "Why does it matter who it is?"

"It *is* her. That's why you're so detached? It seems to be the right word." She was angry, and he didn't blame her to a certain extent, but on the other hand, he'd truly been rail-roaded into this position with Karen. She clarified in clipped tones. "I've just always had this feeling because of the way you look at her."

"I wouldn't mind if we could keep this conversation more private."

"Too bad. I'm shit out of luck then, huh?" She stood up and gave him a tight smile. "I thought this was a long shot from the beginning. You've been polite to me. I will give you that. God, I am so pissed I wasted my time coming here. I'm going home."

Maybe he would have argued with that decision, but that would have been extremely hypocritical. He hadn't wanted her to come in the first place, flat out. He wasn't going to go that route, so he explained frankly. "I've been trying to figure out how to tell you this wasn't going to work out. I'm sorry. I really did not want to hurt your feelings."

She looked back over her shoulder as she walked into the house and shot back scathingly, "My feelings? Don't flatter yourself. My pride a little, but I'm already over it."

He felt bad, but then again, relieved.

He went down the steps and walked past Drew, whose eyes were wide open despite his seemingly relaxed pose on a towel like he was napping in the sun, hands behind his head. "Well," Rob said in passing, "that discussion went well. Not."

"I heard her part of it anyway. I think most of the county did. She has no problem raising her voice. There was definitely a 'hell hath no fury' moment going on."

"I believe I noticed that. I'm going for a swim."

Rob dove into the water. It was cool and cleansing and helped somewhat. He swam vigorously to the point where the lake led into the channel connecting to the next lake, and then turned around. At least she was leaving. The argument was over and resolved. It didn't fix his life but it helped cross something off the list.

Lauren had heard it as well. So be it, what was he supposed to do?

Take a long swim, that's what.

Neither she nor Drew were in sight when he got back and climbed out of the water.

He toweled off and resigned himself to going back up to the house. Not quite the restful afternoon he imagined, but then again Karen's car was gone.

Another uncomfortable discussion was in front of him, and he didn't want to have it either, but getting it all over with at once wasn't a bad thing.

Someone had even maybe had made him a sandwich. Lauren wasn't at the table, and when he came in Drew pointed to a seat. "Lunch."

He took a seat and accepted the plate. "Thanks. Arsenic or anything in this? Tell me Karen didn't leave it for me or else I'm going to make you take a bite first." He was only half-kidding.

"No. She wasn't all that happy when she left but Karen's gone, so just relax. Lauren made it. She's up taking a shower. I think we both waited until we heard Karen's car go to come up to the house. She didn't bother with fond goodbyes to either of us."

"It has nothing to do with you and everything to do with me. I accept full responsibility. You heard. Don't take it personally." He picked up the sandwich and didn't necessarily feel like eating, but knew he was hungry.

"I admire you for being upfront." Drew looked reflective, his blue eyes still holding a hint of amusement. "You have a ton of faults, but you cannot tell a lie. Not effectively. What you needed were three older brothers like I have. I was telling lies at two years old."

"A *ton* of faults?"

"If you deny that, Hanson, you just aren't paying attention."

"I'm not denying anything."

54

"So you didn't lie to Karen. It didn't exactly win you a popularity contest, but you knew you weren't going to get that trophy anyway."

"I wasn't expecting it to be pleasant. It wasn't."

"If you think Karen won't land squarely on her feet, think again. Remember, she's 'already over it'."

"I remember."

"You'll never hear from her again and she'll have already blocked you from every source of her social media."

"You need some work on your counseling skills." Rob set aside his sandwich.

"Hey, I have persuaded a terrified executive onto an overseas flight before cocktail hour. No easy task. My persuasive skills are fine. I'm not talking you off a ledge here — I was pointing out the bright side."

"*You're* relieved she's gone."

"Yep." He tipped back a beer, and then said, "It was tense enough before she came breezing in last night, and off the charts this morning."

It hadn't been exactly the relaxing vacation he'd planned either so far, so Rob agreed.

At least it couldn't get worse.

CHAPTER SEVEN

The blonde had taken her bag out and tossed it in her car with a vengeance.

Interesting, since her plates indicated she'd driven quite a distance for such a short stay. As the observer, he thought she was happy upon arrival, but not so happy on departure.

No, he knew *she wasn't happy on departure.*

Why?

It did make him wonder as he watched her climb in and back out recklessly, narrowly missing a tree.

Well, she was going and would be out of sight and out of mind. Good, he wanted rid of her.

His wish was answered a few moments later when he heard a knock on his door and went to open it.

* * *

"I think maybe we should go out to dinner."

Drew thought they needed a break after Karen's departure and Lauren had cooked breakfast and made lunch. "With all these highbrow houses around here, there has to be someplace nice. I might walk over and ask Heaston if he has a recommendation. He dropped in on us in a neighborly fashion. I don't see a man like him sitting around making

56

a grilled cheese sandwich so maybe he'd have a fair idea of where we could go."

"Let's just drive over and see what he has to say. Otherwise, we can figure it out on our own." Rob seemed on board with it. Drew had a feeling he would be fine if this particular day was over. He couldn't really blame him. Did the three of them really need to sit around staring at each other and not talking about it?

No.

"It sounds good to me."

"I'll drive so you can have a glass of expensive booze."

Rob lifted a brow. "Sounds like a deal to me, but I don't need a whiskey hug. I didn't lose the woman of my dreams."

He didn't have the woman of his dreams either.

Speaking of which, Lauren came into the kitchen, stunning with her hair loose and wearing a light-blue sundress.

"Dinner on the fly?" he asked her. "Something you don't have to cook."

"On the fly? Such a pilot term."

"I am a pilot. May I repeat you don't have to cook?"

"Oh, I caught that part, trust me. It sounds very nice. Almost better than *you* don't have to cook."

At least they were still teasing each other. Some tension still, yes, but working past it. Having Karen out of the picture helped. Everyone felt better.

"Hey, there's nothing wrong with boxed macaroni and cheese. I can make a mean frozen pizza too."

Rob was silent during all of this. He said finally, leaning against the counter, "I'm buying. I think I owe all of us for the drama."

"I don't think you really owe anyone for anything." Lauren looked at him.

The funny thing was Drew agreed. "That was all Karen, but a nice night out doesn't sound bad. Let's drop in on Professor Heaston and ask him where we should go."

Rob agreed. "Should be interesting. I want to see his house. My uncle said he's pretty reclusive, but he had no problem dropping in on us."

"I'm going to guess that house is over the top."

That proved to be true. It was a small mansion situated in a grove of pines and deserved the paved driveway to the top of the hill. Glass and cedar with multiple decks like Rob's uncle's house but toss in a pool with a courtyard and what appeared to be a guest house at the back.

Nice.

Heaston evidently wasn't home or else not answering the fancy faceted front door that had an artistic image of a weeping willow etched in the glass.

Drew checked his phone instead. "Ten miles down the road there's a fork and go left. In Willamette there's a small bistro called Andre's. The chef owns it and does all the cooking and he's French trained. He moved here to relax a little, according to the website. It says he'll come out to your table on most nights. The menu changes every day."

They backed out and followed the directions, and Lauren said in dry observation, "If Glenn Heaston was home, he wasn't exactly gushing over with inviting us into the house. There was a car there."

"Maybe he's not as tidy as he should be when his wife is out of town and didn't want to show us a messy house." Drew thought it was a little odd too, but other than that one dinner, he didn't know the man.

"It's possible he went out with friends." Rob apparently agreed. "Or could be he has the muse going and wanted to work uninterrupted. That's fine with me. I'm pretty hungry actually. Floating around in a boat all day is hard work."

So was breaking up with a girlfriend because you're drawn to someone else. Drew thought it but didn't say it.

The restaurant proved to be glass-fronted and discreetly elegant, but the parking lot was already full, and they sat in the bar for a short while before they were seated at a nice table in a corner. Bottle of wine delivered. All was well.

Except it wasn't. The three of them had a lot to say to each other.

Drew was notorious for weighing in very frankly in almost all situations, but this was different. This was his life, and the truth was, he was no angel either. This was tough because there were facets to the situation that weren't fair to all three of them, but full disclosure now didn't seem like a good decision. He chose to say instead, "Nice place."

It was a chic mixture of country and European elegance, understated but very high-end.

"No beer mirrors in sight." Rob took a sip from his glass. "Hmmm, great Merlot."

"You're buying, so I just ordered the most expensive one." Drew said it with a straight face.

"You'd do that, Fletcher. But in this case, I'm going to let it slide. You made a wonderful choice."

Lauren seemed more relaxed and that he didn't expect. "This was a good idea."

Drew gathered that Karen leaving was a very good thing for all of them, not just Rob. There was nothing like taking a tense situation and making it even tenser. When the waitress bustled back, a young, pretty woman in a stylish black skirt and white blouse, he went ahead and ordered for everyone by saying, "You pick for each of us. We're just going to trust you. Does that work?"

She was taken aback for a minute, but then rallied. "No problem. Any food allergies?"

They all shook their heads.

Lauren laughed and shook her head again as the waitress walked away. "Drew, really?"

He took a sip of wine first before he answered. "Babe, who is going to know better than anyone else what they'd order in a restaurant than someone on the wait staff? I do it all the time in many different countries. I ask them to bring me something good. They do. It never fails. I've eaten some interesting things, I'll admit that, but life is for adventure, right? Those giant cockroach things in the rainforest part of Australia that taste like lobster are great."

"You've eaten *what*?" Lauren stared at him.

He shrugged. "I was there. Why not? Saw it on a travel show."

"I am never riding on a plane with you. You're a cowboy."

"Well, if flying by the seat of your pants is about to come up, get over it. We mostly use instruments but can step in if we need to. Let's see how our dinner goes and then you can comment."

"It had better not be cockroach."

Rob had his back. "Admit he did a good job with the wine."

Drew had to grin. "Wait until you get the bill."

* * *

Dinner was fabulous. Small shrimp in butter, garlic, and asparagus, a pasta dish with lamb in tomato sauce, and duck confit accompanied by fingerling potatoes. The food was delivered with extra plates so they could share and taste all three dishes. Lauren could have sworn she didn't really have an appetite, but she certainly ate more than she expected.

Having Karen gone was such a relief. She wished she hadn't heard their argument, but she had, and some things just couldn't be undone. She didn't really blame Karen because while she would have walked away more quietly, she'd have walked too. He wasn't interested. She couldn't blame Rob either, because if he wasn't, he just wasn't and he'd done his best to express his feelings in a thoughtful way. There are some things that can't be forced.

Or helped.

He looked composed but resigned to the unhappy confrontation that had made Karen leave so dramatically. And he was also not quite as tense now that it was over. In Lauren's opinion — which might or might not be impartial — he deserved points for being as decent as possible under the circumstances. Whatever sexual encounter had — or had not apparently — occurred, he hadn't initiated it. She knew that much.

Unfortunately, so had Karen.

Lauren wasn't about to bring it up and she didn't care to examine her own conflicted feelings on the matter either. She set aside her fork. "That was delicious."

"It really was." Drew lifted his brows. "A round of applause for my ordering method, please."

"Don't be so smug," Rob said wryly.

As if on cue the waitress came back to their table, smiling brightly and holding a tray. "Chef Doumas wants to know how you liked the entrees and if there was a favorite. He changes the menu constantly and is always interested in the opinions of his guests. Now the pastry chef has already chosen for you." She presented the tray first to Drew. "You've started a competition in the kitchen."

Lauren realized right then that the waitress was flirting with Drew, not overtly, but at least a little. Right in front of her, which meant she thought Lauren was Rob's date because she seemed like a nice enough young woman.

"It all looks good." He seemed oblivious to it. "Let Lauren go first. I'm betting on the blueberry cheesecake as her choice."

No, not oblivious.

As for the cheesecake she definitely gave it her vote as an A+. And when they left, she drove since both Drew and Rob had definitely had more than one glass of wine each.

Winding roads and twilight woods made for an unsettling ambiance after a fairly eventful day. And when a deer dashed across the road she had to slam on the brakes because it came out of nowhere and she could swear she missed it by inches. That was all they needed. A car accident would round out the evening nicely.

She thought they were all relieved to pull in and disembark safely. Not because of her driving but because the day was about over.

"I vote we watch a movie." That was Drew as he got out of the car.

"I get to pick."

"Oh, hell, no. You like romantic comedies." He opened her door. "I don't know if I can take it."

"Drink beer," she suggested. "It'll get you through."

He groaned and at least Rob laughed as he shut the car door. "She has a point there. You were planning on it anyway."

"I was," Drew conceded.

"No surprise there, Fletcher."

"Like you weren't, Hanson."

They were funny together, she had to admit it. Grown men still acting like college boys every once in a while, but everyone maybe needed that. She had a couple of close friends from high school and every once in a while they got together to laugh and gossip, but her main confidant was her sister, Jana. They texted or talked every day pretty much but she'd only described the stunning cabin, sent a few pictures from her phone to show how beautiful it was on the lake, and left out the drama.

She wasn't ready to talk about her interesting relationship situation at all, not even with her best friend.

* * *

The flickering images on the screen began to roll to the credits. Probably just because Drew had goaded her into it, Lauren *had* picked a light-hearted comedy with romantic overtones, not that it mattered to him. Rob was so aware of her it was like a physical touch and he'd watch anything right now, even a documentary on the social life of sea anemones.

Drew snorted and pushed a button on the remote to send the screen to black. The media room was just off the main part of the house, furnished with a leather sectional, glass tables, and massive system. Lauren had her legs curled under her, all three of them on the huge couch. "What was that sound for? You were laughing through the entire movie."

"I'm sorry. These chick movies all end the same." He shrugged derisively.

"Why was it a 'chick' movie? Be careful, Drew, you're sounding like a misogynist with a comment like that. Because there weren't a bunch of armed bad guys running around being foiled by the good guys also with guns?"

"Misogynist? Me? I think women are smarter than most men, work harder, and deserve our utmost respect. I am also a true fan of your gender for myriad reasons besides those. But all these movies — some of which are directed by men for your information — all end with the same sappy kiss."

"I thought it was sweet," Lauren argued. "Happily ever after. What more could anyone want?"

"How about an I-want-to-fuck-you kiss?"

Drew had definitely had a little too much to drink.

She gave him a scathing look he probably deserved. "Oh yeah, that's romantic."

"No, no, no." Drew plucked the wineglass from her hand and set it aside on the polished coffee table. "I beg to differ. It's very romantic."

"Hey, give me that back." She reached for the glass.

Drew snagged her wrist. "I'll be more than happy to show you how it's done."

Rob was just going to stay out of this one.

"You're an expert, is that it?" Her eyes narrowed.

"You tell me."

"Fletcher, you are on rocky ground here." Rob said it without inflection.

His comment was ignored.

She looked more than startled when Drew leaned in and went for it, slanting his mouth against hers possessively, because it wasn't part of his makeup to do anything halfway. She stiffened at first, probably because Rob was sitting right next to her, but relaxed after a moment or two.

It was surprisingly erotic to watch her body stance change. Every male understood when a female responded to him and when she really wasn't all that interested, and the reverse was true as well if Karen had been telling the truth.

Rob hadn't wanted the intimacy, and it hadn't — in his opinion — been a bad call to just say no.

"Well," Drew asked with a cheeky grin when they parted, "how'd I do?"

In answer she gave an exaggerated shrug, her cheeks a vivid pink. "That was a good effort, I suppose, but—"

"A good effort?" He took her shoulders and turned her toward where Rob sat on the couch. "This is a challenge. Hanson, let's see how you do."

Whatever Rob was expecting, it wasn't that. He wasn't the only one. Lauren's eyes widened. "Drew, let's not take this too far here."

If he thought about it too much, he wouldn't do it, and if she thought about it too much, she'd never agree either. Rob wasn't exactly sure why Drew had just practically dared him to do what he wanted to do in the worst way, but he wasn't going to argue the point. He asked in a not quite steady voice, "Give me a shot at the best kiss title?"

He just kissed her without her answer, his hands closing over her waist as he tugged her closer. With the first touch of his lips, she gave a betraying tremble but then opened for the brush of his tongue.

Heaven.

The roundness of her hip pressed his thigh and she tasted like warm woman and wine. He chose a different approach and was restrained, the exploration of her mouth gentle yet urgent, and he didn't do anything else except run his fingers lightly up her bare arm in a gentle caress, the other arm encircling her waist.

He was still sure she could feel his passionate hunger. A declaration without words of how he felt and what he wanted.

Best kiss of his life anyway hands down, but then again, he'd really never had a first kiss with a woman he was in love with, so this was uncharted territory. Her mouth was warm and soft, and the scent and feel of her was both evocative and visceral.

She'd definitely participated and when he lifted his head and looked into her eyes she seemed a little shell-shocked. His voice was barely audible when he asked, "How'd I do?"

It took a moment but she finally said, "Have the two of you always been this competitive?" She shook her head and got it together, pulling away. "You both know what you're doing and we'll leave it at that, plus add that I refuse to be the judge in any more ridiculous male contests. I'm going to bed. Good night."

They both watched her leave the room and Rob had to say into the resulting silence, "I think it is entirely possible we've both had a little too much to drink. Why the hell did you do that to me? Why the hell did I do that to you?"

Drew lounged back, a rueful smile on his face. "I really kind of did it to myself too, so keep that in mind. I don't know why. Some measure of guilt for the fact if I wasn't in the picture — and I probably shouldn't be — I think you and Lauren might be really good together."

A confusing declaration if there ever was one. "Good grief, Fletcher, I wouldn't even know Lauren if it wasn't for you."

"You don't understand. I need to just talk to her about something. I've been avoiding it. I find it ironic that you and I can talk about it, but I can't to her. To tell the truth, I've pretty much avoided you on this subject too."

This whole day hadn't made a lot of sense, and that statement didn't help matters.

Rob looked at his friend searchingly, not sure what was coming next. "What? What subject?"

Drew sharply took in a breath. "I'm married."

What the hell?

That was an unexpected bombshell. Rob searched for the right words. As a matter of fact, he searched for any words at all. All he came up with finally was: "Uh . . . you aren't required to tell me every detail of your life or anything, but how could I not know this?"

Drew explained with obvious reluctance. "I started a relationship with one of the female executives I flew regularly and she took charge of that as she does most things. When she suggested marriage, I was free and single . . . it was romantic — elopement to a tropical island, great sex and long lazy days relaxing together, but that isn't real life. Cassandra is a busy professional, and I'm gone constantly. It hasn't worked out. Surprise, surprise. Stupid of me to think it ever would. Everyone makes mistakes, that's a given. We have a house but are just never there at the same time. I moved out and bought the condo more convenient to the airport since the house is what she wanted and picked out. End of story. Divorce is pending."

"How long ago did this happen?" He was incredulous.

"Two years. Unfortunately, I think after the first three months we understood our lifestyles were going to make it impossible. But we hung on for a while, ignoring it was a mistake every time we did get together."

"You didn't tell me?"

"No. I told my father and stepmother just out of courtesy because I don't really communicate with them often, as you know, but by the time I did, I already knew it was not my best decision. Maybe . . . oh hell, I don't even know. I wanted it to work, but it didn't." He looked away, his expression taut.

"Lauren. She doesn't know?"

"No." Drew sighed and rubbed his jaw. "I have to tell her. I thought the divorce would be over and done before now."

Rob smiled humorlessly, still trying to assimilate this new information. "I'm not quite as impartial as I could be, but my opinion is you *do* have to tell her."

"No, you aren't impartial and yet you're correct. I'm not looking forward to it."

CHAPTER EIGHT

He leveled the telescope, saw the cars were there, but they weren't outside enjoying the beautiful starlit evening.

Dark house. He wondered what kind of conversation they might be having . . .

The impression was the trio was regrouping and taking the defection much better than the blonde had done.

Passing them on the road had been interesting. Part of him felt ingenious. Part of him wondered at the wisdom of some of the chances he'd taken, but there truly was a method to the calculated risks and he'd been very careful.

Careful enough was always the question.

He was discovering it was part of the thrill.

He'd always wondered about that facet of the game.

* * *

The dark car pulled in about ten o'clock in the morning.

Drew was sitting on the deck brooding about the night before, trying to figure out his options. He'd told Rob and that was something, but he had no idea if that was the right decision or not.

Lauren had no idea she was sleeping with a married man, and it just wasn't fair. It didn't matter it was over and the divorce pending — it mattered he hadn't been entirely honest.

It mattered a lot. He'd fallen for Lauren but there was a measure of guilt there that took away from that happiness, and if she was torn, and Rob was torn, he was in the same proverbial boat.

Rob was a good-looking, successful young guy and that turned Karen on, which was fine, but what didn't seem to register with her was that he was an old-fashioned farm boy at heart. He and Lauren were probably perfect for each other.

That aside, the new arrivals, what was going on now?

The two men who got out of the car didn't look like they worked in an office even though one of them wore a suit. One was fairly young in his mid-thirties or so, jeans and a button-up shirt, blond hair, a casual air with an athletic build, the well-dressed one older, balding, maybe fifty. They walked toward the house like they had a purpose and came up the steps.

Since he was on the bottom deck, Drew was the first one they encountered and he stood up, puzzled but not alarmed. "Can I help you?"

"Detectives Carter and Bailey." The older one flashed a badge.

Now he was alarmed. He had to blink. "Detectives?"

"Yes. Can we talk to you?"

He couldn't think of a single reason to refuse. "Of course. About what?"

"We tend to ask the questions." It was a pleasant but firm response.

He supposed that was a valid point. "Since I have no idea what you're talking about, go ahead. Ask away."

"You are?"

"Andrew Fletcher."

"How long have you been in residence here, Mr. Fletcher?"

"Three days. Well, this is now day four, I guess. We're on vacation."

A lot had happened in that time period. It certainly seemed longer, but that was correct.

"Would you mind taking a look at a photo?"

"No, not at all."

He looked at it, but didn't recognize the subject. A slender woman, well-groomed, her clothing chic and obviously expensive, middle-aged but attractive. He handed it back. "I'm sorry, I've never seen her."

"Mrs. Heaston seems to have dropped off the radar. Neither her husband nor her sister can get in touch with her. They have both reported her missing in separate jurisdictions."

Whoa, Heaston's *wife*? He digested that. "As in Mrs. Glenn Heaston?"

"Yes, sir."

"He said she went home to Lexington. We got here on Friday but had dinner with him on Saturday and she was gone by then."

"Had he heard from her?"

"He didn't say, but I didn't get the impression that it would be unusual if he hadn't. She leaves him in solitude so he can write." Drew emphasized carefully as he said, "That is only what *I* took away from the conversation."

"What else did you take away?"

"He certainly didn't act like he thought anything was wrong, but then again, that was a few days ago."

The young one, Bailey, asked, "Did he say anything else?"

"Is he a suspect?"

"Everyone is a suspect." Bailey, not antagonistic but blunt, was forthright. "No offense. Part of the job. What were you doing Friday night?"

Apparently, everyone *was* a suspect. It was just disconcerting to be one.

"We grilled steaks and ate dinner." *I made love to my girlfriend, possibly for the last time, but that is none of your business.*

"Dr. Heaston said you have three people staying here . . . can we talk to the other two?"

Nice of them to ask permission, when the truth was, of course they could talk to them anyway. He gave the requisite directions. "Feel free. Rob Hanson is in the house and Lauren Mathews is on the dock."

The three of them — all apart. That was telling. His life was pretty upside down, so this new glitch was par for the course. He really needed to talk to Lauren as well. Trying to figure out how to do it was a problem. He owned what had happened last night.

He really couldn't quite figure that out either, so she had to be wondering what the hell was going on if he couldn't explain it to himself.

Maybe it had been a test of loyalty. Maybe Rob was right and he'd imbibed a little too much alcohol.

Lauren didn't know anything about the disappearance, but neither did Rob, so it didn't matter. He felt bad for Heaston, but it didn't have anything to do with the three of them.

He had some real problems of his own. "I'll go down and tell Lauren you want to talk to her if you want to talk to Rob first." She was in her bathing suit and Drew was sure she wouldn't want to talk to detectives while lying on a towel in a skimpy bikini.

"We'd appreciate it."

"I'll go get her."

* * *

Rob was on his computer trying to clear up a few things at work when there was a light rap on the glass door that still managed to sound like it meant business. Two men, both with badges out, greeted him with their names and he was definitely surprised. Uncertainly, he said, "Hello."

"Rob Hanson?"

"Yes."

"Mind if we come in and have a word?"

"No, I suppose not." He gestured at the table, not certain at all what was going on. "Have a seat."

"Thank you. Wow, nice place." The young one gazed up at the soaring ceilings.

"It belongs to my uncle, but thanks. Can I ask why you're here?"

"Mrs. Heaston appears to be missing and we wanted to know if you have observed anything unusual since your arrival." The one who introduced himself as Carter asked the question, his demeanor friendly but his eyes keen and focused.

"I don't know." Rob sat down and closed his computer. "I suppose I thought it was at least absent-minded of Glenn Heaston to be out in his canoe when a front was clearly rolling in on Saturday night, but I have no idea how tuned in he is to the weather, so unusual might apply or might not. He works from home, so maybe not too worried about it. We invited him to have dinner with us, but that was actually the first time I'd ever met him. It was one of those situations when we were about to eat and it was clear he couldn't leave right then, so why not. He didn't mention his wife was missing or seem worried."

The questions were rapid fire after that.

"Had you ever met Mrs. Heaston?"

"No."

"Not once, not even last summer when you were here?"

Was that an assumption or had Drew told them?

"Not then either. My impression is she doesn't actually spend much time here. In fact, Heaston said she doesn't."

"But *you* were here last summer?"

Why that question? He was certainly surprised. "I usually come at least once in the summer and again in the fall."

The young one said, "Nice free vacation in a great place, is that it?"

"Exactly."

There was a point to this he didn't like. At all. He just didn't know what it might be.

"When last summer?"

"Summer is a term covering months. I'm not sure just off the cuff . . . why?"

"Last summer a young woman was found drowned here and that investigation is open. If you can't help us with Mrs. Heaston, since this is the same lake and we have to talk to you anyway, we wondered if you saw anything then either."

He really did not remember exactly when. "I can look to find out the time frame, but honestly I don't think I can recall anything that stands out. That's last year. If I saw something suspicious and it was alarming, I would have said something at the time."

"If you would look up those dates, we'd appreciate it for our notes."

Good to hear? No. He wasn't sure he wanted to be part of their notes at all.

Just then Lauren and Drew came in. She was wearing only a towel and a bathing suit and looked gorgeous with the sheen of sunscreen on her smooth skin.

Or maybe he was just biased.

No, the universal male reaction seemed to be appreciation for the scenery. Nothing overt and other than polite, but it annoyed him, and probably Drew as well, but he was still reeling from last night's revelation, so Drew's right to be annoyed was open for debate. So was his.

She held out her hand. "Lauren Mathews."

They both shook it with alacrity and introduced themselves. Why was it he thought her interview was going to go better than his?

"We've asked Mr. Fletcher and Mr. Hanson if they have noticed anything unusual during your stay here and wondered if you could also weigh in. Mrs. Heaston has been reported missing."

Surprisingly, she said decisively, "Yes, I have. Dr. Heaston put something heavy in his boat the first morning we were here."

The police officers both looked interested. First Rob had heard of it too. Drew didn't look clued in either.

"And then?" Carter asked.

"He sailed off and I wasn't there when he came back." She paused. "I know this isn't helpful really, but it just sounded weird when he dropped it in. Like dead weight. It could be nothing, but I will tell you, I noted he looked around."

"Did he see you?"

"Yes. I was sitting there reading on the bank."

That didn't make Rob happy at all. "Lauren, why didn't you say something?"

She lifted her slender shoulders. "Like what? All he did was put something in his boat. It wasn't necessarily unusual to me, it was more off-color because it seemed like he was checking to see if anyone was watching. Why would I think something was wrong? At the time I'd never even met Dr. Heaston."

"You had dinner together. Did he say anything about that incident? Ask you about it?" Carter again was the one asking the questions.

"He mentioned he'd seen me reading on the bank and was quite charming in an amusing way about asking if it was one of his books. That's all."

End of story.

The two officers nodded then and departed, leaving their cards in case any of them recalled any more information. He, Lauren, and Drew were left together not by choice but by circumstance.

Awkward silence.

"Was it right to even tell them that? The husband is always the first suspect, isn't he?" Lauren sank into a chair and looked repentant. "I just thought it was weird at the time. Only a little off-color, but still—"

"It was right." Rob sat back down opposite because he'd gotten politely to his feet when she came in. "Their job is to investigate, and while it might seem like nothing to you and me, it might really be something."

"It didn't seem like nothing."

He spread his hands. "There you have it."

"Lauren, I really need to talk to you." That was Drew, subdued but resolute from the look on his face. "And it has nothing to do with Heaston, trust me."

So he was going to do it. He needed to tell her, but this was between them, so Rob got back up to his feet. "I'm going to go cast a few lines. It's a nice morning."

He'd thought this vacation couldn't get more complicated.

It seemed to be headed that direction.

CHAPTER NINE

There was a certain magic to timing. He'd called in the missing person report just when he should have, so that worked.

A method to the madness.

There was every chance Angela's sister knew the truth. Felicity would have no problem pointing a finger in his direction.

She was an unpredictable bitch.

Let her prove it.

She couldn't, and if she tried, she might be very sorry indeed.

He held the cards and had stacked the deck.

* * *

Chris Bailey looked out the windshield, absently noticing the passing scenery as they wound through the county forest headed back to the office in Willamette, but his mind was elsewhere.

There was no evident crime, no body, and no car. He hated these vague cases. The one piece they could maybe use was from a young woman in a skimpy bathing suit who thought she heard a dull thud.

At this point not even a homicide.

The missing woman's husband certainly was not frantic but had explained why. Chris had read the report three times at least. Mrs. Heaston could be shopping on Park Avenue or taken off for Italy and they were wasting their time. She had the money and had been known to do it before.

Chris had done it too. He went impulsively to Florida on a road trip once with some college buddies and forgot his phone charger, so no one really knew where he was. He'd eaten a lot of fast food and stayed at a very cheap motel. His parents had been pretty ticked off at him being AWOL but it hadn't occurred to him it was a big deal.

Not quite the same but the point was it could be that simple.

Carter was a good detective but very old-school. They didn't clash but they didn't necessarily see eye to eye on things all the time. Chris was a lot faster to make up his mind and Carter was more methodical. There was something to be said for both approaches, but it only jelled some of the time.

He looked over at the driver's side. "I don't like Ms. Mathews' rendition of what happened."

Carter drove like he did everything else, carefully. His response was to the point. "You don't trust her, or you didn't like what she had to say?"

"The latter."

"It was inconclusive."

Chris shook his head. "That's not what I mean. She saw nothing, I agree. But Heaston sought her out that night. Why? You've been doing this a lot longer than me. That didn't stand out to you?"

"Oh, it did."

Chris knew Carter was an enigmatic man who really did not want to be partnered with someone so different in age and experience but was intelligent enough to not let it show through very often. They brought something different to the table on each investigation and so far the collaboration had really worked out well when it came to positive results in solving cases. Therefore, mutual respect existed, but not necessarily mutual accord.

"He wanted to know what she saw."

Carter braked for a four-way stop, his right-turn signal on. "Or he saw a very attractive young woman reading and is a novelist and decided to pay a neighborly visit to get a closer look."

"That has occurred to me too." Chris tapped his fingers on his knee as they turned west. "This just feels like a homicide to me. Same exclusive lake with those big expensive houses and while cause of death was ruled drowning and manner of death undetermined by the medical examiner, that first victim had suffered a blow to the head and was probably unconscious when she went into the water."

"That young woman didn't live on the lake. It appears she was dumped there, or visiting someone."

"Appears is the operative word there. If she was visiting someone, why wasn't she reported as missing? She's still a Jane Doe."

"We didn't work that case."

"No, but it wasn't ruled a homicide either. Maybe we *should* have worked it."

"Okay, hotshot, maybe so. But we have other cases and when the ME says manner of death undetermined, the sheriff doesn't necessarily treat it like a homicide. The only reason we are asking questions about Mrs. Heaston is because Lexington asked for us to help on this end."

"It wasn't ruled an accidental drowning. I want to know if Heaston was there at the time and I want to know if Rob Hanson was there. I took algebra and hated it, but common denominators are at work for me."

"Two possible suspects, I agree. But not two homicides. One drowning and one rich middle-aged lady who could be off at a spa somewhere having a facial. It doesn't make for a murder case in either case without more evidence. Same lake, I agree. I don't like it. However, it could easily mean nothing. People drown in lakes. It happens."

"Wasting our time?"

"Wasting our time for now."

I don't necessarily agree, Chris thought grimly.

When they walked back into the office, Doreen, who ran the front office, looked at them both pointedly. "You both have messages on your desks from a woman named Felicity Barrett. She would like daily updates on the case involving her missing sister. I refrained from mentioning you two have other cases and there are only so many hours in the day."

It had to be the Heaston case.

Why was it Chris was resigned to the fact that this was going to be complicated.

* * *

"Let's go out to the deck and talk."

Lauren had a feeling they should because to say she was confused was an understatement. Drew's unusual actions the night before were part of it but she wasn't exactly blameless. She'd not necessarily encouraged Rob, but neither had she resisted that telling kiss.

Truth be told, she'd wondered what it would be like more than once or she would have made more of an argument. Rob no doubt sensed that, but then again, Drew had apparently known it as well.

Should she apologize? Not sure if embarrassed was the right word, but maybe chagrined described her reaction to her own actions. She took a chair, reasoned it was Drew's fault because he'd put her in that position, but maybe she should apologize.

"Drew, I—"

"I'm married." He hadn't sat down, but stood there by the railing, visible tension in his posture.

To say that stark declaration took her by surprise was an understatement of substantial proportion.

"What?"

To his credit he didn't look happy. At all. "I'll clarify. Separated and in the process of a divorce, but in a technical sense still married. I was going to tell you once it was final — it is no deep, dark secret — but I wanted to wait until then. She's dragging her feet now and my lawyer says there's almost nothing I can do to make this go faster."

She was reeling. "Drew."

"I'm in love with you, Lauren. The trouble is I don't think I'm the only one."

No, whatever was happening, he wasn't going to get away with that. "Don't even cloud the issue. We've been dating for months. How could you not *tell* me?"

"I was looking for the right time and just don't think I can wait any longer. Half the time I'm not even in the country, so I wanted us to have an opportunity to really talk about it."

"That's not my fault. I can't believe this."

His expression was brooding. "I thought it would be settled long before this conversation had to happen, Lauren. I swear it. This thing with you and Rob is a lot more on my mind."

She was honestly not sure if she should cry or laugh hysterically. Maybe both would be appropriate. "I have no idea what to say to that."

"That you understand at least a little would be helpful."

"I can understand to the extent that if you had told me you were a married man, I would have walked away before our first date."

"Tell me something I don't know. Why do you think I didn't say anything before now? It's over. I haven't asked details about every single relationship you've ever had. Before now I also have never said anything about you and Rob."

"There *is* no me and Rob."

"Please. I saw that kiss."

"*You* suggested it, and I'm really wondering why now. Are we actually arguing about you not telling me you're married? You have no argument. You lied to me."

"I think I just did tell you."

He had. She tried to calm down. Deep breath in, deep breath out. "Better late than never. I've slept with you."

"We've made love. Different."

"I wonder if your wife would feel that way. I contributed to you cheating on her." She got up on shaky legs. "I'm going back to my book because this morning lends itself to fiction a lot more than reality. I can't deal with police officers and your sudden urge to reveal the truth at the same time."

He deserved that one, but she wasn't exactly blameless either.

Rob was on the dock. She walked down there slowly, wondering if it was a wise decision. He had his fishing pole in hand and turned, took one look at her face, and said, "I'm going to guess he told you."

"Yes."

"I have no idea if you want my opinion or not, but if you do, let me know."

"I'm so furious with him." She meant it and sank down on the warm wood to wrap her arms around her knees.

"I think," he said in a measured tone, "you need to weigh in that if there is one thing I know about Drew it is he is about as forthcoming as anyone can be. If he thought his marriage was viable, he would never have approached you at all. He became emotionally involved with you even though maybe he shouldn't have. He didn't do this on purpose. I can totally understand his duplicity."

She knew Rob meant his feelings for her. He wasn't trying to win a contest with that heart-stopping kiss. He was trying to tell her something.

"The two of you aren't making my life any easier either. Have you met her?"

"Drew's wife? No. I had no idea she even existed. I . . ." He stopped then, trailing off. "Hmm, maybe I have. A woman stopped by his condo once to drop something off while I was there. He didn't introduce her and all he said to her about me was 'this is Rob'. I thought it was a little off at

80

the time, like she might know who I was but I had no clue about her."

"That's hard to believe. You two are best friends."

"But still true. I admit I don't even know how to comment on that. I was pretty shocked when he told me and that was just last night after you went up to bed. He said they eloped and then I guess the honeymoon was pretty much over, so he didn't say anything. Knowing Drew, he was probably gone half the time anyway."

That was an echo of an excuse she didn't want to hear.

"Let's change the subject. This thing with Heaston's wife—"

"I know." He interrupted, which Rob didn't normally do. "Tell me about it. The police also wanted to know if I was here last summer when some woman drowned."

Lauren gazed at him, confounded. "Like you might be involved? Did they really ask you that?"

"Yeah, they really did." He sounded serious. "It was implied, not said outright, that maybe foul play is suspected."

"My impression is you'd catch a spider in your house and then set it free outside."

"I'd like to think I'm not perfect, but pretty harmless."

He wasn't harmless to her peace of mind. Those striking hazel eyes, the dark wavy hair — he was undeniably attractive and she understood Karen's anger over it not working out between them. Maybe not the way it was handled by her, but at least the disappointment. "I don't see you on a wanted poster anywhere in a post office."

"Thanks." His smile was brief and without humor. "Let's hope they are with you on that one."

She hoped for the same thing. No one like Rob could ever be a true suspect. "I'm sure they just wanted to know if you had any information they could use."

"That's what they said. I just wasn't positive I liked the tone of their questions."

"They are detectives, not greeters at a local grocery store. Of course they are concise and to the point."

"Maybe so. Let me operate on the same level. How did you leave it with Drew?"

"I just left it. I walked away so I could think about it. I need to process."

"I can understand that. I'm sort of in the same place. I'm trying to figure out why he didn't talk to me either."

"Well, we have that in common then."

"I wonder if maybe *he* wonders why he didn't talk to either of us."

"It was reckless and impulsive and he was afraid he'd made a mistake right away?"

To her surprise Rob hesitated, but then said offhandedly, "Or isn't quite so convinced it was a mistake. He said they are mid-divorce, and that they had quickly realized it wasn't working, but why he still kept it so quiet is very out of character in my opinion."

That brought clarity into full view. Was Drew not sure about the divorce? How could she even possibly fault him for that? Look at her, at odds over him and Rob.

"Did he say that?"

"No. You are getting my take on it only."

"What am I supposed to do? He's *married*. He never lied to me. He just failed to mention it."

"What you shouldn't do is ask me. I'm not impartial, remember. Oh, I'm trying, but impartial I'm not."

She stood up. "Let's dump this topic also. Teach me how to fish."

Rob looked at her like she'd sprouted wings and suggested they fly off to the moon. "What?"

"Yep, it is supposed to be so relaxing and I could use that. You and Drew think it is definitely the way to pass the time. Teach me how. I want to catch a fish. Use a fishing pole. I've never done it."

"Really? Not even bluegill as a kid? Worm on the hook and a bobber in the water? There's no thrill like having that bobber go under."

"Nope. I want to give it a whirl and not just take your word for it."

"Okay, talking my language. My tackle box is in the boat and you can use my pole. Let's go."

He steadied the boat for her and she climbed in and sat on a flotation cushion in the middle seat. He turned the handle on the motor and they moved away from the dock.

It actually was relaxing, she discovered as they cruised slowly through the water for the next hour or so. All she really had to do was hold the fishing pole in her hand but the scenery was wonderful with the trees crowding down to the shore, and while she didn't catch anything — though there were a few tugs to her line — she had a new appreciation for the sport. It wasn't exciting, but it was woods and water and the sun.

More relaxed but still not exactly ready to deal with it all was how she would characterize her psyche when they got back. Drew was *married*.

"I'm normally so comfortable around him," she said without preamble. "I don't think Drew lies to me."

"Or me." Rob knew exactly what she meant, no explanation necessary. He held out his hand to help her out of the boat after he'd tied it up. "And he hasn't, it was a sin of omission."

His hand was warm and strong and she held on to it even after she climbed onto the dock. They just stood there, looking at each other, his fingers tightening around hers in a gentle squeeze.

"In my case a really big sin," she said emphatically. "Can I move to Karen's room?"

"You can do whatever you want." Rob frowned. "Talk to Drew, Lauren. Like I said, he'll explain. I really didn't ask too many questions I was so taken off guard, and I assume you were probably the same."

"I'll talk to him," she said quietly. Then vowed silently, *But I sure as hell won't sleep with him.*

CHAPTER TEN

He adjusted the telescope and poured a glass of bourbon. He was so surprisingly relaxed he almost couldn't even believe it.

He'd done his best, but expediency was necessary. He'd handled the vehicles separately.

An old, rotting empty barn.

A mall parking lot.

He could move them around later. Perfect. He wished he could sell his wife's expensive luxury car and maybe he could down the line. There were people that didn't ask questions.

No connection. No witnesses.

Time to think about another topic entirely.

The tall dark-haired one, Hanson, had taken Lauren out in the boat and they appeared to be having an earnest conversation on the dock, holding hands. Fletcher was nowhere in sight.

Why?

It really begged the question — trouble in paradise?

The dynamic had changed and he was very intrigued.

* * *

Drew checked on his email and closed his computer when he saw a message from his lawyer. So far they never contained good news. He didn't even open it. A better plan was in order, but he didn't have one.

At all.

When Rob and Lauren came in, he was making a chicken sandwich in the microwave. Not good for you, but he didn't care at the moment. He ate in airports all the time. "Any fish?" he asked, trying to be cordial but not begging for forgiveness either. He was maybe the most culpable, but not the only guilty party in the room.

"I had some bites," Lauren informed him, her tone still cool. "Oh, I mean strikes. I'm still catching on to the angler lingo. But no, I didn't catch a fish."

Rob said, "After lunch maybe you two should go out. It's nice on the water. Lauren learned how to cast in about three tries."

He was trying to stay unbiased. And it couldn't be easy for him.

"He means I didn't hook his shirt on the third try. The first two, he almost went into the lake."

At least she smiled. It was guarded. Drew was really in deep shit, but she tried.

Drew smiled back, mostly in relief. She was talking to him. "I don't think you have the heft to bring him down but go ahead. Toss him in the drink."

"Don't underestimate me." She gave him a very pointed look. "I don't know if you have the nerve to be out in a boat with me. Talk about dangerous."

"Trust me, I have the good sense to *not* be out in a boat with you right now."

"That works for me since if you could cheat at fishing, you probably would."

"Low blow, Lauren," he said reproachfully. "I'm separated and we have filed for divorce. That isn't cheating. I have no idea what she's doing. Like none."

She did relent. At least a little. "Rob thinks I should talk to you."

"I think we should talk about a lot of things."

Rob, he noticed, decided to leave the room as unobtrusively as possible by walking into the den. Drew murmured, "The deck sounds safe enough."

"I could still throw you over the railing."

"Whatever happened to talking?"

She headed for the stairs. "I just don't know what to say. I'm going to leave the talking up to you. I'm going to go change."

He got out a beer and a glass and poured her some wine since the moment definitely needed it, and then went outside. What a beautiful day. Great flying weather. He almost wished he was on a plane right then. This hadn't been a very relaxing vacation so far. He wasn't convinced it was going to get any better, but it had to rank up there with the most interesting.

Lauren came out unfortunately no longer in a bathing suit but a causal top and shorts and barefoot. She was still beautiful but he was partial to more bare skin. She looked at the wine and lifted her brows. "A little early, isn't it?"

"For this conversation, maybe not."

She picked up the glass. "Oh, I can't wait. Then go ahead."

"I get why you're angry but life is unpredictable. How could I know I was going to meet you?"

"If it wasn't for Rob, would you have ever told me?"

That was actually an astute question, but Lauren was bright. He told her the truth. "Eventually, of course."

"When?"

That was fair. "Like I said, the day after my divorce was final probably."

The day I asked you to marry me instead. He didn't say that out loud since this was definitely not the time. Besides, he wasn't sure now he wanted to jump feet first into marriage again. The situation with her and Rob made him even less sure.

"I guess I can see that," she conceded, but hardly let him off the hook. "That would have been an interesting conversation. 'By the way, I'm single now'. I don't think I'd have liked that any better than this one."

"I'm thinking I can't win."

"I'm thinking this is a day I got up and didn't see this hit coming. It could be worse, you could be suspected of murder."

"Where did that come from?" he said, not certain of the segue.

"The detectives asked Rob if he was here during the time a woman was found drowned in this lake last summer. I think coupled with Heaston's wife going missing, they are really sniffing around."

"Not around *him*?"

"I wasn't there for the conversation."

That was just ludicrous when it came to Rob. "No. They are nuts. I'm not doing myself any favors here but he's the nicest guy in the world."

"I agree."

"Thanks."

"Well, you ranked up there too before recent events."

No, not getting off easy for this one. "I'm a nice guy as well. I haven't murdered anyone and neither has he."

"I agree again."

"Lauren, I've apologized but can you see it from my point of view, please? Cassandra and I agree we aren't together. For all intents and purposes, I'm single."

"Oh, that's her name."

"Yes."

Lauren looked away. "Then why is she dragging her feet?"

Good question. He'd wondered over that as well. Cassandra had blocked him at every turn. They'd sat down and agreed on the divorce with a mediator. Her idea. He had no idea what was going on since that meeting. "I'm not sure. I don't think it is to spite me. I'd guess she's too busy to bother with it. I'm out of the country all the time, but then again so is she. It just didn't work out for us. I haven't seen her since just before I met you."

"Do you still love her?"

He'd been expecting that question and wasn't surprised she asked it. "To a certain extent I do, but then again love is not an exclusive emotion. I *do* love *you*. I think you can acknowledge romantic involvement is complicated."

She retorted, "That was a dig I didn't need. I acknowledge romantic involvement with *you* is complicated."

"Right back at you. If we are going to have an argument, should we talk about Rob as well?"

That hit home. She shook her head after a moment, the look in her eyes distant. "Maybe not."

* * *

Chris had reviewed the unsolved file again. Cause of death was drowning. Manner of death was undetermined. In the notes, the medical examiner did say it was possible she'd been unconscious and put in the water because of the suspicious contusion but it was also possible that a boating accident caused the bruises. She'd been wearing a swimsuit. Young, probably mid-twenties, and as of yet not identified.

It was possible, considering the affluence of people who lived on that lake, she was a fatality at a party and there was alcohol involved so no one wanted to admit to knowing her for liability reasons. She'd definitely had some in her system when the autopsy bloodwork came back. No sexual assault involved.

That was good. He hated those cases.

One possible scenario was that a rich boy has a wild party at his parent's lake house and someone dies and suddenly no one knows her. Maybe they don't even remember her getting knocked off the dock or the boat. If she came with an invited guest maybe the owners truly didn't know her name or if she was even there.

But someone . . . somewhere, knew who she was. Yet no one had bothered to report her absence from this earth. Law enforcement had used the media to ask the public for any possible identification and had no success.

Why had no one reported a missing woman her age that they could match? It just didn't make sense to him and he didn't like it when things didn't make sense.

Maybe that was why he'd been promoted to detective.

He was good at it, or he hoped so and he was learning every day.

Any unexplained death bothered him.

There was a story there.

He wrote down the most obvious. *Not from this area. Missing from somewhere else.*

He needed to see if he could narrow down how she got here from there. With no personal information that was difficult. Maybe a girlfriend invited her, maybe a random guest . . . this was a tough one. Swimsuit. That was something. She wasn't just hitchhiking down the road. Nicely trimmed nails — the ME was meticulous about those details if asked — and a tan that matched the suit.

Rich place, dead unidentified girl.

The possibilities were pretty extensive. This wasn't the only lake in the area so she could have drowned elsewhere and just been dumped there. However, now Mrs. Heaston was missing and it was really bothering him.

Two women and the same lake.

There was a connection.

He felt it.

* * *

The voice on the other end of the call asked, "Can I please speak to Karen Foxton?"

Since it was the house phone landline, Rob was surprised it rang in the first place and it was only chance he was there to answer it instead of outside in the sunshine.

"She isn't here. Excuse me for asking, but how did you even get this number?"

"I'm a colleague and she left it on her desk for me because of the important case we are working and she was worried down in the boondocks her cell might not work. No offense on the boondocks remark. Those are her words, not mine."

That sounded like Karen. He glanced around at the expensive surroundings. "I don't know if this falls into the category of the boondocks, but she left in the early afternoon yesterday. She's usually glued to her email and her cell certainly works from home. I'd try that."

"Already did. Thanks. I guess I'll try again."

He hung up just as Lauren walked into the room. Her expression was not indicative of a happy outcome to the conversation. She said, "Don't ask, please. He went out in the boat."

"I won't ask."

"Thanks." Then she told him anyway. "I think I threw his wife at him and then he threw you at me."

He chose his words carefully. "I think you are both justified there and I'm sorry to be part of the equation because you're unhappy."

"Not with *you*." Lauren sank into a chair and sighed. "I'd just go home at this point but I don't want to spend hours with him in the car right now or to cut his vacation with you short. I don't know what to do. I'll adjust to this somehow."

"Well, if it makes you feel any better, I didn't want what happened with Karen either but I wasn't given a lot of choice." He exhaled. "No, wait, I'm excusing myself. I could have just broken it off and I intended to. I thought I could do it more privately since she wasn't going to be part of this vacation after all, but then she unexpectedly showed up. My fault all the way because I should have told her right when she suggested the guest list included the four of us that I wasn't going any further with the relationship."

"Probably." Lauren's expression was reflective. "She wants a good-looking, successful guy and you fit that mold, but the truth is I don't think the two of you want at all the same thing in *life*. I wouldn't say that if I wasn't fairly sure you hadn't come to the same conclusion."

"Oh, I had."

"I'd say she's a downtown penthouse kind of girl and you're a white picket fence in the suburbs sort of guy."

"That about sums it up. Throw in maybe a big dog to catch sticks. I need a lawn to mow."

"I love the smell of fresh mown grass." She looked away and briefly shut her eyes.

He didn't need the encouragement. *That I could give you.*

What he wasn't going to do was press an unfair advantage.

Instead, he told her, "Someone just called looking for Karen."

"Really?" Lauren's fine brows went up.

"A colleague . . . she should certainly have arrived back home yesterday evening." He frowned.

"She'd taken some time off to be here, so who knows what she decided to do with it."

That was a valid point, but it was troubling just the same considering she'd gone through some effort to make sure she was easy to get a hold of because of the case.

"I tried to call her to tell her, but guess what, she declined to answer." Rob's smile was ironic. "Go figure."

CHAPTER ELEVEN

He dropped off a book.

It was a front, as a thank you for the dinner, but a reasonable explanation for just stopping by. He handed it over. "This is for Ms. Mathews."

Hanson was cordial, he'd give him that. "She's in the kitchen if you'd like to give it to her yourself."

She had been there, as beautiful as ever — he was far too fixated — drinking a glass of wine. She'd accepted the book with what appeared to be true appreciation and read the title. "A Poisoned Lady. *That sounds interesting. What a beautiful cover.*"

It was. That was the publisher, not him.

He did his best self-deprecating act. "It is based on the Borgia family and their preferred method of murder. I do find history fascinating, of course. I think that might be obvious given my profession."

"It makes sense to me." *Her smile faltered.* "I'm sorry to even ask this, but is there any word on your wife? I'm not prying, I'm concerned."

He was prepared for questions like that. "No, but I'm not all that worried. She's done things like this before. But it is unusual for no one to hear from her. I am borderline concerned myself. However, that qualifier applies. Enough to call the police, but I hope I'm not wasting their time. Your blonde friend certainly didn't stay very long."

She didn't seem surprised he'd been watching, and he didn't think she would be either. Lauren Mathews was an intelligent young woman.

Very coolly, she said, "She isn't exactly my friend."
That, he already knew.

* * *

Dinner was tense.

To say the least.

Lauren made chicken in a spicy tomato sauce, some French bread and roasted asparagus and called it a day. She'd decided in an encompassing view of how men and women handled bad situations that men still needed to eat, and women tended to lose their appetite. But she was just basing it on herself. A single case study.

For three people who had a lot to talk about, they were remarkably quiet.

At least Rob and Drew enjoyed the food, or they were hungry because they devoured it and cleaned their plates, but maybe once again they just didn't want to talk. Not to each other really and not to her either.

Since she'd made dinner, Rob and Drew took on the cleanup and she went quietly upstairs and moved her belongings to the guest bedroom. There was no need for a grand announcement, Drew would get the message. They'd talked about it — his feelings were clear and she thought her feelings were pretty clear as well.

He considered himself no longer married and in her mind he really still was.

They were at an impasse at this point.

She wasn't sure about her relationship with Rob and she didn't think he had the slightest idea what to do there either, so the guest bedroom made the most sense.

Her bags were moved, and it looked like Rob had set out fresh sheets so she could remake the bed and she made short work of it.

This situation was seriously complicated. And for whatever reason, she felt Heaston realized it and was curious about it.

That bothered her more than maybe anything else. The man brought her a book and didn't seem to be concerned about his wife but was definitely curious about Karen's abrupt departure. His smile had been charmingly apologetic and he explained when he needed a break from his writing he went on the deck to look out over the lake and he'd seen her 'storm into the house' and then leave.

He'd also signed the book he gave Lauren: *To the Femme Fatale*.

At that moment she didn't think that was very funny.

"We're going to sit on the deck in the screen house if you want to join us." It was Drew, leaning against the door-jamb, his arms folded across his chest. She waited for a comment about her changing rooms but he didn't make one.

She just nodded. "It's a beautiful evening. I'll be right down."

The screen house was a protection against mosquitoes and she could hear both Drew and Rob talking after she opened the doors and walked over to join them. No laughter, not that she really expected any.

But the water shimmered in the afterglow of sunset and the tree frogs were singing. She was going to make the best of it.

Two very nice men and stars above? Life could be worse, but then again it could be better.

She could know her own mind.

They could also know theirs, which didn't exactly absolve her, but they were definitely all sailing along together on a ship of uncertainty. Lauren had made herself a cup of tea — she'd had enough wine for one day. She picked a chair and sat down, took a sip from her cup, and asked, "Am I the only one that thinks Heaston is a very odd man?"

Heaston won the day as the safest topic.

"He's on the eccentric side," Rob agreed quickly. "He's awfully calm for a man who has reported his wife missing to the police. I would only do that if truly concerned."

"I find that interesting too," Drew offered up. "But I do think we all deal with things in our own way."

"He just wanted to talk about Karen." It still bothered Lauren he'd figured things out so easily.

"Karen?" Rob looked startled. "They never even met."

"If you think he isn't paying attention, think again." She'd easily come to that conclusion. "He's watching us."

"I think so too." Drew said it with emphasis. "I've seen him doing it."

"He has a solitary occupation," Rob pointed out, ever the reasonable one. "It is natural to be interested in what else might be going on around you when otherwise you are alone all day. My grandmother complains about the nosy woman next door who spies on her when she pulls weeds and waters her garden. I really can't imagine how that could be interesting for the neighbor, but supposedly it happens. Is my grandmother imagining it? I have no idea."

"Heaston certainly seemed to know what was going on here. Maybe your grandmother is right. If pulling weeds and using a watering can is interesting maybe her neighbor is just lonely. He might be as well."

"I don't get that impression," Drew argued. "I think he's studying us."

Unfortunately, Lauren agreed they had a dynamic going on that might have caught his attention, but it certainly had her attention too. "I think so. I'd find the three of us an interesting subject group."

"If you were writing a Shakespearian play." Rob said it dryly. "I think Heaston does something similar with his books, but I don't want to be a main character." He then skirted the subject since none of them wanted to talk about it. "I might have asked him for a copy of a book for Karen's sister as a nice gesture, but I have a feeling she'd have burned it if it came from me."

Lauren agreed with that, but silently. Karen's acrimonious departure had not signaled a capacity for forgiveness, even if there *was* a nice gesture on Rob's part. He hadn't been unkind, he'd just been honest.

Drew was the one who said, "You know, sometimes it just doesn't work out."

* * *

He went to bed alone.

For someone involved with two women, that was an interesting feeling. Drew lay there in the dark, arms folded behind his head, all by himself.

The odd thing was he wanted to contact Cassandra to talk about this, but that was such a risky idea on so many levels he wanted to laugh. That woman was a problem solver, brisk and upfront, but she was part of the problem, so maybe not a good choice. They hadn't talked for a while. They were cordial enough but at odds over the process.

It wasn't like he blamed Lauren for her outrage but he still didn't understand why Cassie was stalling on the divorce. It wasn't money. She made more than he did and he wasn't asking for a dime. They weren't arguing over that at all. The financial part wasn't an issue.

They really weren't arguing about anything. They were just in agreement it wasn't working out as it stood, and neither of them seemed willing to change anything.

So he called her anyway. He actually didn't know where she was, but it turned out to be Florida, so at least the time frame was reasonable.

"Fort Walton Beach. Beautiful here."

"I'm in Tennessee. It's beautiful here too. Wooded hills, big log cabin on a scenic lake, the works."

"Sounds nice. Why are we having this conversation, Drew?"

That was so her. All business. Cut right to the chase. "You aren't signing the divorce papers."

"I wasn't aware there was any hurry."

"How long are we going to postpone this? I'd like to get on with my life."

"You've met someone else." It was a statement, not guess.

"Haven't you?" He really didn't know.

"Not like you."

He wasn't sure how to take that. "I've met someone, but I neglected to tell her I was still married. That didn't do me any favors. It doesn't help that Rob is into the same woman. There, that's the summary of my situation. That's not common information by the way."

"Rob? The tall, dark-haired delicious one?"

Oh, that made him feel better. "I suppose. He's just a friend of mine so I don't really think of him in those terms."

"You aren't female."

"I'm glad you noticed that."

"Oh. I did. You've got some serious competition going on there, my friend."

They *were* friends, which is why he hadn't pushed harder since she was pushing back. And she had met Rob once, just by accident when she'd stopped by the condo to drop off some of his clothes. He'd merely taken the box and said, "This is Rob. Thanks."

He hadn't introduced her either, just casually set the box aside.

"Tell me something I don't know," Drew continued. "I would label it a minor disaster to any romantic possibilities to have two good friends interested in the same female."

"And you called me? Oh, it must be."

"The laughter is unappreciated."

Her tone changed. "I've quit my job and taken another position that won't require all the travel. Just so you know. I'd like to give it another try between us, your dilemma aside. I'm doing my part."

Silence on his end.

She certainly registered it. "It's your turn to comment right now, honey."

Oh shit. Drew tried to regroup. "What exactly are you saying? You've changed your mind about the divorce?"

"Let's say I'm no longer sure it is our *only* choice."

He didn't need this wrench in the already faulty clockworks or whatever the saying was. "Were you ever planning on telling me this?"

"I called your lawyer and said I needed to talk to you. He said you were on vacation but he'd try to contact you."

He'd skipped that message. This moment was his fault on that front. Drew asked carefully, "He tried. How serious are you?"

"Drew, I resigned as a vice president of a Fortune 500 company. I'm very serious. Acknowledge it."

For her that really was *very* serious. "Shouldn't you have talked to me first?"

"No. Otherwise you wouldn't have believed me. Put your money where your mouth is. Declaring intent is just a bunch of words. But action is different."

She had a point there. Maybe he wouldn't have believed her.

"Way to make a statement, but really?"

"I was losing my mind traveling constantly and my single attempt at marriage went south because of it. Executive decision to call it quits. I'll control my own life. My new job will have me sitting at a desk and overseeing projects, not switching time zones every few days. I might even get a cat. Will you think about it?"

"I'm somehow not picturing you in a pair of fuzzy slippers with a cat sleeping on your lap."

"Well, I'll skip the fuzzy slippers, you've got me there. Tell me about her. This girl. Are you sleeping with her?"

"Not currently — you were kind of a deal breaker. I'm thrown off balance here. And give me credit, she isn't a girl, she's a woman." Certainly, the other side of the bed was empty, so he wasn't lying. "Let's keep in mind we are legally separated."

"That is easily solved. And I can tell you are off balance. But guess who you called. You called *me*. That says something right there."

Undeniable.

"Talking was never our problem. We just didn't really have a life together."

"Maybe now we can. Like I said, think about it."

End of conversation. She just hung up. Typical Cassandra. He stared at his phone and then reflected that he might just need to move to a desert island and wear a loincloth and spear hunt fish to cook over an open fire for food. A simpler life held some appeal. His current one was way too complicated.

There was no way he was going to get any sleep now.

He got out of bed, jerked on his jeans, and went downstairs.

Rob was still in the screen house, sprawled in a chair, and maybe that wasn't surprising since Drew had stayed in bed a whole twenty minutes maybe. He got a beer out of the cooler, wondered if he wasn't drinking too much on this vacation and then decided maybe he wasn't drinking enough, and went to join him.

"Sleep isn't happening for me. I guess not for you either."

"No, not really."

"I just talked with Cassandra. She isn't positive the divorce is what she wants." He unfastened the cap on his beer. "This explains a few things but is the last complication I need."

"What about you? What do you want?"

Good question. And Rob was, after all, a lifelong friend. Everything else set aside, if he needed to talk to someone, Rob would be his choice.

"I'm not quite sure what my options are right now. I'm aware that isn't a good answer. This change of heart on her part has kind of thrown me off."

"Are you just going to take Lauren home then?"

"She's pretty pissed at me. All those hours with an angry woman won't be fun."

"I can take her or she can just drive my truck and I'll rent a car."

"I don't know what she wants to do. I don't even know if I should talk to her or if you would be a better choice to ask about how she wants to handle it. She didn't ask *me* to take her fishing."

"I catch more fish. She's an intelligent woman. It's logic not preference."

"Yeah, right. You do not catch more fish."

Rob unsurprisingly changed the subject. "I've been sitting here thinking about something else entirely."

"Let me know what it is unless it involves my personal life. I don't want to talk about that anymore."

"It doesn't. You know, life isn't all about you, Fletcher. Remember that weird sound we heard that first night we were here? We thought it was a bird. What if it really was a woman screaming?"

CHAPTER TWELVE

The police officer was young, polite, and far too intelligent.

He began the conversation with a simple question. "Tell me again about the last time you saw your wife."

Glenn didn't dissemble. This wasn't the time. "She told me she was leaving five days or so ago. That isn't unusual. She thinks the house here is pretty but boring and that's a quote, and I don't blame her. For me it is perfect but she craves a more social environment."

"No mention of a destination?"

"She said Lexington. We have another home there. I went through this before with you and the older detective."

"Anything happen that evening you found unusual?"

"No." He frowned. "Like what?"

"We're just following through since we have some new information. We'll keep in touch."

"What new information?"

"If we find out anything, we'll keep you informed."

Evasive.

Glenn thought about it after the young man departed. He also thought about Lauren Mathews and how she'd been there on that bank reading her book, observing him load the boat.

It seemed an easy assumption she'd mentioned it.

Not good news for him.
Or for her.

* * *

It wasn't unusual for Chris to make notes during lunch or dinner, and breakfast wasn't out of the question either. He was unfortunately busy, even if this was what they called a quiet neck of the woods.

People still killed other people, even here, though he didn't just handle homicides.

Maybe that was why he was so interested. In a place that was beautiful and tranquil like the hills of Tennessee, it shouldn't happen, but it did.

He'd pulled up to the boat access earlier and taken a look around. Beautiful water, clear and serene. That dead girl had been found floating right there, so it really was plausible she'd been dumped.

He wasn't so sure. So he'd stood there and really pictured it.

If you spent time on the lake, he mused, *you'd know this was a good spot*. It was interesting introspection but any good detective reflected on occasion about if you were the one committing the crime, just how you would pull it off.

Put the body here at the public launch site. That way it could be anyone. A practical and calculated answer. There were no houses in view, the turn-off from the road was on the top of the dam leading down to the water and out of view of anyone driving by.

So she was dumped but was it from this lake or somewhere else? Just because she drowned didn't mean it was in this body of water.

That was quite the question.

He stood there and thought about quietly floating to a death where water invaded your lungs because you weren't conscious but still breathing, and guessed it happened here.

She was insensible, hence the blow to her head, and put in the water to drown. He felt it.

That was his gift, if he had one. He could feel a crime. It was the difference between him and Carter. Give his partner a case and he dissected it like a surgeon, but he handled it differently.

It was like Chris could sense the scene. Picture it, smell it.

He'd always asked himself if fear left a residual aura. Animals could sense it, so why not humans?

So it was true, she was dumped in the water still breathing but not conscious enough to fight. Water in her lungs because she wasn't aware she was drowning until it was just too late — if she ever did. He didn't like the image but there were a lot of things in this world he didn't like.

One of them was human beings killing each other. An animal killed out of fear or a need for food. Human beings were different. Motive was more complicated.

That's where he lost the bloodhound track.

Carter had already told him he wondered too much about why when all he needed to do was concentrate on who and how. Motive was usually the weakest part of every case because you might never understand it. He didn't discount that, but it did interest him.

Mrs. Heaston must be the only person in the country who paid with cash for everything because she hadn't used her credit cards for as much as a tank of gas or a soft drink. It was possible, but improbable. *If* she was still alive. Anything could have happened between here and her home in Kentucky, but her car hadn't turned up either.

He was treating her disappearance as another possible homicide.

He set aside his cup of coffee and wrote:

1. *Rob Hanson, Glenn Heaston, Andrew Fletcher.*
2. *Hanson at lake at the time of unknown girl's death? Fletcher there also?*

3. *Heaston's boat. What did he put in there and is it even pertinent to the case?*
4. *Is Hanson's phone call just an attempt to deflect suspicion? He and Andrew Fletcher think it is possible they heard a woman screaming the night they arrived. They put it off as a night bird of some kind, but conveniently remember it now.*
5. *Mrs. Heaston is alive and well, and the Jane Doe's death just an accident.*
   End of list.

Chris hit save on his laptop as his lunch went cold, and thought it over.

That was it. All the clues they had. Not much to go on, but at least a glimmer of the truth might be in there.

For whatever reason, he was sure Mrs. Heaston was dead in the water, somewhere.

* * *

Rob stopped in town and since it was his turn to cook, got some hamburgers and buns, potato salad, and a deli cheese-cake. That covered it for now.

Two days and they'd be heading home. Friday to Thursday had been the plan because Drew had overseas flight plans.

He had some seriously mixed feelings about that. Everything had changed and how he, Drew, and Lauren would go forward was really going to be interesting. This new issue with Cassandra sure didn't help. The way Drew described it he wasn't sure if he agreed with her or disagreed. Saying you are ready to give up and then changing your mind wasn't fair, but maybe it implied a greater commitment to the relationship than anticipated and perhaps it had surprised even her. He didn't know her, so it was very hard to judge.

Right now he would not want to be Drew. He'd lost the woman he thought he had, and gained back the woman he thought he'd lost. It was an interesting tailspin turn of events.

Right now, he would not want to be himself either, Rob discovered, when he pulled into the driveway of the house. A now familiar dark car — unfortunately — was there.

What the hell?

He should probably not have made that phone call.

But how could he not. He parked next to it and got out, retrieved his bag of groceries, lifted it in his arms and smiled without a lot of sincerity. "Detectives. Nice to see you again."

"I bet you don't think it is nice at all." Carter returned that same false smile. "No one likes to see us, so we aren't offended. We want a statement from you in reference to the call you made. Mr. Fletcher already gave us his version of what happened. Ms. Mathews says she didn't hear it but she was inside and the air-conditioning was on."

"I'll do that, no problem. I take it still no sign of Mrs. Heaston."

"We'd appreciate that statement."

No reciprocal agreement for an exchange of information, he noted. Maybe if he had their occupation, he wouldn't do that either.

"All I have to say is what I reported on the phone. It sounded like a woman screaming, but both Drew and I decided it could be a bird like an owl. The sound stopped and I haven't heard it again. I have no idea if it has any significance or not. I thought I should mention it."

"The acoustic properties of water are tricky," Bailey pointed out. "Any idea of the direction?"

"Maybe the far side of the lake but it sounded closer."

The only acknowledgment he got was a nod after both of them recorded what he said on their phones and he gave the date.

That seemed to be it. They got in the car and drove off.

When he went inside the first thing he said to Drew and Lauren was, "I should have just left it alone. Go ahead and say it."

Lauren disagreed. "No, because living the rest of your life without saying anything would not be a happy journey. I think it was the right thing to do."

Drew was on board. "We both heard it."

"But it still could have been a screech owl." Rob deposited the groceries on the polished counter. "I don't know if I accomplished anything, but we are sure getting to know the local law enforcement." It was hard to be jovial about it, but there weren't a lot of choices.

"We seem to be." Lauren came over to peer into the bags. "What do I need to do?"

"Relax. I've got this one. Trust me, I've kept it as easy as possible. Take the evening off."

"Tell you what, I'll set the table. If I know the two of you, we'd just eat from the containers."

She had a point there. Drew admitted, "In college Rob and I used to store pizza boxes under our beds and just pull those out and eat what was left over from the night before. We lived. Here we are."

"That given due consideration, we are still eating off plates." It was said firmly. "I'll set the table."

She went to the cabinet and took out placemats and truly Rob thought it gave her some sense of purpose, so he didn't argue the point. Normalcy was something he valued as well.

As far as he could tell it was the only way to handle the situation.

Nothing was normal.

He said, "I'll start the grill."

"I'll join you." Drew got up with alacrity, beer in hand. He was probably drinking too much but Rob didn't blame him at the moment. Back to work, back to his life — and his wife maybe. Who knew what would happen.

A rumbling in the distance was set off by a glimmer of lightning. "Another storm coming in but so it goes. You can't fault our weather so far."

"What exactly did you tell them?"

"We heard something like a woman screaming and decided it was a bird and left it alone."

"Me too."

106

At least the stories matched.

"I got the impression they came in person hoping to interview us separately."

"Then they got their wish."

"My wish is for a peaceful night without more screaming, no more inquisitive detectives, and no revelations that make me wonder if I am paying attention to the world around me." Rob opened the grill. "I'm not passing judgment, for the record. I just thought with the marriage thing, I might be the first person you'd tell."

"You know, you *were* the first person I told, Hanson, beside my parents and then only because Cassandra wanted to meet them. I waited for that, too." Drew looked resigned and a little weary. "Dammit, it was fun at first. A clandestine romance, but while there was plenty on the romance side, we are mostly talking sex. I don't have the slightest idea what to do. I don't know if either Cassandra or I know how to live a normal life in the conventional sense of the term, but then I wonder if maybe that doesn't make us perfect for each other. She wants to settle down now. Lauren has always been grounded and she will be that way her whole life. Cassandra is more like a tropical storm blowing in from the gulf. It could all change course in the blink of an eye. I've flown over a few."

"Is Cassandra going to turn into a hurricane?" Rob lit the flame and set the plate of burgers next to the burner. "Please understand I want you to be happy, I'd like to be happy myself. I want all of us to be happy actually."

"Hurricane C? I don't know. She is a force to be reckoned with."

"Is Lauren going to be out of the path of the storm?"

"Cassandra isn't one to hold grudges as far as I can tell, she just wants to win the fight if she's decided to take it on. I didn't give names or affirm or deny anything. I want to repeat to everyone, we were legally — and still are — separated before I even met Lauren."

"So she isn't gunning for a rival, she's focused on you?"

107

"I get the impression that's how it is. Like I've said, I have no idea who she's been seeing either."

Rob almost asked if there was any jealousy involved but left that one alone. "So the executive wants to be a housewife?"

"Oh, I doubt that. She's just taken a less high-powered job."

"Which she took for you?"

"For her too, I imagine. I just fly them from here to there. As far I can tell, her life was all meetings and negotiations. Every single last one of those executives seems tired on the trip back home. I know she was wound up, but essentially exhausted each time. She fed on it, but it all also fed on her."

"I am really not sure what to say except that I hope it works out for the best for both of you." He put on the burgers. "I really cheated on dinner, but not as bad as you did with your aunt's lasagna. I take full responsibility for the deli cheesecake coming from the supermarket, and hopefully it will be edible."

"I'm pretty flexible. Do you really think the detectives are looking at you?"

It was bothering him. Rob had to say grimly, "Just because of the location and timing, I think I'm a person of interest to those two, yes."

CHAPTER THIRTEEN

The screaming.

Trust Angela to screw everything up. He hadn't expected much of a fight. She'd surprised him there.

Maybe he was more transparent than he thought. He'd never had much respect for her intellect but in retrospect, she hadn't really been caught as off guard as he anticipated.

And she really had a vocal objection to her murder.

He claimed to be working and listening to classical music as was his usual routine and that he didn't hear a thing. The detectives seemed to take that at face value and left.

He had wondered once he realized the Beautiful Trio was in residence next door if maybe they'd noticed the unusual sound in this quiet setting. At the time, he hadn't even known they were there.

Evidently, they were very there.

Evidently, they had noticed.

Lauren Mathews had noticed his ritualistic delivery of the body as well.

He'd written a novel years ago where the doomed heroine perished on the ship due to a virulent fever that sparked intense fear in the crew and she was wrapped in a shroud and sent to a watery grave.

It was his first literary attempt, never published but still sitting in a drawer in his desk. He often wondered if that venture into the

fictional world hadn't just shaped his life but his psyche. He'd titled it:
Buried at Sea.

It was a very pertinent question, but luckily no one but him had ever read it.

* * *

It was more difficult than she imagined waking up to the sound of Rob taking a shower in their now mutual bathroom. Lauren rolled over in bed.

His cell phone was ringing. She could hear it, and it wasn't like she would dream of answering it for him, but it was kind of early in the morning.

This arrangement was better than sleeping next to Drew given their current controversy, but not exactly comfortable either.

The phone stopped so she went and rapped on the bathroom door. Rob answered in just a towel wrapped around his lean waist.

"I thought I'd tell you someone just tried to call you."

"Now? It's like six in the morning."

"I'm aware of the time. That's why I told you." He and Drew had discussed an early fishing expedition.

He looked alarmed. "My grandfather has been in the hospital off and on lately. Thanks for letting me know. Sorry if it woke you."

She didn't tell him sleep hadn't happened much for her anyway, so no problem. Seeing him without a shirt certainly wasn't going to help her drift off now. Nice well-muscled chest, but she'd seen him in just swim trunks frequently enough she could visualize it anyway. "I hope everything is okay."

"Me too. I guess I'll go find out."

He fairly sprinted toward his bedroom and she decided to cross her fingers for him and just went downstairs for a cup of coffee. Drew was there of course, in worn jeans and a T-shirt with foreign letters on it, eating a bagel. He didn't pull any punches, but then he rarely did.

"Looks like you slept about the same as I did."

Maybe she should have at least run a comb through her hair. She tried her fingers instead and went over to the fancy coffee maker. "I was a little restless."

"You look beautiful, don't get me wrong. I missed you, by the way."

His voice was very quiet and his demeanor subdued. Lauren selected a coffee blend, put it in the machine, and pressed a button. "I missed you too, but my new perception of our relationship has taught me something. I don't think I realized I was this old-fashioned."

"And here I knew it all along."

"Drew."

He did have an infectious smile even if it was fleeting this morning. "I'm serious."

She waited for the coffee, added creamer and then went and sat down at the table. It wasn't like she wasn't speaking to him. There were still feelings involved. "You should have informed *me*."

"I think you've known all along, too."

True enough. She shifted topic. "Rob is on a phone call. I hope everything is fine."

"It isn't." Rob walked into the kitchen. "God, I need a cup of coffee to deal with this."

"Your grandfather?"

"No. It was about Karen."

Lauren had to admit she was startled. She stared at him. "Karen? At six in the morning?"

"I don't know if it is a long story, but it is a story anyway. Give me a minute."

He did look unsettled.

Both she and Drew gave him that minute. It seemed like he needed it since he was a bit pale. When he joined them, hands white-knuckled around the mug, he said tightly, "Karen is missing. That was her colleague, the one who has already called me. The police called *him* because he'd tried so often to reach her his number came up first. They've found her car, her cell phone and her purse inside it, in a mall parking lot, but not her. Guess where she was seen last. Apparently here. The car has been there for a while."

Utter silence. Lauren certainly didn't know what to say.

Rob went on, his expression bleak, "I guess a young woman who had parked next to the car heard her cell ringing in the morning and when she went to work the next day, heard it ringing again. She contacted security because the car hadn't moved and, in this day, and age, no one goes without their cellphone that long. The security guys agreed it was an unattended vehicle after keeping an eye out and called the police. They ran the plates. The detectives are going to love this."

Another missing woman? That was just bizarre and scary. It was Drew that pointed out forcefully, "You have an alibi. Lauren and I both knew you were swimming in the lake when Karen left. We saw you dive in the water. We heard her car start up and pull away."

"Who is to say I didn't swim to the cove because I knew she was leaving, climb out under the cover of the trees, and somehow intercept her in the driveway. That would literally have taken me less than ten minutes. I didn't do that, but in the time it took me to finish that phone call, get dressed and walk down here, it occurred to me that was possible. If it registered with me, it will with law enforcement as well."

It was terrible that Lauren thought he was probably right. "Maybe nothing has happened to her. Maybe she got out of her car somewhere and it was stolen."

"If so, I get the impression she sure didn't report it."

That her car was stolen was possible, but that she wouldn't contact anyone really wasn't, even if her cell phone was a casualty. She could easily find someone to call for her if she was stranded. Most people would at least take a second to dial 911 for a woman in a panic. At least Lauren wanted to think they would, but maybe she had a distorted view of humankind in general. She was starting to think so.

So where *was* Karen?

It was already warm out with the sun coming up, but she was cold. "I can't explain that."

"Unfortunately, I can't either." Rob drank some coffee and shut his eyes briefly.

Drew argued, "We have no idea how police departments operate. Think about it. Where was this mall?"

"You've seen it. It's the strip mall right next to the place where we ate dinner out the other night."

Drew swore softly. "You are shitting me."

"I'm not exactly in a kidding mood. I used my credit card there. There are now no doubts about me knowing the location if our two favorite detectives do their homework, and somehow I think they will."

* * *

They went fishing anyway.

Lauren sat quietly in the back of the boat, her expression remote, open book on her lap, and she was ostensibly reading but not making a good show of it.

Drew had checked the calendar on his phone. He wondered how long it would be before he was asked some interesting questions himself.

Not long probably.

Though it hadn't come up before now, he'd driven down for a little R and R once last summer between flights. He didn't think for one minute Rob would mention it to the police, but Cassandra knew. She'd called him about something and he'd answered from the lake. Not to mention he'd landed the jet in Nashville, so there would be a flight record.

Considering that and not knowing the timeline of the first victim, maybe he was just as much a solid suspect as Rob.

That wasn't exactly a welcome revelation.

He said carefully, "Hanson, I think we are in the same boat."

Rob looked at him, rod and reel in hand. "Since we are sitting in the same boat, I have to agree with that and add something intellectual like what the hell are you talking about?"

"Not what I meant. If that girl drowned when you were here last year, I was here too for at least part of the time, and certainly have been here all this week."

Rob digested that for a moment. "There's a cheerful thought. Off the hook because instead they suspect my best friend? What a relief."

"Hey, sarcasm does no good in this situation. I was the last person on this lake to Karen climb into her car and drive off. That is, according to what I know."

Rob cast into the water, looking troubled. "I get what you are saying, but she wasn't involved with you."

"I'm just saying it isn't implausible."

"Fletcher, here's some advice, don't ever be your own defense attorney because you are making a case for the prosecution."

"I'm hoping it will never come to that, I'm just pointing out the investigation into you could be just as much about me now that I checked the date you gave me. We were both here. And we are the only two that heard the screaming. Being each other's witnesses probably doesn't hold much weight."

"I don't want there to be an investigation for either one of us."

"I can second that. The good news is we didn't do anything and have no idea when that woman drowned."

"Karen and I parted not on the best of terms but I certainly don't want anything to have happened to her."

"I don't want that either." Just because Drew hadn't cared for her particularly, it was still disturbing to think she might have joined the growing roster of missing women. Surely someone out there was missing that first drowning casualty and whether it had any connection to recent events he had no idea. "If she was abducted from the mall, it could be anyone."

"Too much coincidence for me," Rob argued, shaking his head. "If they locate Heaston's wife alive and well, that would change everything, but I also think Karen would be hard to abduct. She's very self-aware."

Drew didn't disagree. Karen was a lawyer and a savvy woman no doubt well versed in the darker edge of society. He did observe, "I'm hoping she's fine, but anyone can be taken by surprise."

"I don't discount that, but she'd be more difficult than most."

"Maybe so."

"It's Heaston."

That was Lauren, utterly quiet before now, speaking from the back of the boat. "If you two are going to have the discussion, here's my slant on it. He put that heavy object in his boat. He came over to see if I would mention I noticed it. He spies on us, and I just plain think he's very offbeat in a nice enough way that still hits the wrong note. He's much more likely to have intercepted Karen's car than either of you without any of my personal feelings coming into play. I know he watched that argument before she left because he told me he did. Take it into consideration."

Drew listened because Lauren was as intelligent as she was beautiful and that was saying something. He found Heaston's interest in her disturbing. "Why the hell would he do that?"

"Who knows?" she said succinctly. "Unless he's hiding it, he's very . . . disconnected."

"I see you are wearing your psychology hat."

She took a moment. "I find him too intense."

Rob said, "How so? That of itself is not a sin."

"No," she agreed. "But you just asked for my perception. He's too dismissive of his wife's absence and was far too interested in your relationship with Karen. I think the balance is disturbing. It comes down to the fact I just don't like him and I don't know why."

"I don't disagree. Let's leave tomorrow morning instead of waiting for noon like we planned. I thought this would be the vacation that would let us all relax and unwind, but it hasn't worked out that way."

Drew had to chime in. "Uhm, I'm thinking that's not going to happen. For some reason I think Bailey and Carter are going to want us to stick around for at least a few more days."

"I think we should." Rob was obviously solidly opposed.

"I have to leave the country very early on Friday morning, so I have to leave tomorrow. Do you think they'll agree to that? I don't want my license suspended for even a few days." Drew was dead serious. "They could actually do that if they felt they had probable cause. A judge would have to agree, but it would really suck for me."

"You are both speculating on something that might never happen." Lauren set her book on the seat, her hair ruffled by the wind. "They should of course talk to us. And maybe I've read too many suspense novels, but the husband is the first one they suspect when a woman dies or disappears since usually it is because he has the most to gain."

"That is one hell of a house," Drew said, "but who is to say he didn't pay for it all, despite marrying a rich woman. He's a professor, yes, so that doesn't probably make a fortune, but he's also a bestselling author and that might."

"Motivation right there, either way." Lauren wasn't giving an inch. "He either wants her money, or he doesn't want to give her half of his."

"Could be," Drew acquiesced. "Or there is some other predator out there."

CHAPTER FOURTEEN

At sixteen I made the high school football team. No one was more surprised than I was except maybe my father. He wasn't an easy man to please, but that did seem to make him happy. I was hardly a star, and any and all efforts in the classroom were ignored, but one blocked pass won me some approval. I honestly think I just stepped the wrong direction and it hit me and bounced away from the intended receiver, no skill involved. Still, it was blocked.

We are the sum of our parts. Sports are not involved in my makeup. I'm more an intellectual.

I quit after the first season and my father really never spoke to me again. He even skipped my graduation on some flimsy excuse.

I got the message but never really forgave him. When he died suddenly, out of petty revenge, I skipped his funeral.

* * *

The killer was on a learning curve.

Chris sat with chin on fist, staring at his computer. It was getting late.

The map of the lake was comprehensive because it was an aerial view and included water depths and all the houses and size of the lots. None of which he could afford in his lifetime, but personal wealth had never been a goal anyway. His simple little house was adequate for a place to sleep and eat, and was in a quiet old neighborhood close to work. He was amazed at how many of the houses on that lake had swimming pools, but maybe women like the sophisticated Mrs. Heaston didn't want to dip their toes in lake water but just wanted to float on a raft or sit in a lounge chair in the sun.

So, where was she?

His vote was the east side of the lake where it was at least thirty feet deep or even deeper. The killer had just thrown the first one in. What if he'd sunk her body there too?

If there even was a killer.

Maybe he was just wasting his time. It wasn't like he wasn't working other cases. A man had been killed in a town nearby in what seemed to be a bar fight, but it could be motivated by jealousy and they were investigating. Everyone was conveniently absent of any memory of the event. Alcohol was involved, and a brawl that got out of hand, so it was proving a challenge. Manslaughter maybe, but someone was dead at the end of it.

This wasn't the same though. The vibe was different.

This was calculated murder. He knew it.

He had some evidence to justify a search of the lake. They needed divers. Those guys knew exactly what they were doing. He just needed Carter to agree with him so they could put in the request, but his hunch Mrs. Heaston was the key to solving the other case too wasn't enough. Just because he operated off his gut didn't mean everyone did.

At this point that missing woman could be anywhere. A shallow grave in the woods or blowing some serious coin in New York on a new purse and expensive shoes.

His instincts screamed she was somewhere close.

* * *

"Can I talk to you?"

Rob had been in bed for about two minutes before that soft question was asked. It wasn't Karen coming into

118

his room this time, it was Lauren, dressed in a T-shirt and pajama pants but somehow still managing to look sexy. She didn't mean it that way though because she explained with a wan smile, "This news about Karen . . . I can't go to sleep. Do you mind? If I wasn't so ticked off at him, I'd ask Drew, but I am. I don't usually subscribe to the big strong man nearby theory but I'm having no luck drifting off on my own. I don't feel safe. Every small noise has me sitting up. In a place this size there are a lot of them, take my word for it."

How could he say no? Luckily, he was wearing boxers which he didn't always do. "Well, yeah, sure, but Drew won't like it."

Now he'd be the one not able to sleep, however, he did to a certain extent understand her unrest. Drew *really* wouldn't like it.

"I think he might want to ask his wife if she had a problem with him sleeping with me. I'd love to hear the answer to that question." Lauren sat down and then sighed as she settled on the bed. "Sorry, I'm not trying to be a bitch, I swear, but I just sounded like one."

"I've never thought that you were anything of the kind." He could smell the sweet scent of her hair already or maybe it was body lotion, he wasn't sure, but he sincerely hoped just having her so close wouldn't give him an erection. She wanted safe, not a sexually aroused male next to her, though how she couldn't know that climbing into bed with him would affect him was a mystery. She was well aware of his interest and this wasn't exactly summer camp. "I think we are all off balance."

He had no idea if Drew had told her about his conversation with Cassandra. What he did know was he wasn't going to be the source of that information. That was between Lauren and Drew. He was merely an observer but yet had a vested interest in the outcome. The delicate balance between his relationship with Lauren and his friendship with Drew was undeniable.

If he really had a relationship with Lauren at all. Of course, they were now essentially alone in a bedroom together and that had been one satisfying kiss the other night, but he was so uncertain about what was really going on he wasn't going to make any assumptions. "I'm so concerned about Karen — for several reasons — I doubt sleep is in my future either."

"*I* am off balance for sure." She looked at him very directly. "Why wouldn't you go to bed with her?"

"You mean just sex." He fielded that one easily enough. "This sounds like I'm handing you a line, but I just knew I wasn't going to fall in love with her. Since we are trading pillow talk apparently, I know supposedly we don't, but guys do have standards. Not fair to her, or fair to me either if I took advantage of the opportunity, because then I wouldn't like myself very much."

"Not everything in a short skirt, is that what you're saying?" Her smile had nothing to do with humor.

"That kind of sums it up. I think our real problem was she'd figured it out too, but that didn't bother her. That's a very basic personality difference hard to overcome for me."

"I guess I'm having the same problem with Drew. I would never have kept it quiet if I was married. I would have told him flat out from the beginning."

He knew Drew. He said carefully, "The difference is he truly cared about your reaction because he cares about you. I'm not agreeing necessarily with how he handled it, but it makes some sense to me. We aren't at all talking about the same thing. If I had to call it, he was looking forward. It hadn't worked out. His wife was walking backward, and you were the future. He thinks that way."

"Maybe our problem is he and I don't have a similar outlook on life, as you pointed out about you and Karen."

Silence.

He was definitely shaken about the news about Karen. Mrs. Heaston was a little different in that he didn't know her personally. "I expect tomorrow will be interesting."

"What if Drew is right? It isn't Heaston but someone else?"

He'd considered it too. "Maybe. We live in a world of hidden monsters."

* * *

Lauren wasn't lying — she simply couldn't sleep and Rob was a tempting option for conversation being right across the hall. It was hard to decide what might be more upsetting — the thought of Heaston or that there was an unknown presence out there.

Heaston's attitude bothered her more than anything. He'd done nothing really suspicious except dump that package in his boat and look around, but his interest in Karen during their conversation struck the wrong chord. He seemed so intrigued about the quarrel when he should have been worried about something else.

Like his missing wife. But maybe he was right. It was perfectly in character for her.

But Rob was correct, this *was* a world of hidden monsters.

Lauren said quietly, "You aren't one of them. I don't believe that."

"No, I'm not. I'm hoping all involved agree with you."

Every muscle in his body had tensed. She felt it. Was she doing this to get revenge on Drew? Sitting this close in the dark?

I want you to hold me in your arms.

She almost said it out loud. It was a treacherous temptation. She was hurt, and more than a little confused, and it wasn't just Drew's fault either.

Rob didn't offer that embrace but she wasn't surprised. Ethics were at war with betrayal right now and she had a glimmer of insight at least over what Drew probably had felt when they'd met.

She didn't mean to try to forget it for just one night. That wasn't worth it.

Rob was undoubtedly on the same page. He'd turned Karen down.

Not to mention he was evidently a suspect in a murder case.

So was Drew if his speculations were correct.

"What are we going to do now?"

"The two of us?" She wasn't even sure how to ask.

He shook his head. "No. The three of us."

That was true. She had no idea what Drew was thinking. It left her adrift and Rob was definitely a solid win as someone to lean against.

After this evening she had no definitive idea what she was doing either.

"As far as I'm concerned, Drew has forfeited his vote on what happens next." The initial affront had passed, but she'd considered the situation. "I understand you are friends and it complicates things, but I think he and I are going to disagree on this forever."

"Trust is hard earned and easily lost." Rob's eyes were shadowed by long dark lashes. "I hope I had nothing to do with it if you go your separate ways."

"Maybe a little." At least she could respond to that honestly. "It isn't retaliation, but it isn't betrayal either. He's just as guilty of that. Our relationship is apparently built on quicksand rather than bedrock."

"I don't think innocence one way or the other is a question."

True enough. "Drew and I are in a strange place," she acquiesced. "But he isn't exactly the man I thought I was falling in love with."

"No, he *is* the man you fell in love with, he's just maybe a little more complicated than he seems. Drew is good-natured but under that smooth facade are some problems from his past he's never addressed, like his mother's death."

"He was a child."

"He was twelve. You aren't a child then and yet you aren't a man. In the Civil War he could have marched with the infantry."

"What happened? It isn't like he talks about it." She was truly curious.

"I don't even want to tell you."

"Do it anyway." She jabbed him in the ribs, but added quietly, "Please."

"She drowned."

Was he serious? One look at his face told her he was. Rob shook his head. "I haven't asked for details and Drew has never offered them, so don't look to me. They were on a summer vacation, that's all I know."

That was horrifying.

She said, "He's never told me. It was generic. He just said she died when he was young."

"I understand. If he doesn't want to talk about it, he won't. I wouldn't. He and his father aren't close either."

Of course, he wouldn't talk about it. He was male. Though, women kept secrets too, just not as well in her opinion. "I really didn't know. If the detectives find that out, they really might take some interest in him in a psychological way."

"That occurred to me as well. I don't want them to take an interest in either one of us." Rob sighed. "I want to go back to my life and not worry about them knocking on my door again one day, but like you, I think Heaston is an interesting guy."

Interesting was right, she thought with an inward shiver.

"He's enigmatic." That was the best way she could think to put it. "I don't know what he's thinking. There's no transparency."

"Well, to my knowledge you've only met him twice."

"Spoken to him on two different occasions," she corrected. "I think we've met a bit more often than that if you count other forms of engagement. I'm going to bet he knows I have a mole on my right thigh."

"You still think he's shamelessly people watching and we are the only people to watch?"

"Well, you have to admit we are kind of interesting. I'm not positive any of the three of us know what we are doing."

"I'm going to have to agree with you on that."

She stood abruptly. "Good night."

If she stayed, she was going to do something impulsive, and this was just not the time to start a new love affair.

CHAPTER FIFTEEN

Was it the last night?

Maybe.

They'd mentioned a week or so for their trip. Almost there.

He couldn't just let them leave.

This book outline was just getting to the point where he was riveted and he needed them. He especially needed Ms. Mathews. Her role was beyond important. She was the fascinating main character.

The epitome of historical fact and legend, she'd inspired him to begin to write what he thought might be his best book yet. The face that launched one hundred thousand words.

Except he didn't know how the story ended yet.

* * *

"Are you ever coming to bed?"

Chris started, glancing up from his screen. Sara's long dark hair framed her elegant cheekbones. She was of Spanish descent, had a volatile temperament, and he knew that tone.

"Complicated case." But he shut down his computer.

"Yours usually are. It can wait."

She was wrong. One woman was dead and another one missing. He and Sara were live-in lovers and though

125

he wasn't purposely ignoring her because he'd thought she was asleep, apparently she wasn't. She was a financial advisor and very pragmatic, which meant she liked direct, so he just asked, "Sex?"

"I've been thinking about it and kind of waiting for you to wander in and follow through with that hope. I swear you *are* Sherlock Holmes or someone very similar. Abstracted is the word I would use."

"I don't like mysteries. I want to solve them."

"I don't like it when the stock market does something that doesn't fit the model either." She had a swimmer's body with slightly square shoulders but long shapely legs. She could — and did — run marathons, something that he wasn't interested in, but if she was, he wasn't going to argue one way or the other. She was always in training for something or off to the gym, so they suited each other fairly well, their paths not crossing all that often, which seemed to work out for them both.

In bed she was passionate and vocal, and he was glad they had rented a house instead of an apartment. They had done so because Sara had a dog. That intelligent animal left the room when it realized clothes were coming off, which Chris found amusing.

The dog scampered off when he shrugged out of his shirt and he went to close the window so no late-night pedestrian got an earful.

The resulting athletics were a satisfying sensual experience but when Sara drifted off afterward, he slipped on some sweatpants and went back to his computer. Alexa, the little furry mix of who knows what because she resembled a mop, came to sleep at his feet.

The real problem was both Heaston and Hanson were very smart men. He'd researched them online and met them both. They weren't the only candidates, but access to the victims was key to this investigation. Connecting the two cases was important but the longer Mrs. Heaston was gone, the more he was convinced something bad had happened to the woman.

Something bad had happened to Karen Foxton. Hanson had dated her and been to that strip mall location. Heaston had been right next door to the lake house where she was last seen. They were in a tie for lead suspect. Both had been on the lake last summer.

Then there was Fletcher. His mother had drowned.

Multiple killings were ritualistic.

Carter had sent him an email. He was instantly riveted by the content as he read it.

Well, damn, that was interesting.

* * *

Mist drifting over the lake . . . last morning out. Drew gazed out over the view and decided he might not miss everything about this vacation but would miss this. The scenery was stellar. Still water and trees, birds calling, and no one else in sight . . . perfect.

Except Rob, who sat across from him, line in the water, his expression distant.

They were both distant from each other at the moment.

He'd heard them talking last night, first Lauren's light tone, and Rob answering her. Not the actual conversation but the acoustics of the big house were such that from the second-floor bedroom he could hear them up on the third floor having a discussion of some kind.

From the same bedroom.

It felt very strange to not be able to ask the burning question on his mind but he couldn't see how he had the right, especially after his conversation with Cassandra. That was the reason he'd been sleepless in the first place. It was safe to say Lauren wasn't dating him any longer, so the way things stood she was free to make her own choices. Jealousy wasn't an option. He *was* jealous to a certain extent, but then again, he'd probably forfeited that right.

What to say? He chose: "I'm going to have a very hard time leaving this place."

Rob shot him an incredulous look. "After everything this week?"

"Yeah."

"Fletcher, have I ever mentioned you're an idiot?"

"You aren't exactly a rock star in that department so don't throw stones. I think we both managed to lose our girlfriends in the space of a few days. Whatever happened to our quiet fishing trip?"

"The hell if I know."

"Here's your answer. Women."

"I suppose." Rob paused. "I want us to walk away from all of this still as friends."

Drew thought that was maybe *his* answer right there. It was somewhat of a bitter pill to swallow, but then again, here he was, not sure what to do about Cassandra either so he was at fault. "I'd prefer that myself. Listen, Lauren's life is hers. She's a grown woman. She can make her own decisions."

All Rob said was: "I think you are both in accord on that."

"But not in accord with anything else right now."

He had turned the boat toward the house. "I bet she'd agree with you that the car I can see now sitting at the back of the driveway does not belong to her two favorite people. Fuck it, Drew, I knew it. It's Bailey and Carter. Again."

Carter should come first just by virtue of seniority, but Bailey was a lot more dangerous. That was one observant man.

"We should have made a swift exit this morning for Ohio."

"It is barely seven o'clock."

"I was joking. I'm guessing this is an important call. They must not care that some people actually sleep in on vacation."

"I think if they worried about suspects and their tender sensibilities, they wouldn't be doing their jobs. Apparently, they don't take early mornings off either."

128

Drew thought that was true enough but didn't like the word 'suspects'. He asked darkly, "Could you please refer to us as persons of interest. 'Suspects' just has a bad ring to it."

As a joke it fell flat, but then again, he wasn't in a jovial mood.

He wished he hadn't taken the time to look up the article on the drowning victim. Yes, he and Rob had been at the lake around that time, give or take a couple of days. He'd driven over from Nashville in a rental car, so that also could be traced back to him via credit card.

It depended on how thorough they were and as of now it wasn't a murder case as far as he knew, just one unexplained drowning and more missing women.

But those two homicide detectives seemed very intent.

Rob docked the boat and Drew jumped out to secure it. He was sure neither one of them really wanted this conversation, but both thought it best to get it over.

Their arrival was duly noted, and Carter, looking decidedly better than they did at this early hour in their fishing clothes, met them on the porch. His shirt was nicely pressed, and Drew was sure he'd worn his faded jeans two days in a row. What the heck, he was supposed to be on vacation, not worrying about laundry.

"Gentleman, good morning. We have a few questions. Do you recognize this woman?" He handed over a picture obviously printed from a computer but the image was clear.

Karen, of course. That hadn't taken them long.

"We both do." Drew handed it back. "I don't even need to let Rob see it. Karen left a few days ago, and yes, she was pissed off. But she drove off on her own and Rob was swimming and Lauren and I both saw her leave absolutely alone."

"She didn't say where she was going?"

"She didn't even say goodbye." Drew wasn't going to back down. "So, no, she didn't except she declared she was leaving and I assumed she meant to Ohio. I'd like to be more helpful, but I can't be."

Rob had stowed the fishing poles and he walked up behind him. He was truthful. "We had a disagreement, but it was like a high school breakup. She'd pretty much invited herself along on this trip in the first place."

Bailey must have gone to the door and knocked and talked to Lauren because he came out of the house and down the steps. He was cordial but brisk as he joined them. "I assume Detective Carter has let you both know about the recent disappearance."

Rob said, "We knew already something was wrong. She's a pretty busy attorney and her colleagues have touched base with us, asking about her not answering calls because she gave the house phone number in case her signal was weak here."

"The last call she made, according to them, said she'd be back in the office on Monday. It was made from here or near here according to tower signal records."

They *had* been busy.

"I don't know what happened and if I could help, I would."

Bailey didn't look convinced. Neither did Carter. At all.

Okay, maybe Carter was just as dangerous but just seemed lower key. Something to think about. He asked, "She was 'pissed off' — and I am quoting you, Mr. Fletcher — about what?"

Both detectives were looking at Rob, who simply told the truth. "I declined to make it more intimate between us. The lady took offense. She isn't unappealing physically but can be more than a little pushy. I think I'm a more traditional guy than she anticipated. It wasn't serious as far as our relationship stood, so I wasn't going that direction."

That summed it up and was as forthcoming as necessary. Drew didn't see how hearing the actual dialogue would help them.

"So she got angry at the rejection and left?"

"Pretty much."

Bailey didn't pull any punches. "You do realize we aren't going to take your word for it. When we find her, if your DNA comes into play, what you just said will count for nothing."

When we find her.

"It won't come into play." Rob's voice held positive conviction.

"I actually believe you." Bailey looked introspective. "We appreciate any help we can get. Where would Ms. Foxton go if she wanted to disappear on a voluntary basis?"

"No. Didn't happen. She'd never leave behind that cell phone. She was chained and padlocked to it." Just as much conviction right there and Drew agreed.

"So you think she was abducted."

"I have no idea, but I can say I don't think she'd leave her phone behind. Even though we didn't part on the best of terms, I'm worried about her."

"I believe that answers my question."

Drew wasn't sure it did, but he wasn't a detective. "I think it makes us very uncertain about the circumstances of her being missing."

"We are on the same page there. Ms. Mathews indicated you three might be leaving soon. We'd like to ask you all to stay in this county for a few more days as we sort this out."

Drew muttered a very bad word.

Rob stepped up for him. "I can arrange it since I can work remotely from here, but Drew has to fly out due to his job. I'm more than willing to help and stay, but his work can't be done anywhere except in the cockpit of a plane."

Neither Bailey nor Carter looked happy about it, but Drew doubted happiness was on their agenda this morning.

Drew said evenly, "I'll submit flight plans if you want, but Rob is right. I have to go. A plane needs a pilot unless you have a solid reason, I can't do it."

That was a gauntlet.

"No. No solid reason at this time," Carter said it coolly. "But we will take those flight itineraries."

Bailey said, "We'll be in touch."

They left and as they watched the car pull out, Rob said, "That actually went better than I expected."

"We aren't done."

"Nope. Persons of interest? Oh, we are interesting to them, that's not in doubt."

Drew said tightly, "I appreciate you helping me out."

"Just told the truth."

Lauren came out to the deck with a cup of coffee and sat down, her expression taut, still wearing pajamas. They joined her at the table, all three of them just looking at each other for a moment. Drew could usually come up with a smart-ass comment for anything, but not this.

She spoke first. "They have nothing." Lauren said it with conviction. "You went fishing, and so did they. If they did have probable cause, they'd have taken you in for questioning. They can keep you for twenty-four hours but that's it. You know, Heaston can back us up. We know he saw the argument and Karen storm off, and that's a direct quote."

"You mean suspect number three?" Rob probably wasn't trying to be sarcastic, but it came off that way. "I'm sure *he's* a viable witness at this time."

She argued, "He could confirm you've never met his wife, and he saw Karen leave. I'm fairly sure he could confirm he saw you swimming in the lake and Drew lying on the dock."

"And admit to being a Peeping Tom of sorts?" Drew shook his head. "I wouldn't. I agree he could, but—"

"He already has to me."

"All he has to do is deny he ever said it." Rob eyed her cup. "I think I need clarity on what is going on because it escapes me this morning. Excuse me for a minute while I go make myself some coffee."

That left him and Lauren ostensibly alone. Drew asked cautiously, "Sleep well?"

"No, not particularly. You?"

"Nope."

"Are you going to be able to leave? I know you have a flight scheduled."

"They didn't say I couldn't and the question was asked."

"This is so surreal."

"I couldn't agree more. I can rent a car if someone will just take me to the closest place where that is possible. Feel free to drive mine home."

"Rob will take me back. There's no need for that."

"Sweetheart, Rob has been politely asked to not leave this county for at least a few days. Because of Karen, I think he moved into suspect number one."

"Are you serious? That's ridiculous. What about Heaston?"

"He didn't know Karen. Rob did."

"Rob doesn't know Mrs. Heaston."

"Lauren, prove it. That is what it comes down to. He comes here a couple of times a year. They could so easily make a case that he'd at least seen her and certainly knew she was there at the closest house on this lake. Karen is his real problem. By his admission, they had an argument. You and I both heard the confrontation. The police know it is why she left. Now she's not to be found."

"Not because of him."

"You don't have to convince me. Bailey and Carter are another story."

"I don't have to convince anyone. I guess I'll just stay a few more days then. I can work from here."

"Because you are so ticked at me or because of Rob?" He knew better than to ask but did it anyway.

"Some of both."

"I'd rather you were far away from here, Lauren. Women are *disappearing*. Wherever we are on a personal level, I'm not comfortable leaving you."

"That isn't your decision to make, now is it?" Then she apparently relented. "Drew, I'm so conflicted I'm not sure what to do, but leaving Rob here alone and not knowing what is happening is not a very good option for me."

"Or me either, but I have double your problem. I don't want to leave either one of you here. But I'd better go pack."

CHAPTER SIXTEEN

It was on the news at noon.

A very curious thing to hear Angela's name linked with that of another missing woman.

Her picture flashed on the screen, her disappearance much more the focus of the story since they'd found her car, due to her cell phone.

He hadn't thought of that.

Without it the vehicle might have sat there for some time, unnoticed since there were businesses all around it, but while Angela could have not even been in the state when she went off the grid, the plea was more for any information about Karen Foxton.

He'd put his wife's vehicle in that abandoned barn, so it was invisible. Nice day for a stroll on a country road to get him home.

So far so good.

Almost the perfect crime.

They'd find it sooner or later. He'd never thought they wouldn't.

* * *

He was gone.

There just wasn't an easy solution to the current situation. Lauren was trying for it, but the wicked wind was blowing two different directions. Drew had kept it pretty

134

neutral as he stowed his suitcase in the trunk and shoved it shut, but then again, what choice did he have. "Just so you know, none of this went like I expected."

That made two of them. Or the three of them actually, because Rob certainly hadn't planned any of this happening either.

"I know." Her return smile was probably not very convincing. "Trust me I won't be going for long walks in the woods alone. It will be more like working inside with the doors locked and Rob within screaming distance."

"You could still go with me."

And meet your wife? She didn't say it, but it occurred to her to make the comment. Instead, she shook her head. "The detectives asked only for a few days. That I can manage. I'm going to see what happens."

"I don't think I have much bargaining power right now or I'd insist."

He had zero bargaining power at the moment. "You're flying out, Drew. I could sit at my desk at home wondering what is going on, or just be here and know."

"With Rob."

That point was hard to argue. "You tell me," she said in a level voice, "just what we are supposed to do. They want us to stay, so we're staying. You have an excuse we don't have."

"They want *him* to stay."

"We've been over this."

"This is difficult for me. Just don't disappear when I'm gone. I don't want to be exonerated that way. Lauren, I do love you." He touched her cheek. "Be careful. I have no idea what is going to happen next in our lives, but losing you isn't an option."

"I'll stay close to Rob, don't worry."

His expression was wry as he pulled out his keys. "I kind of figured that one out already. I'll see you soon."

He drove off in his expensive car and she wasn't sure if she was relieved or upset to see him pulling away.

Yes, she'd be with Rob but she doubted Drew would be alone either.

"So he's off." Rob slid back the screen and came outside, putting his hands in his pockets. "I thought I'd give you a minute or two alone."

"I think in a figurative way, we just said goodbye."

"I absolutely have no comment that will sound impartial."

She walked up the steps to the deck and sank into a chair. "I can't go on a vacation with one man and leave with another. That is not how I live my life."

"The entire circumstances are on the extraordinary side." He seemed relaxed but maybe like he was dealing with internal conflict too. "I can't say if I'd rather be him, or me. I want to be here alone with you, but he just got to walk away from the major problem. Why don't you qualify your comment by saying: I can't believe I arrived with one murder suspect and ended up with a different one? Why didn't you go? I know he just asked you again. Or I would have, in his place."

"For more than one reason, but mostly because I didn't want to just leave you alone."

"Hell, Lauren, I want to protect *you*, not the other way around."

She glanced around and said firmly, "I'm not unaware of the situation. I think that is the usual problem. What you don't see coming your way takes you off guard. Heaston has to be fascinated. I have the feeling he's in the same quandary as we are, wondering if we are going to go or stay." She rested her chin on her fist. "I trust Bailey and Carter. I believe they want to sort this out, not just assign blame."

"I hope that's true. That they just don't want to pin it on anyone handy. I'm handy."

"No, they want the truth." She was convinced, and why she didn't know, but she was. Maybe it was Bailey. That was one intense man. There was some faith there on her part.

"If we are stuck in this situation, I hope that is how it works out." He paused. It was there. She felt it and heard it. "I never wanted anything bad to happen between you and Drew even though I was having some less than angelic thoughts about you."

She hadn't really expected that declaration, but maybe in a way she had. She was emotionally involved with Drew but needed to admit her feelings for Rob were serious in a different way. Then again, he was a different man. "At least we are on the same page there. I wasn't fooling Drew either. However, he who lives in a glass house shouldn't throw stones as they say." She equivocated, "I'm being unfair. He explained, but I wish he'd done it earlier."

"I think he was convinced he was handling it the right way. Since we are here for a few more days, should we make a trip to the store? I'll cook dinner, just don't expect gourmet. They said don't leave the county, not don't leave the house, but I really am reluctant to have you here alone."

She wished she didn't agree, but she did. "I can make dinner, no problem. I like to cook. I just didn't want to be *the* cook all week. We'll go together. I'm uneasy enough a small sound would probably make me head for a closet, which as far as I can tell, is the worst choice ever according to every horror movie I've ever seen."

He gave a humorless laugh. "We can drop off the flight plans Drew printed, maybe staving off an impromptu visit from the police which I would prefer to deflect during my meal. Doing our civic duty will save taxpayer dollars."

"Now wouldn't that be a nice change of pace." She rose. "I'm on board."

"It's a beautiful day, so a drive through the countryside sounds okay with me anyway."

"I could use the sunshine and I'll avoid the police station if you don't mind."

"You can wait in the truck."

"That's a deal right there. Liquor store next. Let me get my purse so I can replenish some of your uncle's wine supply. I've drunk my fair share of his this past week."

"He won't care, Lauren," Rob assured her.

Given the expensive house, he probably wouldn't, but she did. "I care."

* * *

It was a county sheriff's department in a rural area and he wasn't exactly senior staff, so Chris was there with one secretary and a deputy when Hanson walked through the door. Everyone else was out including Carter who was handling a hit-and-run down near the state park. Not really a homicide probably, but if the guy didn't make it at the least vehicular manslaughter. The term detective was broad enough they covered all kinds of different investigations.

"These are for Detectives Carter and Bailey."

Chris got up from his desk and took the papers himself. "Thank you, Mr. Hanson. All quiet on the lake?"

Rob Hanson gave him an ironic smile. "So far so good, but it's only early afternoon. Those are the flight schedules for Drew. It looks like he won't be back for a while except a day here and there between trips. I can stay for a few extra days, but at some point, I need to at least pick up my mail and Lauren has obligations too."

Chris understood. "We are doing everything we can. The older evidence gets, the harder it is to use. Give *us* time. I barely slept last night." It was true, he'd gotten maybe three restless hours.

"No word on Karen?"

At least Hanson seemed sincerely concerned. Too bad Chris didn't discuss cases with suspects. "We'll be in touch."

"Okay, thanks."

He left and Doreen came over to give him a fax. "Now where's he been all my life?"

"Who?"

She pointed at the door. "The one that just left."

"Oh. Around, but in Ohio mostly. And he's twenty-eight. I have his profile committed to memory. Not your whole life."

She was sixty if she was a day. "That's harsh, you rascal." He didn't mean it that way but luckily, she had a good sense of humor. "True enough. Damn, all you hot ones are so young."

"I think you're gorgeous."

"Keep on talking, Detective. I'm all ears."

He was laughing as she walked away, swinging her ample hips. He called Carter.

"How is the case going?"

"The hit-and-run? It isn't. No one saw anything and if someone did, they aren't talking."

"If this brightens your day, I have the flight schedules for Fletcher. Hanson was just here to drop them off and he seems edgy to me. Should we bring him in for questioning?"

"On what basis? We just don't have enough to justify it."

"He could easily implicate Fletcher."

"That is the direction you're leaning now? Fletcher?"

"I checked tower log records for local airports. Fletcher was in this area when the drowning victim turned up. He flew into Nashville and didn't fly out for five days. He rented a car. I haven't been able to prove Hanson was here yet but give me time. So for now, Fletcher seems more likely to me of the two. Good-looking young pilot meets a girl, kills her either intentionally or by accident, and knows just where to dump the body quietly and efficiently because he's familiar with the lake . . . he flies all over the world. I wonder if we could hook up more disappearances to him."

"That's ambitious. Let's solve this case first."

"There's something else. Let's not forget his mother died in an accidental drowning."

Carter paused before saying in his careful voice, "Accidental being the key word there."

"He was twelve, I was just thinking out loud about the possible emotional ramifications."

"You've considered federal law enforcement, haven't you?"

"What? For the case?"

"No, I meant applying for a job with them."

Yes, Carter *was* sharp all right. He admitted, "I wouldn't mind being a profiler eventually."

"You'd be good at it. You want to get in their heads, and I want no part of that."

It was true. Carter was all meticulous cop and very little imagination. He added, "Keep working it and we'll circle around. I was thinking Hanson is much more likely but maybe you have a point about Fletcher since you did some homework evidently on that."

"Like I said, I couldn't sleep. Don't break Doreen's heart and tell her you are thinking Hanson for the culprit. She's in love."

"Thanks for the information. I would never break Doreen's heart. She'd break my arm or poison my coffee." Carter actually chuckled.

He didn't think the man was capable of it. A chuckle? They ended the call and Chris checked his email. The report was there from the techs on Karen Foxton's car, because they were currently treating it as a crime scene. No blood, a few prints that weren't hers but could be from anyone, none of them on the steering wheel because it had been wiped, and the summary was she wasn't likely to have been killed in her car.

Then . . . where?

If she was killed at all, though he thought it unusual she'd leave behind her nice car, her purse, and her cell phone in a strip mall parking lot.

Or wipe the steering wheel.

He wrote down: *Likely homicide.*

With Mrs. Heaston he wasn't as sure. No car, but no credit card trail so she wasn't out shopping Fifth Avenue unless she had wads of cash, which most people didn't use in this day and age, but maybe she did. He noted: *Homicide or maybe just left her husband and is with a friend.*

Heaston seemed only mildly concerned. Chris had picked up on that.

Unidentified victim, he wrote: *Who are you?*

The facts were few.

Young and probably pretty but morgue photos were never flattering, nice body, and inconclusive head trauma that hadn't killed her except leaving her in a state that allowed her to drown.

That was all they knew. He sat and pondered it for the hundredth time. Had it been his case he'd have a sample from the lake and the fluid in her lungs tested to see if they matched, but it hadn't been his case and there was no way now to find out if maybe she drowned somewhere else.

Frustrating, but then again, even if it could be proven it was somewhere else there were not resources enough to go around testing every lake, river, and pond nearby, so practicality had to come into it. Besides, if she was a victim somewhere else, it would still be difficult to prove who dumped her body in the lake.

Back to square one.

No identity, no suspect, no real leads at all. But with the recent surge in interest in tracking down relatives through a simple DNA test there was a database and they'd tried it just in case someone related to the victim popped up.

Nothing.

It was a cold case.

CHAPTER SEVENTEEN

Midnight was his favorite time of the day, but a ways off.

He usually used the time to write, listened to the wind sighing through the trees, and held off the demons that way, but they still lurked in the shadows and he knew they were there.

Waiting for him. Laughing in the dark.

Twilight soon.

Fletcher had left. He'd seen him go in the early afternoon.

That caught his attention.

So Hanson and the femme fatale were alone now. Had she gone for the sensitive, tall, dark and handsome hero instead of the charismatic pilot?

It changed the book's direction a little.

The triangle had held his attention, but one on one left no mystery. Maybe they had resolved it but he hadn't.

This was a problem.

He needed to know.

* * *

Lauren kept it simple with just grilled chicken tacos and some guacamole — both easy to make. But it was delicious and Rob seemed to agree, eating his dinner with appreciation, and afterward they sat on the deck sipping margaritas.

They might as well act normal even if the world was completely off-kilter. It was pretend enjoyment.

Nice sunset. Nice evening all around but there was some rumbling in the distance.

"Storm headed in. There's a chance of one for the next few days in the forecast. Typical summer here."

The cumulus clouds had formed an ominous anvil-shaped background gilded by crimson during the course of the evening. "It smells like rain," Lauren agreed.

"We've had some beautiful days but also our share of dark skies."

"Are we still talking about the weather?" she asked wryly. "As a metaphor it works."

"I suppose it does."

"I always thought life would be simple. Grow up, go to college, get a job and a house, fall in love with the right person . . . simple, right?"

Rob shook his head and took a drink. "You're such an optimist. I find it endearing as someone that hasn't found it simple at all. Nothing could be more complicated than falling in love."

"How often do you fall in love?"

"Just the once." He took a sip from his glass and looked at her pointedly.

That was nicely done. She didn't know what to say and finally settled for: "I find that hard to believe."

"At my advanced age, you mean? There have been a few serious relationships, but nothing that lasted because obviously that chemistry just wasn't quite there."

"Your advanced age? I'm not far behind." She raised her brows. "Watch it, Hanson."

His voice was soft. "You are heart-stoppingly beautiful."

"You aren't too bad yourself."

"How someone looks isn't enough and we both know that."

She agreed. The purple martins were out over the lake, flying in graceful circles and she watched them swoop up and down, wondering who else might be enjoying this still lovely evening.

"How come I think Heaston is watching us right now?"

He accepted the change in subject. "Intuition. Prior experience? I don't think it is out of the question."

"I bet he is."

"You really don't like him."

"I don't like *that* about him for sure."

"Considering his profession, he has to have an inquisitive mind."

"I think he has a disturbing indifference to his wife's absence."

"You've made that clear."

"It doesn't bother you?"

"We all cope differently. Maybe he doesn't want to face it. She wasn't my wife or was ever going to be, but Karen's disappearance is bothering the hell out of me and I'm not sitting around talking about it."

A valid point. She'd give him that one reluctantly. "Maybe he just wants to forget about it if there's nothing he can do, but I'd be frantic."

"Every relationship is quite different." He didn't exactly shrug but it was there in his tone. "I've never understood my parents. They are civil but absolutely have no mutual interests. They don't even vacation together but seem happy enough with the arrangement. I don't think it would be like that for me. My mother gardens and my father plays a lot of golf. They have a separate existence. For all I know it's a match made in heaven."

"It did produce you." It was her perfect opening to turn the tables when it came to compliments.

He smiled. "I'm not sure if everyone on the planet would applaud that, but if you do, that's important to me."

"My family is a little different. My parents argue constantly but I think oddly enough they are on the same page most of the time, so it is labeled friendly bickering and all of us laugh about it."

"Three of you, right?"

"Four. All older than me, two brothers and my sister and I are best friends."

"I assume then all potential suitors are carefully screened."

Lauren countered, "I know you have a sister. Answer your own question."

"I always get an opinion on whomever I'm dating, that's true. Men take each other's measure, that's for sure, but tell me women don't do the same thing."

"We do," she conceded. "We just are more subtle about it. Your gender doesn't hide their feelings nearly as well."

"I don't discount that, but not to split hairs, we have a harder time not just being upfront. If another guy doesn't like you, we just walk away from each other. You all get your feelings hurt but politely pretend not to show it."

"I think you are inferring women can be two-faced."

"I suppose, since we are having this deep philosophical discussion, my politic view is that women are just more sensitive."

"Very diplomatic."

"I try."

He really did have a smile that did interesting things to her. She said, "You do pretty well. It's nice out here, but can we go inside? I swear I can feel him watching us."

She could and it made her very uncomfortable even if it was just imagination. It easily could be. There was no evidence that Heaston was anything but a nice man, except her gut feeling that maybe it was a facade.

Intuition was very valuable in her opinion. In retrospect, she'd known Drew was holding something back from her. He'd never mentioned her meeting his family, which had seemed odd to her, but maybe not now that she understood where he stood. Surely his parents knew he was married, so introducing a girlfriend would be awkward.

One mystery solved anyway.

Rob was more serious about it. The minute they walked inside he caught her around the waist and pulled her close.

When he lowered his head she melted into him, no holding back. He kissed her with a hunger she could feel. Nice and lingering and at the same time intense.

They were both breathing unevenly when it was over.

He stared down at her. "I wanted that with no one watching, not Heaston and not Drew. Just me and you. Sorry if I took you off guard."

What had really taken her off guard was her response to that impetuous kiss.

"Uhm . . ." It was about all she could manage.

"I agree."

"I can't . . . I mean we can't . . ." She fumbled for the right words.

"Go to bed together? I didn't ask for that, now did I?" He murmured the words against her lips. "Maybe when this is all settled and that discussion comes into play, we can cross that proverbial bridge. I can settle for a goodnight kiss."

Or two, she found.

Drew would never have been there for a child, she found herself musing. Financially he would, of course, but he literally would never *be* there because he was gone so much. She'd always known it, and it had made her very cautious.

Rob would be there every step of the way. She knew that too.

Her life was evolving and it was unexpected and fast-paced. He was right there now holding her against him and, considering everything, she felt surprisingly positive about the situation.

"We are both insane, you do realize that." Yet she rested her hand on his shoulder and didn't pull away when he finally lifted his head, just gazed into his eyes.

"I think that's how it works." His fingers drifted down her back. "Men and women, it makes sense but yet it doesn't."

"Of course it does." She decided on levity, even if her voice was breathless. "We're right and you're wrong but we put up with your gender's nonsense. My grandmother always said that."

146

"Wise woman."

"Oh, she is. And when you taste her famous chocolate tart, you'll fall head over heels for her and forget about me."

"I don't know, you're kind of unforgettable, but I'm willing to try that tart."

"She won't even give me the recipe. Her own granddaughter."

"Probably because she wants to see you, so she uses it as bait maybe."

"Maybe," she conceded. "It works actually."

The sharp rapping on the door came clearly enough. Rob let her go and muttered, "What the hell?"

* * *

There was no one there.

Rob wasn't too excited to answer the door in such a secluded place when it was getting dark outside and, to say the least, some questionable things had been going on that had caught the attention of the police.

He flipped on the outdoor lights and he stood there, unwilling to open the glass door mostly because if it was just him, fine, he'd walk out there. However, as it stood, Lauren would be vulnerable if he was taken by surprise.

So he stood there wondering what the hell was going on. "Who is it?"

Lauren was wide-eyed, her glossy hair rumpled, but that was probably his fault. Running his fingers through it had become his current fantasy and he'd just done it during that second memorable kiss.

He responded grimly, "I don't know but I'm going to tell you, I'm not opening that door to go check it out. I'm standing here wondering if that might be what whoever it is wants. If I go look, which I normally would out of curiosity, they might just shoot me or jump me — we don't know — and you would then be alone and unguarded."

"Could it have been a woodpecker or something?" She looked hopeful but there was doubt in her eyes.

"Not unless they peck on glass and last I checked they don't. No." The last time he and Drew had assumed the culprit was a bird for an odd sound he was now fairly convinced they had been wrong about it. "Someone knocked on this door on purpose. Why? It's getting late and is almost full dark."

This wasn't exactly a city neighborhood either, with people walking by on sidewalks and kids maybe playing ring-and-run pranks. This was a lake cabin and the only way to get to it was by boat or in a vehicle. They hadn't heard either one.

For the first time in his life, he wished he owned a gun and knew how to use it. His uncle was a firearms fanatic so maybe one day he'd take him up on the offer of a few lessons but that wouldn't help right now. There were guns on the property but he wasn't at all skilled in using them, which probably made them more dangerous than helpful, and he was fairly sure they were in a safe. "Someone is messing around out there."

Truer words never spoken.

The sound of shattering glass sent his adrenalin spiking and it was fairly high already. He grabbed Lauren's arm. "Stay with me."

Someone was definitely breaking in.

"No worries there." She didn't resist, her voice thin. "I don't think I'm a fainting heroine but there's nothing wrong with my sense of self-preservation."

He dragged her down the hallway. "I don't know if I want to go down in the annals of history as someone who staved off an invader with a canoe paddle from probably the Lewis and Clark era, but the office is close and there are two of them on the wall in there."

"I bet the Vikings did it all the time."

"I think the Vikings were the invaders. Lock the door. God, I wish I'd grabbed my phone."

Except he remembered there was a landline on the desk. There had been no need to use it before now except to answer the calls from Karen's office, but at least he could call 911. He grabbed it. Dial tone. Thank God.

"What's your emergency?"

"Someone is trying to break in, or has broken in." He unfortunately couldn't give the address, once again it was in his phone but he didn't know it by heart except for the road. "Can you trace the call for this exact address please and also contact Detective Bailey of the County Sheriff's Department to tell him Rob Hanson called in an intruder. I have his card but not on me. I think he'll be interested."

All he actually had on him was a pair of jeans and a T-shirt. He'd even taken his shoes off out on the deck. The only thing worse than a man defending himself with an antique canoe paddle was a bare-footed man with said paddle locked in a den, but once again, he wasn't letting Lauren out of his sight.

"Is anyone hurt?"

"Not yet," he replied grimly to the dispatcher and thought, but let them try to come through that door.

He went and took down those paddles from that fancy rack and handed one to Lauren. "Don't be shy if it is necessary."

CHAPTER EIGHTEEN

Sophia sensually rubbed his naked back. "You are my Adonis."

"Am I? Who is he?"

"A Greek god."

No, she misunderstood. He was referring to her other lover. "I know the reference. I mean my rival."

For a moment, and it passed quickly, she tried to pretend confusion, but then sighed and gave him his answer. "A warrior prince, capable of anything except utter devotion. I know he has other women."

"When you share his bed, how are we different?"

"You can't ask that!"

"I just did."

She stretched sensuously, the tips of her breasts brushing his bare chest. "He takes what he wants, but you give."

He didn't like it. Too contrived and he was a better writer than that in his opinion, so Glenn sat and thought about how he needed more inspiration. He reread the words, looked at the screen and thought they were not a perfect fit for the erotic tone of the novel, not even close. Then he abandoned his desk and went out onto the deck. Flashing blue-and-red lights, men in uniform, and using the telescope he could see Hanson out there talking to them.

Police officers. Two of them, in uniform and then they went into the house, obviously looking around. The place was illuminated like an *attraction at an amusement park and he had to admit it added interest to his evening.*

Between his wife's absence and the Beautiful Trio, he was having an eventful week.

Why had he broken the window?

Pique perhaps, he wasn't sure. Were the trio still intact or had Fletcher lost the battle? He thought he had because when he'd gone up on the porch, intending on an exploratory visit to see if he could gain any information, he'd seen Hanson passionately kissing his prize.

The surge of possessive jealousy took him by surprise.

That was his heroine, his own femme fatale. An incomparable muse.

* * *

Chris parked his SUV next to the squad car and climbed out into a humid Tennessee night. Frogs were singing in the trees, crickets chirping, and the water moved gently under the moonlight.

A gorgeous night. No rain. That threat had passed without fulfilling the promise.

He could have declined to address this call and left it to the patrol officers but had a feeling he should just set sleep aside for now. If one venture into the night could solve three cases — at *least* three of them — he was on board.

The uniformed officers were just coming out the front door as he got out of the car. He knew them, so he greeted them without much in the way of fanfare. "What's going on here, guys?"

"Detective." One answered with a nod. "Not much. A warning knock on the door and a broken window. It really was broken from the outside and even if they hadn't called it in the alarm would have gone off. Someone wanted to get in. The owners are freaked out."

"Three ongoing investigations of possible murders in the area make the caution understandable."

One of them whistled. "Okay, that makes more sense now since you just showed up. We answer the calls, but the dispatchers don't really tell us shit. All we got was that there was a possible intruder."

"We have a drowning and two missing women."

"Here?"

"Connected to this lake, yes."

They glanced at each other and Chris certainly caught that interaction. "What? Something I should know?"

Falk, the senior officer, said, "Maybe. We responded to a call out here once before. A few months ago. It was to a house on this lake but not this one. Domestic violence. Even with all these high-end places and money floating around it still happens in this area, you wouldn't think it, but it sure does. The girlfriend went off in an ambulance because there was blood everywhere. We arrested the guy for battery and he was one unhappy camper. It was a close call on a resisting arrest charge, but you know what, he turned out to be a lawyer, so maybe for the best he didn't push us quite far enough for that. I hope she sued him for her broken nose and other various bruises and his rich ass lost because she had a better attorney. Just saying."

That really *was* interesting.

"I'll look into the report. I appreciate the tip."

Another suspect? Maybe, since there was a history of violence toward women. It did raise a red flag. Worth the trip maybe, but he still had some pointed questions for Rob Hanson.

But the first order of business was a very important one for Lauren Mathews.

Hanson answered the door barefoot, looking tense and unhappy. He said, "Detective Bailey. Come on in."

"I do have a few questions."

Lauren Mathews was drinking a cup of tea while sitting at the kitchen island, looking about as pale as the polished marble counter. She was composed and greeted him politely. "Sorry we interrupted your evening."

"No problem. You called in and you should have. Where was Mr. Hanson when you realized someone was trying to break in?"

At that abrupt question, she looked taken aback. "Rob? Right next to me."

"Never out of your line of vision?"

"No. He was holding on to me actually when it happened because we'd just heard the knock on the door and not much longer after that someone broke the window."

Holding on to her? He really wasn't surprised, even with the admission Foxton had joined the vacation group to be with Hanson. "What room were you in? Kitchen, great room, bedroom?"

"Kitchen," Lauren supplied, but color crept back into her face at the reference to the bedroom.

Chris nodded, aware of her embarrassment but then again, he needed to know. "I just want a clear picture. If Mr. Hanson could have snuck out and broken that window it would change this investigation."

"I didn't." The man in question wasn't combative, just declarative, his jaw set. "Look somewhere else. We'll be leaving tomorrow. Lauren can't stay here."

Chris understood Hanson's point of view, but he wasn't positive he agreed with the location change either. "Andrew Fletcher switched out his first scheduled flight for tomorrow with another pilot. I really appreciate you bringing in those itineraries so promptly. Are you sure he ever left the area? Did you know about this sudden change in plans?"

He let it hang in the ensuing silence, the implication obvious.

"You can't be serious," Lauren Mathews said after a moment, the words careful. "It wasn't him. Drew wouldn't ever break a window. He wouldn't need to do that. He could just make a call and we'd let him in without question. Both of us trust him." Then she amended, "In that regard."

He'd already gathered the relationship might be complicated.

So he chose his words. "Jealousy can make anyone do strange things. It doesn't look like the vandal really wanted to get in the house — he just wanted to ruin your night. Your personal life isn't my concern unless it is complicating the investigation. If it does, I will ask questions."

Ms. Mathews looked chagrined over that observation. Rob Hanson didn't look happy either. He said evenly, "Drew wouldn't. I've known him for a long time. If he had something to say to either one of us, he would have just said it."

Maybe, maybe not. They knew him better than he did certainly. But his conclusion made sense.

"He was here for the recent disappearances, and also for the drowning last summer, or at least in the window of the victim's death, since it is very difficult to gauge time of death when a body is in the water."

"You can't mean he's an actual suspect. I was here too." Hanson wasn't really defensive, just pointing out the obvious.

"I know. Why do you think I asked where you were when the window was broken?" Chris smiled thinly.

"No stone left unturned? I am not under that stone you are looking for. But neither is Drew Fletcher. He wasn't ever on his own from his arrival until today, and neither was I. We can vouch for each other in that regard, for what that might be worth. Both of us can't be guilty."

That was an unlikely scenario, true enough. He thought about the lawyer who knocked around his girlfriend. Not everyone was as innocent as they seemed. "Who else do you see on this lake?"

"Not too many people. A boat or two comes into view now and then, mostly at the other end past the point. People are on their decks having drinks or enjoying the sun occasionally when we go out fishing, sometimes children in the water, swimming. Usually, it is quiet as far as I can tell. The houses are vacation homes, so there's some weekend occupation but that's about it."

"Dr. Heaston is here a lot, and often alone, he's told us that." Lauren had an edge to her voice. "He likes to watch us with his telescope."

First of all, she was worth watching from a purely male perspective. Second, he'd already gotten that she wasn't a

154

huge fan of the writer from a comment or two she'd made. Chris said, "That really isn't a crime unless he's peering in your window."

"Don't even say that. I don't want anyone looking in my window. That's not real life, that's a nightmare." She gave a mock shiver, but he had a feeling it wasn't at all feigned.

"No one does, that's why it is a crime." He kept his voice very even. "You didn't hear a vehicle or a boat before the knock on the door? Nothing?"

"No." Hanson paused. "But I wasn't exactly paying attention."

Enough said. With the undeniably attractive Ms. Mathews he might not be either. She confirmed hollowly, "I didn't hear anything."

It could be as simple as a would-be burglar checking to see if anyone was at home and when he realized there was movement in the house, he abandoned the plan. Chris decided to take a pragmatic view rather than be alarmist. "Any number of scenarios might apply. As you pointed out the houses are known for being vacation destinations. Someone might have just been trying to see if there was anything valuable inside. When they realized someone was here, they left."

"Or else it was whoever caught a glimpse of Lauren at one time or another and came around for another look." Hanson pointed it out with vehemence. "All this past week she's been reading outside or sitting on the dock."

That was certainly possible given the tie of the women to the lake. "Welcome to my world. I am always trying to second-guess what the bad guy is thinking. I win sometimes, but it isn't always a slam dunk."

Hanson said grimly, "No offense, but while I appreciate what you do, I want no part of your world."

"Just sit tight for a few more days, please. I think you two might be the key to all of this more than ever now. I'll ask to have a county deputy swing by a couple of times a day."

He did think they were central to the case. Was it Fletcher? He wasn't as convinced as they were that it wasn't.

It was only too plausible. Malicious but not an actual threat. Pissed off he had to leave and maybe lose the girl.

Something to consider.

* * *

Drew wondered if he was making the mistake of his life — again. He was essentially giving up fighting for a life with Lauren on the off-chance his wife really meant it. But then again he wasn't sure he was going to win Lauren anyway. Rob could offer her the life she wanted — solid, secure, a father to take his kids to the park, maybe coach a softball team, attend school events. Drew had come to the conclusion he wasn't ready — or maybe ever would be — to be that kind of husband. He could fly them to the Grand Canyon or any amusement park they choose, but he would not be there for the day-to-day.

Mowing a lawn? No thank you. That wasn't him. He'd hire a service.

It was pulling him apart.

He pushed a button on his phone after he pulled into his driveway. "Long drive but I'm back in Ohio."

"Good," Cassandra responded. "I was thinking dinner at Bella's in celebration of our old times, and hopefully new ones. I made a reservation when I got your text."

That was pulling out all the stops. The place they'd had their first date. Well, if he was going to do this, he should be all in. He'd shuffled his schedule to meet Cassandra and arranged a later short flight to D.C. instead so he could take his time with this evening. "Sounds nice. That is always a winner. I'll meet you there."

"You aren't coming here to pick me up?"

It might be the gentlemanly thing to do, but he was handling this cautiously. "We are in the middle of a divorce. Let's meet and have dinner and talk first."

He should probably mention he was a potential person of interest by a certain police department in Tennessee, but he left that out. This was complicated enough.

Luckily, she didn't argue. "Fine, we'll meet at eight o'clock. The reservation is under our name, of course."

Our name. He'd always known she was one determined woman when she wanted something. He'd experienced it firsthand. She'd insisted on the expensive house they still owned and she'd paid for most of it herself. He was gone so much the condo suited him just fine once they separated. She'd been on that same track when they first met with her hectic schedule, but things change.

And he wasn't as ready to go with the flow as he had been before.

The restaurant was upscale and pricey but casual on purpose, appealing to young professionals, and yet he dressed carefully. Which might be an indication of his feelings . . . it was hard to tell.

He wasn't anxious or excited to see her. He was calm and controlled, just off balance. All of this wasn't happening to someone else, it was happening to *him.*

He drove to the restaurant and was a little early. He was seated at a table he could tell she'd asked for specifically, ordered a cocktail for her and was sipping on a light beer when Cassandra walked in.

Heads turned.

Lauren was captivatingly beautiful, but Cassandra was more understated. With a chic haircut at her jawline, the dramatic sense of style — this time a sapphire dress — but mostly it was her confidence that caught his attention. Cassandra glanced around and spotted him at their table. Her smile was compelling as she came over and he stood politely, pulling out her chair.

She kissed him, a calculated move, as well he knew. Her hand lingered on his shoulder. "Hello."

"Hello."

Nice kiss, discreet but with a liberal dose of erotic mixed in. She knew how to play nice.

She knew how to play *very* nice. He hadn't forgotten.

But she also knew how to get exactly what she wanted. He was well aware of it and if she'd decided their marriage was on the list, he was going to get the full court press. There was never going to be a time when he claimed he understood women entirely, but he did know that about this particular female.

She sank gracefully into her chair. "How was Tennessee?"

"Eventful," he answered truthfully, taking his own seat. "I just planned on sitting in a boat, communing with water and trees, and due to my superior skill with a hook and line, catching more fish than Rob did. That wasn't exactly what happened."

"He caught more fish?" She took a sip from her cosmopolitan, eyebrows raised, looking amused.

"No, I think we ended up about even there. Tell me you want the calamari for an appetizer."

She clearly knew full well he was deflecting but chose to let it pass, maybe as a gesture of conciliation. "Sounds wonderful. That sauce is magic."

There he had to agree. "Over the top. How do you like the new job?"

"It is more challenging than I thought it would be. In a strange way, I think I stepped up more than stepped down. I'm much more connected to the people who work for the company. I think I'm good at it."

He could see that but was surprised she would recognize it. She'd climbed the corporate ladder very quickly due to her intelligence and determination and had liked the position of power, he'd known that. Her goal had always been to go nose to nose with her male counterparts and hold her own. She also liked the money, no doubt about it. If Lauren was the artistic girl-next-door type, Cassandra was the razor-sharp sophisticated executive with high-end tastes.

He needed to stop comparing them.

"Never a bad thing." He said it neutrally. "You look great. I like the dress."

She tilted her head, studying him. "You do too. Nice tan. You must have gone out on the boat some of the time. Do you want us to sell the house? I know you really never wanted it in the first place."

Right down to business. If there was one thing about her, she wasn't reticent.

"That's up to you. I was going to give it to you in the settlement." He would have signed a pre-nup but she hadn't asked and for that matter, he hadn't either. "I'm gone so much, and you were gone a lot as well, that I thought we'd be better off with something simpler to manage. Maybe your perspective has changed."

"Let's keep it. My perspective *has* changed. I want our marriage to work. And I want children."

The waiter arrived then with their menus and he about dropped his on the floor, but managed to rescue it. "What?"

Cassandra's response was composed, and if not rehearsed, certainly she'd at the least anticipated his surprise. "I know I said I didn't think we had that on our horizon, but I'd like to have a child. Our child."

He really had no idea what to say.

"It made me reassess everything." She essayed a smile. "Tell me about her, this woman you're involved with. Are you willing to consider us instead?"

* * *

No sleep in sight. Maybe three hours, and a fitful attempt at best.

Lauren wasn't going to waste her time, so she got out of bed. Rob was at the dining-room table, she discovered, working on his computer. He looked up from the screen.

She sat opposite and said wryly, "I see I'm not the only one who couldn't sleep."

"No. I tried, it just wasn't happening. I dozed for maybe a few minutes here and there."

"No success for me either." She was succinct. "He can't really think it's Drew."

"Bailey? Well, there's an argument to be made if he does." He picked up a coffee cup and took a sip. "How could you and I not know he was married? It makes one wonder. I defended Drew — you heard me — and I still would, but I wish he'd never been the one to tell us he might be suspected. That alone is suspicious."

She wished that too. "I thought he was crazy. I was wrong."

"I was worried he was right. I've got to be suspect number two now."

"You didn't break that window tonight or knock on the door." She said it forcefully. "I was right here. I can vouch for you."

"No, I didn't. But, like with Drew, the incidents could be unrelated."

"Then Bailey had better figure it out."

"I get the impression he's really trying to do just that."

She did too. "Are we going to leave or stay like he asked?"

He ran his fingers through that thick, wavy dark hair. "I don't know. You tell me because it is your decision too. I'm wondering if we wouldn't just be stuck explaining it all to a different set of officers if anything else happened. I keep telling myself the police here at least know what's going on. If you are being stalked for some reason, who is to say they can't travel to Ohio?"

There was that. But was this about her? Hard to say.

"This house has a high-end security system." She was thinking out loud.

"It does." He didn't argue. "But we can't turn it back on until the window is fixed."

Drew would definitely know where she was, not that she bought into that theory anyway. "I vote just stay here and cooperate. It's beautiful and peaceful, they were very quick to respond, and we aren't sure of anything."

"No, we really aren't."

160

"So . . . here?"

"If that's your decision. Beware that I will be your shadow, but no hardship on my part there."

"I have an ulterior motive, but it has occurred to me that you'd be right here with me so I might be safer than by myself at home."

He looked wary but interested. "Ulterior motive? Okay."

"I want to start spying on Heaston. Fair is fair. He certainly does it to us, as we well know."

He lifted his brows. "You want a telescope?"

"No, I want a trail camera. The kind they use to track animals. They aren't that expensive and will record whatever happens near the house even in complete darkness. Night-vision feature. What's more, they record it, so we can prove it happened, not just us saying we saw it and making someone take our word for it."

"That's actually a pretty good idea." Rob smiled at her, but he still looked troubled. "Why didn't I think of it? Maybe women *are* smarter than men."

"Goes without saying." She smiled too but it was probably just as hesitant. "The local hardware store should carry them. I'm not a woman on a mission really, but I am concerned for everyone involved."

"Me too. We'll go get one tomorrow morning." He glanced at his screen and grimaced over the time display. "Or I guess it would be *this* morning."

CHAPTER NINETEEN

Not a whisper of light yet.

His head ached. There was no sense of what time it might be.

There was very little doubt he was drinking too much.

Taking a deep breath, he realized he was slumped in his chair by his computer. Maybe he remembered last night, or maybe he didn't.

There was a dark-red streak on his right arm.

Blood from a scratch he couldn't recall.

Wait, yes, he did. The broken window. He remembered watching the show when the police arrived, drinking scotch — probably should monitor his alcohol intake more closely — and enjoying it immensely.

* * *

"Is it safe?"

He was decisive. "I can't live my life that way. Surely after disrupting our evening, whoever visited us has to sleep sometime. We couldn't, so he accomplished his mission if Bailey is right, but maybe a cruise at dawn over the water will fix the situation. Our shadow can't follow us without us noticing, so that's something. The water carries sound. Besides, all I could do was stretch a beach towel over the broken window and tack it in place. A four-year-old could still get in so we aren't safe in here either. Hopefully we can arrange for someone to come replace it this morning."

He was right. She really couldn't live like that either. "I'm going to get a cup of coffee to take with me."

It was disquieting to walk to the lake in the dark, but the chirp of the frogs was peaceful and Rob brought a flashlight.

The lake like glass, the scent of the trees, the utter quiet . . . Lauren didn't realize how tense she was until they left the dock and though she wanted to talk about everything, a contradictory part of her just didn't. She'd managed to get in the boat without spilling her beverage which was a miracle. "What a glorious morning. You weren't kidding about the moon still being up."

"I agree. How nice, and unless James Bond is out there, no one is following us. I am paying attention."

"The vigilance is appreciated." He'd held her hand every step of the way from the house down to the dock.

Sweet, but necessary? She wasn't sure.

"I don't have a choice and you don't really have one either because I would do it regardless. For that matter, so would Drew."

He would. She knew it, and even though she had a suspicion Drew's marriage might not be as over as he'd thought it was, she believed he had serious feelings for her.

She made a helpless gesture. "How can I be involved with you and still care for Drew?"

"I think I'm asking myself the same question."

She sipped her coffee, watching the lingering moonlight dance off the lake and feeling the gentle rock of the boat. "There are a lot of unanswered questions hanging out there."

"Oh, there are." Rob had chosen to row rather than use the electric motor, the soft splash of the oars soothing. "For instance, what happened last night is interesting. What did he want? Or she? I suppose a woman is capable of knocking on a door and breaking a window."

"Glad you brought that up. Look at history and my gender is certainly guilty of a lot more than that. Let's talk

Bonnie and Clyde which was the subject of one of Heaston's books. Since I have a copy now of *A Poisoned Lady*, let's mention Lucrezia Borgia. Heaston finds women who kill fascinating apparently."

"Yeah, it does make you wonder."

It certainly made *her* wonder.

She said slowly, thinking out loud, "It would be interesting to know how he met his wife."

Rob caught the nuances in her voice. She liked that about him. He was very quick on the uptake. "Why?"

"I'm understandably curious. What's her story and why isn't he more worried? Is she just the wife of a rich man or is she the wife of a man who became rich thanks to her inheritance?"

"And the repeated femme fatale reference sets you off on this tangent?"

It did. "It seems to be a theme with him. I hate to break it to him but, this week aside, I live a pretty sedate existence. Get up, go to work, come home and fix dinner, and mow my lawn when it needs it. Occasionally I go out to dinner with friends. I'm pretty boring."

"There's nothing boring about you in my opinion. Drew doesn't think so either, and evidently Heaston has noticed we both feel that way."

She was well aware Heaston had picked up on it. She looked up at the star-studded sky. "If I had killed someone, he might write a book about me. I think we can both guess what the title would be."

"As long as it isn't me," he remarked dryly. "I mean in the starring role as the dead guy."

"Well, don't tick me off. It's a warning, Mr. Hanson."

"Duly noted."

At least he'd smiled even if it was a bit grim, because this was not a light-hearted trip so far, but the boat outing was a good idea. She pointed out, "We have a broken window. You stated he can climb right in."

"For some reason, I think those deputies might be cruising by now and then to see if I'm maybe murdering someone else, more than for our protection. When Bailey asked where I was when the window was broken, I have to admit to a certain sense of shock."

He was correct. Bailey was paying attention. "I could tell." Then she said, thinking out loud, "I wonder if his wife somehow inspired him for one of his books. The inside of the copy he gave me has a list of 'Other titles by Glenn Heaston'. He's obsessed with women who have murdered people. One of them is titled *Deadly Heiress*. I think it is his first book."

* * *

Rob stopped rowing. The boat drifted. Water was rippling, shimmering . . . the world felt surreal. Lauren's face was shadowed. "I'm asking this cautiously. Where did that come from? You think it's about her?"

"Who knows, but I wonder if in doing his research he stumbled across something that attracted him to her. It was written quite a while ago and is the only book he's ever written that doesn't have a specific historical character in mind. This is pure speculation and quite a reach, I admit, but was his initial interest stirred in her because of something dark in her past?"

In the slanting light it was hard to read her expression and he said nothing for a long moment. "It *is* a reach, but maybe you should suggest it to Bailey. I bet he'd be inclined to look into it. She is missing and it is his case. If Drew and I are people of interest, Heaston had better be under the microscope as well."

"If he isn't, I think he should be."

So far, he thought Lauren had been remarkably collected over all the unsettling events of their not-so-relaxing lakeside vacation.

She'd obviously been really considering that aspect. "Whoever it was was trying to scare us, that isn't in question."

"Good tactic since it worked. I go on full alert at the sound of breaking glass. Now I owe my uncle that window.

I can't see how this is my fault, but I do. I came here on vacation . . . I just thought we'd all hang out by the lake. Drew and I would fish. It seemed pretty simple."

"It really hasn't turned out that way."

"No."

"If this was a classic novel, I'd compare it more to *The Shining* by Stephen King. I don't know if he used an ax to break that window, but maybe he did."

Rob stifled a laugh. "You are in a literary mood this morning. Okay, can't argue that one. At least there's no snow in our version."

"I'll give *you* that one. We've had warm weather." Her fingers wrapped around her cup. "And I still haven't caught a fish. It is a personal goal. I don't care, despite everything this is nice. I'm trying to focus on something positive here. You're right. Out on the water, no one can take you by surprise."

"I still have to arrange for someone to repair that damn window. That is not in my skill set. I could fix a computer program in my sleep, but the window needs to look as good as new. I'm not positive I can achieve that." His smile was rueful. "There's glazing compound involved, I know about that much. How to apply it, not so much."

"No help here, I know even less. Do you think he'll be back?" Lauren looked at him.

"Whoever did it? Who knows."

"I think coming by water is the way he got here."

He did as well. "My guess too. Electric motors on boats are practically silent. But they could have parked someplace and walked through the woods."

Lauren gazed at him in reproof. "Rob, that is really not a picture I want in my mind. Someone creeping through the dark woods is as bad as the face-in-the-window nightmare."

"At the risk of sounding sensitive, if you don't have them already, I do," he countered. "How did we land in the middle of this?"

"I hate to break it to you, but you *are* sensitive. It says nothing about your masculinity. And I wish I knew the answer."

"I'm not all that worried about my masculinity, I'm more worried that I sense 'something wicked this way comes' to quote Bradbury since that's our theme this morning. What's worse, to be of interest to the police, or of interest to someone who might be a killer? Both sound bad. I'd just as soon get out of line and let someone else take my place."

"The trouble is, maybe Karen just had car trouble and was ticked off because she didn't get the vacation she expected, and so she called someone to pick her up until she could arrange to have it fixed. What if Mrs. Heaston really is shopping in the Hamptons, and maybe last night was an attempt at a break-in by someone who knows there are a lot of expensive and usually empty vacation homes here. There are reasonable explanations for everything, even that girl that drowned. Alcohol and a late-night swim might be one. I hate to think about fatal mistakes, but that could be one of them."

But why did no one miss her. That's what got to him.

Karen's phone. That also spelled out clearly something was wrong, but it was possible she carried one for work and a personal cell as well. Possible, but not likely, and if so, why wasn't she answering the one she took with her?

He knew Lauren was right on all counts. "I understand their job is complicated, but I admit on a personal level, I wish for all involved, the police would figure it out and not include us. So many loose ends."

"There does seem to be any number of scenarios that are possible."

"I agree. I'm game on for fishing later by the way."

"I'm writing a proposal for a new project." She looked out over the water. "I'm finding it a little hard to concentrate on this trip for some reason."

For some reason. Both he and Drew were part of the problem, everything else aside. "I can empathize. My relaxing vacation went a little off the tracks as well. You and the fish are the good part."

Her mouth twitched. "Such elite company. I'm flattered."

"You should be. Anglers are notoriously hard to please."

"I intend to become one, so that's good to know."

"Sweetheart, when you dipped a line with a hook on it in the water you became one."

"But I haven't caught a fish yet, remember?"

Rob had to grin. "But you've had a strike already. My grandfather had this crusty old friend named Harry and they used to go on fishing trips together. For whatever reason, my grandfather caught all kinds of fish from bass to walleye to perch, and Harry never did catch much of anything. As a kid I remember them arguing over it when they played cards in the evening at an old rickety table and insulted each other. It was pretty amusing." He glanced around. "Uh, trust me, that old cabin was nothing like this. But I loved those trips. They cooked outside and I slept on a cot in the corner of the one room while they each pitched tents on the hill. They argued over that too. The bathroom was an outhouse. Bathing took place in the lake. It was fun, believe it or not. I learned some colorful language on those trips."

Lauren smiled. "It sounds like fun actually. Don't get me wrong, this place is amazing, but as a child the adventure of a rustic camping trip would have appealed to me. Now I want hot water and internet access and to be able to use a blow dryer."

"I don't think those two old outdoorsmen would have approved of this place. Too posh. Wielding an ax for a camp-fire or netting a big fish, yes, but air-conditioning? No way, that was a stiff breeze blowing across the lake. Remind me to tell you when we are in a more festive mood the tale of their ill-fated excursion to northern Wisconsin to go bear hunting one year together. It involves buckets of lard and some stale dill bread as bait to attract the bears."

"Hunt bears? I didn't even know you could do that. I think I'll stick with catching a fish."

He wasn't interested in bear hunting either. "I'm with you and not anxious to sleep on a floor in a sleeping bag ever again. Go ahead with your proposal and I'll see if I can arrange for that window to be fixed and then we can go get that camera."

CHAPTER TWENTY

Inspiration came from various sources. He'd learned to listen to the inner voice, but not question it.

He'd passed the 20k word count on his novel. The book was really writing itself because that was just a few days of work.

And he dreamed when he'd finally fallen asleep.

Black cool water and his body floating in a gentle current but he couldn't breathe and he was getting deeper and deeper . . .

He woke up gasping in his chair and stood to shake it off, trembling and dripping wet from sweat.

That wasn't an experience he cared to repeat.

* * *

Chris got a call from Carter who was supposed to be on a short vacation. He'd just left that morning.

"I do think we have another suspect in the lake case. Registered sex offender lives right down the road. Not close but close enough."

He'd checked that too, but with no bodies — except for the drowning victim, and that could easily have been an accident — there was no evidence of a sexual crime link to these cases.

Chris wasn't buying it as a lead. "He was eighteen when he slept with his fifteen-year-old girlfriend. Her parents were rabid about pressing charges. I agree by the letter of the law he was an adult and she wasn't, but I don't really think that makes him anything other than a typical young man with a pretty willing girl. She said it was consensual. She testified in court it was. That young man got a tough judge. He isn't our guy, or at least I doubt it. I'm really considering the lawyer more closely, the one that beat up his girlfriend. Neither Hanson nor Fletcher has a whisper of that on their record. They don't have a record at all, either one of them."

"Neither did any number of the serial killers I can name that just were smart and efficient and didn't get easily caught. The ghost of Jack the Ripper is still out there and it only took them over a hundred years to figure it out."

"Oh, I'm all cheered up now. We don't have a hundred years."

"I wasn't put on this earth to cheer you up. I agree about the sex offender by the way, but it was worth mentioning. What else do we have? Your text said some interesting developments."

"Fletcher canceled his flight. I don't like it. We don't have any evidence to hold him, but he left ostensibly because of an international flight early in the morning, and then another pilot took it. I only know this because I am keeping an eye on him as a literal flight risk. Even private airlines cooperate when you mention you are a detective."

"So we don't know where he is."

"No, we don't. I know where he's been, but that is about it. He did pilot a later flight to Washington, D.C. this morning and went back to Ohio later, but the fact remains he didn't follow his itinerary, which was his excuse for leaving here in the first place, so we don't know where he was last night. He has a residence there. In fact, he has two different addresses and that's a red flag. Maybe he's packing to leave for good."

"I know about his name on the deed for two properties. I'm looking into it from here."

His partner was all business. Chris said mildly, "Hey, aren't you supposed to be lying on a beach somewhere? Don't send me a picture by the way. I don't need to see you in a skimpy bathing suit."

Carter did laugh and it rarely happened. "No worries. I don't do that, but I do have a tee time tomorrow afternoon, so maybe one of me with a beer in a golf cart. I don't like this case. It's so muddy."

"I think considering it one case is part of our problem. Here's my take. Fletcher is number one, the lawyer very worth looking into, Hanson is third now because he didn't break that window, and Heaston is also a possibility."

"And this could also be a random offender from anywhere."

"That is unfortunately true."

Carter swore softly. Then he said, "See if you can keep tabs on Fletcher, go interview the lawyer, and I'll call tomorrow afternoon. I'll also try and make par on at least one hole during my golf game but I think that is my only hope. Don't take bets on it. I'm playing against my wife and she's better than me. She'll birdie most of them. Is there anything more galling than that?"

"If it will make you feel any better, she'd probably beat me too. I'm a tennis player but golf isn't my game. I'll do both things you just suggested and send an email with the results. You don't need a ringing phone all the time. If something big breaks, I'll call."

"I'd appreciate it. This case is on my mind."

It was on Chris's mind too.

He did better when he wrote things down.

It wasn't some kid who'd had sex with the willing young girl and paid the price for not paying attention to the rules more than his hormones. No. Off the list. He was unlikely to be the one.

If this was a matter of two different cases, they were leading themselves astray trying to make a connection that didn't exist.

But still he thought they might be linked and he just wasn't seeing it.

Crime Blind. Not a great thing for a detective. Working off instincts was fine, but knowing you were missing something was frustrating. On a cerebral level he did better writing freehand, just jotting things down. His colleagues made snide comments, but then again, it worked for him. Handwritten. Not everything had to be on a computer, so he'd taken the notebook.

He also thought with more clarity when he wasn't hungry. So he went out for pizza to a little place in the touristy downtown section.

Deep dish with the works and he felt better once he'd had a slice. There was a nice breeze, people passing on the street . . . he might be in a relationship, but he definitely operated independently and Sara was out with girlfriends. The moppet puppy might be lonely at the moment, but he'd take the rest of the pizza to the house, defy the rules — no people food — and give the dog at least a piece of crust to chew on while the two of them were alone, and continue to try to work this all out.

Why did Fletcher cancel his flight?

He flat out didn't have enough to hold the man before that move, but maybe he did now thanks to that. That canceled flight was suspicious. Taking Fletcher in for questioning was at least an option. Hanson might know where he was, but maybe not cooperate.

Carter was right. Keep track of him.

He logged in and punched up the lawyer the two officers had mentioned.

Interesting man. JAG with the US Army for starters, but no longer enlisted. In private practice now and there was no mention of a court appearance on the battery arrest, so maybe ultimately the girlfriend declined to press charges. If it wasn't for those two deputies, Chris would never know the incident had ever happened.

Police work was part diligence, part intuition, and undeniably part chance. Financial advisors didn't always hit the stock market just right either and highly trained doctors didn't nail a diagnosis the first time without fail, so it was true of everything.

Yes, the lawyer was a visit he needed to make, but if he was a good lawyer, it was doubtful he'd incriminate himself.

Chris also needed to call his mother, he thought with an inward groan.

It was never a call he wanted to make for a variety of reasons, one of which was that she disapproved of his living arrangements because he wasn't married to Sara and they had to have that discussion every single time. The daughter of a minister, his mother had pretty firm opinions on the timeline of how things should go between men and women.

He had to wonder how she'd view the situation with Fletcher, Hanson, and Lauren Mathews.

His mother would have a field day with that scenario. Two good friends vying for the same woman . . . Hanson had admitted the reason Karen Foxton had left was because he'd declined making their relationship sexual, but somehow Chris doubted he'd turn down the lovely Ms. Mathews.

At least his love life was the least of his problems, even if his mother didn't approve.

CHAPTER TWENTY-ONE

The book might rival Tropic of Cancer *or* Lolita. *When erotic fantasy collided with reality then true genius kicked in. He wrote with a ferocity he hadn't experienced in some time and would mourn that energy when it was done.*

Cathartic.

Or maybe his demons were just in charge. He never knew. Was it art or a dark psychological compulsion? The latter most probably but he always wrote about real people, using his imagination to fill in the blanks on how they felt as events unfolded.

All he knew was readers connected with his writing so there were quite a few people out there just like him, willing to immerse themselves in someone else's life. He often wondered if it was an avoidance tactic to not examine a less than perfect existence.

No one was perfect.

How fortunate for him in many ways.

Upon reflection, his life had been a mixed bag.

Privileged childhood but a detached father. He'd tried but their conversations had been decidedly one-sided. No pets ever allowed in their house so eventually he'd given up begging for a dog. It was ironic that now he could get one if he wanted, he had no desire for a pet at all. Not even a cat to curl up near his chair in his den and make him the quintessential writer.

Solitude was his best friend instead.

* * *

She didn't accomplish a thing.

At least not on the project.

Instead, she called Jana at work. Her sister was an accountant and it was fine to talk to her now, but in tax season forget it. Midsummer it was a little different and she actually answered. Lauren said, "Hi, it's me. Bad time or good time?"

"I can talk for about fifteen minutes then have a client walking through my office door. How is Tennessee?"

"Well, I'm learning how to fish, maybe I'll have to try bear hunting in Wisconsin someday with my newfound outdoor skills, and Drew and I have essentially split."

"What? God my life is so boring. So you're back in Ohio? It sounds like we need to have lunch at least. What happened?"

"I'm still in Tennessee. That will need to be a three-martini lunch by the way."

"Uh-oh. Sis o' mine, you don't drink martinis."

Lauren said grimly, "I might start."

"That bad, huh. What happened with Drew?"

"Between me and you — and I mean that — he's married. And before you ask — and if you did, I'd be insulted — no, I didn't know. He finally told me."

"What?"

"You heard me."

"Married? You've been dating quite a while."

"That was pretty much my reaction too. He said they are in the middle of a divorce, but I'm getting the impression maybe she doesn't really want it. The situation is extremely complicated. Drew had to fly out."

"So you stayed in Tennessee anyway?"

"Yes, Drew left, but Rob is still here."

There was a telling pause. "I'm getting a little confused."

"Join the club. Just try being me right now." She looked out over the water but didn't really see the view.

"I admit I think I am getting a hint of what is happening but don't want to assume anything."

"Don't. Let me repeat — *complicated*. I could toss a homicide detective into the mix. Let me make that two." Carter deserved a nod.

"Lauren!"

She said quietly, "There have been some disappearances around here. I don't know what's going on but we're on edge. Last night someone tried to break in. They knocked on the door and then broke a window in the back of the house. Thank goodness Rob *was* here."

"Did they catch whoever it was?"

"No, but I'm putting on my sleuth hat and just let him try to get in again."

"I haven't seen that hat. Here's a thought, come home."

"I'm only still here because I'm truly emotionally invested in this situation, but also because the police have asked us to stay."

"Why did they do that?" Jana sounded taken aback.

"I'll explain at our proposed martini lunch. How is Chloe?" Her niece was a toddler and a handful. "I'm not trying to change the subject, I truly want to know and I really don't have a straight answer right now to your question."

"Chloe is demanding, bossy, and yet so cute I forgive her for both of those things, how's that for an answer, at least from me. Her favorite word used to be *no* but has been replaced by *why*. In short, business as usual. Can you keep me updated, please?"

"Once *I'm* updated, I'll give you a call."

She pressed a button and made the decision to just forget work for the moment.

That was fine, the deadline was still a ways off and her mind was elsewhere. A little digging would be — or could be — at least semi-productive.

A search on her computer revealed some basic details about Glenn Heaston's wife. Angela Barrett-Heaston was indeed born into a wealthy Kentucky family, the classic distillery and racehorse bluegrass type of lineage that garnered her expensive eastern private schools. She'd married Heaston twelve years ago in a lavish ceremony attended by the governor of the state.

The part that really caught her attention was the mention that they'd met when he was researching a book.

It didn't say which one, but she knew where to look and struck gold.

The book *Deadly Heiress* was based on Angela's grandmother, who had been involved in a publicized case involving the murder of her husband's mistress back in the 1940s.

Mrs. Heaston's ancestor had been acquitted, but the trial was a sensation and it had dragged on for over a year.

The victim had drowned in the pool on the family estate and been found by her lover, ostensibly when Elaine Rothberg-Barrett was out of town, but could not provide a true alibi as she had dropped out of sight for the crucial time period of when the crime was committed. It was decided by the authorities at that time to be a murder because the victim had been knocked unconscious and presumably dumped in the water.

It was a warm afternoon, but a chill ran down Lauren's spine. She'd been seriously trying to not think about it, but as every minute passed, she did more and more and now she'd found this. Bailey certainly knew Heaston was an author because a husband was always considered carefully in any case — not being law enforcement, even she knew that — but this, this, was a true connection because of the nature of the cause of death.

Wasn't it?

And in keeping with her theory, as off the wall as it might sound, maybe she found one small indication her suspicion was not completely unfounded. The connection was just too macabre. That drowned girl last summer with a head injury in the very lake where he owned a house?

If it hadn't been for the night before maybe Lauren would have been more skeptical, but doubt was fading into belief.

It was Heaston.

He could come by water. He could walk through the woods. He was the reason the detectives were showing up because his wife had gone missing, he'd asked about Karen leaving . . .

It circled back to him.

And Lauren had had dinner with him, shared a bottle of wine, and one of his books sat right now next to her computer.

He could be a murderer.

It was hard to comprehend she could know one firsthand.

It was an opportune time for Rob to come outside, eyeing the horizon. "Last night it passed us by but I doubt we're going to get that lucky again. There's bad weather on the way. Thunderstorm watch. If we are going to run to town, and buy the camera and pick up something for dinner, I think right now might not be a bad idea. At least the guys came and fixed the window so I can turn on the alarm."

She closed her computer. "Okay, since I need to talk to you and ascertain if I'm really just so rattled, I'm jumping at shadows, or if you think maybe I might have just stumbled on something that is significant enough to tell Bailey and Carter."

Hazel eyes took on a glimmer of interest. "I'm all ears. You know how to throw a hook, Ms. Fisherwoman. All electronics inside and you can talk while I drive, deal? Give me your computer and I'll lock up. I'd like to beat this weather."

* * *

Pearson Drysden greeted him with a sincere smile and did not at all look like a thug in shirt, tie, and pressed slacks, but Chris reserved judgment always. Nice-looking with thinning brown hair and a firm handshake, he exuded goodwill, but it could be a front.

The man had broken his girlfriend's nose and sent her off to the hospital.

Charges might not have been pressed but the arrest report was there.

Domestic disturbance and battery.

He took the offered seat of a nice leather chair on the opposite side of an oak desk and decided to open with nothing but: "I'm interviewing people who own properties on the lake where you have yours, due to some disappearances in the area."

Drysden frowned. "I heard about Angela Heaston on the local news. It just said growing concern over her absence."

"Do you know her?"

He wasn't slow on the uptake. Understanding dawned in his eyes and he settled back. "No, I don't. You are talking to me because of that damn incident, aren't you? Look, I was sorry then, and I'm sorry now. She threw a plate of food at me, and I admit I'd been drinking. She was a lot more ticked off than I was and we had a simple argument that got out of hand."

"I'd say so, but I'm not here to judge you, just to find out if you know anything that might help this investigation."

"I caught her with my elbow as I was trying to defend myself."

Chris said coolly, "I've read the report but, counselor, whether your account of it is relevant or not, you aren't really answering my question. You know how this goes. Any small piece of information could help us. I'm not accusing you of anything. I want to know what you know. With the girl that drowned in this lake, Mrs. Heaston not to be found, and a female lawyer going off the grid, I need some help. Karen Foxton's car has been found."

A calculated move.

It paid off.

Drysden's brows shot up. "Karen Foxton? I actually do know her to the extent that when she worked for the state of Ohio's attorney general's office, we exchanged some emails on a case, but that was a few years ago. Why was she here?"

"Visiting a friend. She drove away, but now is missing."

The man looked convincingly disturbed. "I had no idea, and I highly doubt she had any idea I own property on this lake either. Like I said, professional acquaintances. And the dead woman who hasn't been identified that I'm aware of? No idea. You can't even find a lead? That happened quite a while ago. Why has the investigation gone stale?"

The assumption Drysden could query him on that was grating. "This isn't a courtroom. In case you haven't noticed I'm asking the questions. Where were you last night?"

"At the house. I inherited it from my parents. I live there all summer. It is worth the drive to have the water and the trees."

No one had given him a lake house, but Chris thought philosophically that he was fairly well off overall with a roof over his head and enough food, not to mention Sara and the moppet, so he was in good shape. "Sounds nice, but is there any way you can verify that?"

"Last night? I was alone, if that is what you're asking. I watched a movie."

So a big no.

"What movie?"

"How does that matter?"

"If we come down to it, it might matter. All details matter I've found."

"I watched *A Few Good Men*. One of my favorite movies of all time. Shall I outline the plot for you?"

The sarcasm was unappreciated but at least understandable. "I've seen it, so not necessary. All summer? So you *were* there at the time of the drowning. See or hear anything that struck you as off-key?"

"There were people out on the lake late probably, but that is hardly 'off-key'. That's why we come here. I admit I haven't exactly memorized when that girl died."

"I have committed it to memory."

"I don't have your answer."

Chris weighed his response. "What family wouldn't report a disappearance? I would hate to think no one would miss me."

"And now you're looking at me like I know something," Drysden said flatly. "Well, I don't."

And if you did, you wouldn't tell me, Chris thought as he rose. It was an unsatisfying interview, but most fell into that category on the first pass. When the suspect got nervous, they were more forthcoming. Cornered they sang a different tune.

He didn't like Drysden despite that initial affable smile. Not at all, but that could just be a personal thing. Not all men liked each other, nor did all women for that matter. He didn't believe for a minute the elbow story because it didn't jell with what the officers wrote in the report.

The girlfriend had clearly stated he hit her on purpose, and Chris didn't like the lie at all. The different versions of the truth weren't new to him and he didn't always side with the victim, but in this case, he did.

"I'll probably be in touch." He didn't want the man to have a good night's sleep, he didn't think he deserved one. Drysden he didn't like.

"Oh, I can't wait, Detective."

The dislike was obviously mutual, yet Chris left the office feeling like he at least accomplished something. There was a link between Karen Foxton and Drysden. He'd probably only admitted it because that could easily be traced. Not as strong as her tie to Hanson and Fletcher, but a connection anyway. It didn't move him to suspect number one, but he was really in the running now.

Chris didn't have to be detective to figure out it was going to rain. The air smelled like it.

Hell, he needed to mow the lawn. That would have to wait. There was bad weather on the way and the wind was picking up. Howling like an Irish banshee, as his grandmother used to say.

His cell phone rang and he answered it, eyeing the darkening sky as he pulled onto the road. "Bailey."

CHAPTER TWENTY-TWO

Was it an ill-wind that bodes no good?

He had to wonder.

There was no question he'd underestimated his intake of scotch and the last bottle was empty, which was disappointing.

Brandy wasn't the same, but he wasn't averse to it. That expensive vintage Angela had insisted upon was palatable, and at the price, at least he should enjoy it.

Louis XIII. Close to a thousand dollars a bottle.

The weather was not amenable to a trip to the liquor store just now.

He dug out a snifter.

Why not sit and watch the light show against those high windows.

At least he wasn't out on the dead water.

He decided to listen to Bach. Baroque music complemented expensive brandy, didn't it?

* * *

The storm rolled in like a freight train, picking up speed. Thunder growled in the background, but then it gained momentum, so it truly became a rumbling presence like the artillery from an advancing army.

At least he had the two cameras, Rob thought grimly as he and Lauren sprinted toward the car. And they'd stopped at the local butcher shop and bought two duck breasts which he would have no idea what to do with. Lauren promised him she did and from what he'd tasted of her cooking so far, he believed her.

The first of the rain came pelting down just as they reached the car. Lightning cracked and lit up the afternoon sky.

Stormy weather indeed. No fishing for now.

That would be as stupid as Heaston coming over in his canoe for the night they had dinner together. Not that Rob thought their eccentric neighbor was a stupid man. He was more concerned he wasn't at all and absolutely planned it so that he could stay a little longer than for a friendly hello. A calculated move?

Maybe. Hard to say.

Right now, the cloudburst was in full force and Rob needed to maneuver through wet roads and some serious wind lashing the trees. Lauren said, "I don't know how anyone survives a hurricane."

He swerved around a fallen branch that raked across the road right in front of them. "We seem to have hit the typhoon season here. I don't ever want to figure out firsthand what a real one is like. This will pass quickly."

"Well, we don't have to endure it for days anyway. Summer in Tennessee."

"It appears so."

"I called my sister this morning while I was trying to fool myself into believing I could actually work. Jana was pretty taken by surprise about Drew's revelation."

"We could form a club. I was too."

"There's a thought." Her smile was wry.

"You can be president."

"I'd rather let someone else assume that title."

He laughed. "Fair enough. Feel free to tell me it's none of my business, but what else did you tell her? I admit I'm not sure what I'd say to any of my family at this point."

A crash of thunder deafened her answer, and then she tried again. "All I said was Drew had left and you and I were still here. I could tell she was a little confused, but then again, so am I."

"I understand to a certain extent how you feel. I'm not exactly indefensible in all of this since I fell for my best friend's girl. Drew fell for you too, so how can I judge him? It's fitting we're in Tennessee because it sounds like a country song."

"And I don't think my attraction to you was exactly the secret I thought it was either." She sighed. "So we aren't exactly angels in this triangle, are we?"

"I never aspired to be an angel anyway, just wanted to be a decent person. I can't speak for him, but I've known him for a long time. Drew is decent. He had no part in last night."

"With a slight advantage for being able to keep a secret better than you or I can apparently, I agree, as you know."

He gave a humorless smile as they gained the driveway. "Look at it this way. I'm more transparent than I thought. Both Heaston and Drew saw right through me when it comes to you. So did Karen."

"I'm sailing on the same ship. I'm not impressed with our navigational skills."

"We found each other anyway. That's some common ground."

"No. Since we are being poetic, I think we ran aground and crashed into each other on a rocky beach."

Neither of them mentioned there hadn't been a word from Drew. Rob didn't like the silence, but then again, he might have flown out and be in a completely different time zone at the moment.

He viewed the dark sky and wet windshield after he parked the truck. "We'll have to make a run for the house. It isn't letting up."

"I'm getting used to it. I'll carry the grocery bag if you will sprint with the wine."

"Done deal."

Plus, he'd enter the building first and thought that was best. He'd set the alarm but if someone was determined to break in, they'd get in. Despite all the security in the world there were still robberies and home invasions and his trust level was at low tide.

Like ankle deep at best.

He went first and unlocked the door and it seemed quiet as he stepped inside. Good sign. Lauren followed, raindrops on her dampened hair, going straight to the kitchen to deposit her bag in the refrigerator. "All clear?"

"Seems to be. I hope so since you just walked inside right past me."

"I figured he'd get you first thing when you opened the door." She was joking, but he understood the levity was forced.

The place went dark suddenly and that was certainly no surprise. The wind outside was brutal, buffeting the tall windows.

"Generator," he said briefly. "Give it fifteen seconds."

Sure enough it roared to life in the background and the lights came back on. Bless modern technology and that his uncle had spared no expense in the name of security and comfort. It was run off a propane tank and tucked discreetly off to the side of house. It was loud, but then again so was the storm.

He uncorked some wine, poured two glasses, handed one to Lauren, and sat down at the table. He watched her deftly make a salad, chopping vegetables like a chef, and then start on the dressing.

Mostly he just enjoyed the smooth fall of her hair brushing her shoulders, the soft curve of her lips, and the clean line of her profile as she prepared the meal. The lashing sound of the rain added to the moment, and the wine was a supple Merlot with deep blackberry overtones — or so the label said, he was hardly an expert, but it was certainly a nice complement to a stormy evening with a beautiful female companion.

It was hard to believe he was actually enjoying the moment, considering everything.

She was creative and he was analytical and that might or might not be a match made in heaven, but only time would tell. Embarking on a relationship in their situation was hardly ideal.

Far from it.

* * *

The owner of the property waited in a pickup that had rusted panels, at least three lawnmowers in the back, and what appeared to be a big English sheepdog in the passenger seat. There was a patrol car there as well, the officer inside, which was a good choice because it was coming down in buckets and the trees were bent over like old women due to the high wind.

The barn doors were open and he parked as close as he could, the storm not doing any favors to any clues that might have been on the outside of the car, but hopefully the inside was untouched so any potential evidence was intact.

Because he sure as hell didn't think Angela Heaston parked her expensive sedan in that decrepit structure on purpose. It was weathered to gray, with a roof covered in lichen, the walls crawling with vines, and had a generally abandoned appearance, the one side window Chris could see was broken out with just a jagged shard of glass sticking up from the bottom of the sill like an obscene tooth.

If not the missing Mrs. Heaston, *someone* had left it there and walked away.

The rain pelted his car and he sat and contemplated that this truly was a homicide case now in his mind, but his gut had been telling him that all along.

After ten minutes of waiting, the deluge slowed enough for Chris to face the fact he was going to get wet, and he shoved open the door of his vehicle and sprinted up a small slope toward the barn, glad he always carried a flashlight in his car, not to mention an evidence collection kit.

Whether it was male pride or sitting in their vehicles made them just as impatient, both the other men did the same thing. The young county deputy arrived first, shaking moisture out of his hair. "Detective, I kinda wondered if I'd be seeing you when I ran the plates on the car and made the name connection to the lake."

"Good call. Now I just need a body," Chris agreed with grim humor, recognizing one of the officers that had answered the call on the break-in next door to the Heaston property. "What's the story?"

"I'll let Mr. Filmore here tell you what he told me." He turned. "Ed?"

Filmore was a lean older man as weathered as his barn, wearing muddy boots, overalls, a well-worn shirt, and an old cap with a seed emblem on the front. He had light-blue eyes and a pouch of tobacco protruding from his pocket. Quintessential old-school Tennessee farmer. He nodded. "I called because I am not interested in people trespassing on my property without permission. I don't really use this barn anymore. I only came out here so I could store those lawn mowers until I can get to repairing them. I do that as a sideline." He pointed at the car. "Look at what I found instead. Wouldn't mind keeping it, but then again, that's an expensive machine and someone left it here for a reason. If I had to guess what it might be, I'd speculate so no one would find it."

"When were you out here last?" Chris pulled on a pair of latex gloves.

Filmore creased his brow. "Huh. A month maybe?"

"Anyone know you just visit infrequently?"

He gave a short snort. "Anyone who pays attention would be able to figure it out. The building isn't exactly well kept and it is unlocked. Nothing to steal. I never dreamed someone would *put* something valuable in here. I opened the doors and there it was."

"But you saw nothing?"

"It's pretty far from the house."

There was his answer. "We appreciate you calling it in. I'm going to take a look and then we'll have it towed and get it out of your hair."

"No problem. Guess I'll head on out then. Gregg there has my number if you need anything else."

Only there was a problem, Chris discovered, even if the barn wasn't locked, the car was. Not a huge issue usually, but he stood in a decaying barn in a rainstorm without recourse.

Then the deputy said mildly, "Allow me. Don't ask why, but I'm damned good at this. Just give me about two minutes." He pulled a slender file from his pocket and put on gloves. "The alarm is going to go off, but you can get in."

It took less than the promised two. Chris cocked a brow but nodded a thank you and opened the door because he appreciated it and didn't question the proficiency.

No keys, but he didn't expect any. At first glance it looked fairly undisturbed, like the driver had parked and gotten out and walked away.

But then he saw the purse. Rather like Karen Foxton's car, it sat on the floor, like a dropped shoe, abandoned and forgotten.

No wonder she wasn't shopping in Milan, or relaxing on the Riviera, he thought grimly. No credit cards to use. Angela Heaston had evidently left her purse behind. Voluntarily? He doubted it.

No, drawing conclusions was against the rules — he wasn't going to walk that path, but so far it pointed in that direction.

First things first, he found the button to open the trunk, not sure if he was relieved or not to find it empty except for a folded flannel blanket and what appeared to be a portable luggage roller. No body and, as far as he could tell, no evidence that one had been transported in there.

The deputy somehow managed to turn off the alarm, which was a relief since it was a decent-sized building with tall rafters that seemed to echo the blaring sound. The resulting silence was tempered by the steady rain hitting the tin roof.

"Glad to see there's no one in there."

"It's a good–bad thing," Chris agreed. "We still don't know where she is or what happened to her, but she's been missing for a week, so at least Mrs. Heaston is not in the trunk of her car. I'd just as soon skip that experience."

"Working homicides would not be for me." Gregg shook his head, his expression set as he gazed into the empty trunk. "I see enough with traffic and boating accidents."

"Luckily we don't have very many."

However, Chris had three open investigations right now, not any of them designated murder cases, but all of them probable. One dead woman still unidentified, two still missing but under suspicious circumstances.

He ran his fingers through his damp hair in a gesture of resigned frustration. "I hate to say this again, but if Mrs. Heaston is not alive, I really need a body."

* * *

Dinner was subdued, but it would be under the circumstances. Lauren chose the music — Satie's 'After the Rain', the soft sound appropriate to the mood, the French composer one of her favorites.

Only it was still raining, not with the earlier violence, but a determined downpour just the same. The generator was still running which meant the power hadn't been restored, and that didn't exactly surprise her.

The atmosphere was romantic with an isolated lake cabin, the sound of the subsiding storm, nice wine, an undeniably attractive man across the table . . .

She wished she could reconcile her desire to spend the night in his arms with her moral objection to having two different lovers in such a short time period. The nice girl in her said to wait, although the way he'd kissed her the night before shook that resolve. Thanks to Drew's revelation, she was finally free to acknowledge the desire that had existed for quite some time.

"I think you should definitely talk to Bailey and Carter." Rob's face was shadowed, his expression reflective. "There's only so much they can know from simple interviews in which people reveal only what they want to tell law enforcement. I highly doubt they realize much more than the fact that Glenn Heaston is a successful author. If he hadn't given you books and paid such special attention to us, would you really look at anything except the factual information that might link him to his wife's disappearance?"

"No."

"Bailey especially might appreciate the insight. He has more imagination."

She thought so as well. Her smile was rueful. "I suppose the real question is do *I* have too much imagination?"

He considered it, but she wanted him to think it over. "At first, when you were telling me about the case of her grandmother as we were driving to town, I said to myself that perhaps he was doing research for his book, met his future wife, fell in love with her, and there was nothing sinister about it at all. Just two people attracted to each other and that's natural enough, it happens all the time, even if the circumstances were unusual."

Look at the two of them. He didn't need to spell it out for her that she'd come on this vacation with Drew and would be leaving with him. That wasn't exactly a normal course of events. Still, Lauren said quietly, "But?"

"I can't quite get past the fact that the crime that led Heaston to Angela Barrett was a drowning and the young woman that drowned here also had a blow to the head and was put in the water while she was still alive. As a coincidence, it could be just that, but it seems to really raise a red flag for me. I just doubt the detectives know about the circumstances of how Heaston and Angela Barrett developed an interest in each other. I'm not an investigator, but I would look into financial aspects, and if people around them noticed a problem in their marriage, things like that — but how they met would be immaterial to me unless something set off a warning bell."

She agreed, one hundred percent. Resting her chin on her fist, she ran her fingers down the stem of her wineglass.

"If he hadn't been persistent with the femme fatale theme, it would not have ever occurred to me either. At first, I was just embarrassed because I thought he was referring to some sort of lover's triangle, and maybe he was. There's no doubt in my mind he was watching us, but hopefully femme fatale doesn't have anything to do with Karen's disappearance."

It had obviously occurred to Rob too. He blew out a short breath. "Our problem is trying to make sense out of something that doesn't make sense to either of us."

She would have agreed but at that moment a business-like knock on the door interrupted them and considering the weather and recent events, she didn't blame Rob when he muttered, "What the hell? I really don't want a repeat performance of last night. Stay here and run for the canoe paddles if necessary."

He was only half-joking, but it turned out to be a more welcome visitor in the form of Detective Bailey, who had been out in the storm from the evidence of his damp hair and wet shirt. He came with Rob into the kitchen where she'd carried the plates and said with wry humor, "We haven't seen each other in so long I thought I'd just drop by to say hello."

The moment of levity passed quickly enough. "Mr. Hanson, I just need to show you a few pictures and ask a couple of questions."

His face changed when the detective pulled out the first photo.

"You recognize her?" the detective pushed.

Rob looked wary, but she could hardly blame him for that. "I believe I've cooperated as much as possible so far."

CHAPTER TWENTY-THREE

Police next door again.

It was difficult to know what to make of it and the deck was slippery with wet leaves ripped off by wind and rain, so he didn't move because he was carefully paying attention.

The pendulum was going to swing eventually. He knew the weight of it, but the direction was the mystery.

Had something happened?

Maybe . . . he must have missed it, but then again he remembered the storm.

Then he'd had a revelation about the book and noted it down, so he'd been distracted, even writing the epilogue ahead of the rest of the book.

The ending was tragic, but all his books had a tragic conclusion because, after all, he manipulated true life into his fictional version of the events, but they were based on fact.

Reality was always hard to face.

In the end, death was a serious player.

* * *

Early flight, but those were easy, so he never minded.

Drew got the text right before boarding to do the pre-test. He would have normally ignored it, but the message made it impossible and it was from Rob.

Do you recognize him?

He was supposed to leave in twenty minutes. He looked at the picture, drew a blank but then enlarged it and took a second look.

He texted back. *I think I've seen him somewhere. Why?*
What about her?

The second picture was not at all pleasant. The young woman was obviously dead, her pallor and open glassy eyes more than unsettling. He almost recoiled but collected himself.

It's a little hard to tell. Thanks for the unpleasant image. It made my morning. Not. Once again, why?

You can thank Bailey. I tried to call last night so I could ruin your evening instead but you didn't answer. Didn't we see that guy out in a boat with a girl with long dark hair last summer when we were fishing? Could it be her?

The drowning victim?

Drew cast back, wasn't positive he could say yes, but . . . it was possible. He texted back. *It might be. We talked to them, I do remember that. It could be her I suppose.*

Long dark hair.

That woman on the unforgiving table of death — because this was an autopsy picture even if he wasn't an expert and had never seen one firsthand before — she did have long black hair.

I couldn't swear to it.
I can't either.
I've got a flight in a few minutes. I'll think about it.
Tell me you have a good reason for canceling your flight and an alibi for Thursday night.

What the hell? How did he even know? The answer was easy. Bailey and the flight itineraries. He'd checked.

I do.
Good. Have a safe flight.

Alibi? He had a lot to think about already, including Cassandra. He was still married to her, but there was the worry she'd caught baby fever and he was just convenient. Undying love for him had never been declared.

But she wanted children. With him. She had said that much and certainly seemed sincere.

That had blindsided him.

He wasn't sure how to react. Lauren wanted a family, he'd always accepted that as a given and they'd even talked about it, but just a mention, not a heart to heart. To be truthful, he didn't know where he stood on the subject. But Cassandra had surprised the hell out of him.

What else didn't he know about her?

She could probably manage a family with the same efficient expertise that she'd exhibited at her job, but she didn't seem like the maternal type. He didn't see her baking cookies or know if she even knew how to turn on an oven. Usually they ate out. Maybe he was selling her short because she was the one that suggested they get married. Romantic at heart? He wasn't going to go that far, but he'd said yes, and hadn't really regretted it because she'd understood his lifestyle very well. They'd lived apart mostly and he thought she'd been fine with it.

She was proposing something very different from what he'd envisioned she wanted.

A life, not just a relationship of sex with interludes of them enjoying each other's company but then going their separate ways without being truly intertwined day to day.

It was a definite adjustment in his thinking when it came to her and when it came to the future, so he had Lauren to thank for that. If he hadn't met Lauren, he would have been happy in his bachelor-style life, even if he wasn't technically one.

He absolutely couldn't think about that dead girl.

* * *

It was impossible to not take a moment to ask — even though the lake was peaceful now. It was beautiful out on the deck in the morning sunshine since the rain had traveled east, but Lauren really was curious and hadn't been part of the conversation. "What did Drew have to say?"

"Nothing really. They were prepping for take-off. He was not really able to talk."

"And you don't want to show me those pictures Bailey gave you when he stopped by for his usual visit last night."

Neither of them had slept the night before really, so they'd just not discussed it.

"No." His voice was quiet. "I don't. One was of a potential suspect and one was of his possible victim. If I thought you could help, maybe I would have, but I just can't see how, so why do it? If I can help Detective Bailey, it is in my vested interest to do so and Drew certainly feels the same way, but you weren't here for that drowning last year and that was the underlying purpose of this last encounter I had with the police."

It made sense — or about as much sense as any of this did. All too true. She folded her hands together. "*Were* you able to help?"

"I don't know. I think I recognized one person in the pictures he showed me. That means nothing except maybe Drew and I saw him with the dead girl. That picture of her after she drowned . . . I might never sleep again."

It must have been awful. His expression said it all. Lauren appreciated he didn't want her to see it, because she didn't want to either. "They still can't identify her?"

"Not that I'm aware of. Though Bailey and Carter want information, they don't hand it out necessarily."

"That's understandable. Think about their job."

"No thanks."

She didn't disagree. "I meant they aren't supposed to as far as I understand it."

"Especially not to me."

"Having met them both, I doubt they would leave you here alone with me if you were a true suspect, Rob."

He lifted a dark brow. "They'd have to have at least a shred of proof and they don't. There isn't any, which is why they let Drew walk out of here, but someone is out there."

The other night proved that.

Someone is out there . . .

Because of that kiss between her and Rob she thought she knew the answer to her next question. "Now that you've talked to him, did Drew explain? He went to see his wife, right? That was why he traded his flight."

"He was pressed for time so I didn't ask, but that would be my guess. He said he had a good reason for changing his flight and an alibi for the night before last."

"She's pushing back on the divorce." Statement, not a question.

"You okay with that?" Rob looked at her keenly.

Was she? She took a minute. "I am. Drew and I are no longer together. I'm very okay with it. In fact, I hope it works out for them if that will make him happy."

His shoulders relaxed. "I do too, but while I'm still ticked off at him for not mentioning something so significant in his life, I guess since I've known him for so long, I'm not really that surprised. Do you want a dog?"

Lauren blinked. "What?"

"Well, I do, and I want to have this important conversation. I was thinking a lab mix, big but friendly. Let's settle that right now."

The man was insane. She gazed at him, searching for a response and finally came up with a smile. "You have a nice house with a big yard, so if you want a dog—"

"Things have changed," he interrupted, his voice even. "I'm not eighteen. I'm almost thirty, so could we talk about this? I fell in love with you pretty much the moment we met, not a phenomenon I believed in before it happened to me. From my perspective, any decisions I make that affect my life, I'd like to consider them with a hope they might also affect you. I'm thinking maybe we could get a dog with an eye to a possible future situation where we lived together. So your input is important."

Lauren was so off balance.

It didn't help that he hadn't shaved yet this morning and the slight shadow on his lean jaw and his tousled hair somehow made him even better looking and that was a high bar. The night before they'd gone once again to bed together but she'd known they were both considering an entirely different arrangement involving clothing strewn all over the floor and sleep not necessarily the top priority.

He was right, things had changed. Ironically Rob had Drew to thank that she'd ever even considered it. He'd certainly had to coax her into loosening her inhibitions over sex, and she'd gained an enlightened outlook on an activity she'd previously thought highly overrated.

Jana was right. She did lead an interesting life. At least at the moment.

"Is this a negotiation?" It was a cautious question on her part.

"Of sorts, I suppose." His smile was persuasive. "We've known each other for half a year, and no, I can't think of a more unusual beginning to a romantic relationship, but then again I have to subscribe to the sentiment life is full of surprises. That house is too big for just one person, so if you are at all interested, I know I am."

She did rent and had started looking around for something more permanent to buy like a cozy bungalow on a quiet street, so the offer was tempting. She also loved dogs. "Yes to picking out the puppy. I'm a little iffy on commitment issues right now. Look at Heaston, not even concerned about his missing wife."

"We don't know that."

"Do you think he is?"

"I'm truly not sure," he conceded. "He certainly doesn't seem like he's sitting around worrying about it, but people handle things in their own way. If you were gone, I'd be frantically looking for you, but that doesn't mean that's how he'd react."

That was even better than *I love you*.

Lauren said, "I'd look for you too but you aren't looking for Karen."

"No, I am at this point leaving that to the police. Lauren, she wouldn't appreciate it if I did. I'm worried about her and

I've cooperated, but I don't know what's happening, so I'm just trying to not interfere with the investigation. They are supposedly good at it and *I'm* not Sherlock Holmes."

It was probably a good decision, but she was inclined to contribute just a little bit. "I call it dabbling not interference. We have those cameras now."

"The cameras were a good idea." His expression was still strained, and she understood. Karen's continued absence was escalating from worry to a grim resignation that there wasn't going to be good news of any kind.

The cameras had been surprisingly easy to set up and Rob had used a pull-away wall mounting unit designed for Christmas lights, so he didn't have to drill holes in his uncle's house. Maybe all they'd catch was the sight of an occasional deer wandering by, but who knew. Someone had broken that window.

It was her idea but he'd done all the heavy lifting.

"We will find out. I'm hardly a surveillance expert."

"But technology is your thing."

He shook his head. "It might be, but this isn't the same. They were easy enough to mount but where to place them wasn't."

"Think like a criminal."

"It isn't as easy as it sounds for those of us who actually are law abiding." His smile was rueful. "I've never cased a joint before. I was at a loss when deciding where I'd break in because I wouldn't."

"Cased a joint?"

"Hey, I know the jargon, I just don't have the technique."

"There's nothing wrong with your technique."

He did grin at that, a boyish curve of his mouth. "Thanks. Good to know as long as I interpreted that correctly. This time of day is perfect for fishing. Interested?"

"Is that your solution for everything?"

"Fishing? If possible. It isn't always. I'm trying to focus on normal, even if nothing seems to be that way."

"I'm determined to vanquish this goal, so that sounds fine with me. You'll take it off the hook, right? Note how optimistic I am."

"The key to fishing is patience." He amended. "Actually, the key to fishing is to love the water and being outdoors. It helps with the patience issue because unless you use depth finders and other fancy equipment which takes away from the sport, in my opinion, just wait for that tug on your line and enjoy the scenery. And yes, I'll take it off the hook for you."

Relaxation hadn't been the order of the day so far, but she was willing to try. She had managed to make a couple of sandwiches for lunch, and she picked up the plates. "Let's go. I'll be right back out after I put this in the sink."

Fishing wasn't on the cards.

The sunny day after the storm turned into a horrifying dream as they went down toward the dock.

The body was there on the shore, still half-submerged, face down. Rob stopped so abruptly Lauren careened into his back on the stairs and then she saw it too. He turned around and caught her arms, urgency in his voice. "Go up and call 911. I'll see if there's anything I can do."

There wasn't. She knew it with a horrifying fatalistic sense of the surreal as she ran up the stairs to where she'd left her phone on the table on purpose so maybe she could relax for their small excursion.

Things were going from bad to worse.

That was Karen on that bank. She recognized the red blouse she'd worn when she so furiously departed like a scarlet stain of blood on the wet landscape.

Lauren's hands were shaking as she picked up her phone and called.

CHAPTER TWENTY-FOUR

It was ironic the body washed up where it landed but there were times when he had to acknowledge he had no control over the universe.

Fascinating.

Fate or Kismet . . . what did one call it?

He was a scholar. Born to study people and their different facets. Hanson tried, he'd give him that. He dragged the body out and tested for a pulse, but it was clear he knew it was futile.

He wouldn't want to walk a mile in that young man's shoes today.

That thought sent him straight back to his computer.

There was nothing like inspiration.

* * *

Chris thought that the next time *he* went on vacation Carter had better get a slew of similar calls so they could break even. He'd talked yet again to Felicity Barrett that morning, and she'd made it clear with every passing day she was more convinced something bad had happened to her older sister.

He was sure of the same thing but simply tried to reassure her they were doing their level best to find Angela Heaston.

Now he had to deal with the body that had actually turned up. The coroner and a crime scene tech had arrived, so he stood with his hands in his pockets, watching and waiting to interview Hanson. The coroner was a doctor who would not do the autopsy but could pronounce the victim dead since there were no known witnesses to any crime *if* she was a homicide victim and it was, in his mind anyway, a forgone conclusion.

The similarities were building up in all the cases, and unlike some investigators who had clues but not suspects, he had clues but too many suspects. Four strong contenders, and the chance it was an unknown perpetrator, operating with this lake as a picturesque but deadly background.

Dr. Loren was efficient. Sandy-haired and middle-aged he looked like he should be coaching a high school track team instead of examining dead bodies like this, but he did his job well. He walked over to where Chris stood, stripping off his gloves. "I'll do the paperwork and I'm not surprised you're here, because there are signs of head trauma that disturb me. I am going to guess the opinion you get on cause of death is drowning or a blunt force injury and, on manner of death, homicide when the ME gets out his knife."

There was no way he could hide the wince. "Could you not put it that way?"

"The knife part?" Loren just raised his brows. "Detective, you aren't squeamish or you wouldn't do what you do."

Wrong. The thought of cutting someone open was completely unappealing in every way and he had to visit the morgue all too often. "I catch killers on a good day. I don't dissect their victims, just the crime."

Loren shook his head. "We use science to a good cause. *You* have to crawl inside the actions of someone who would intentionally cause death. I worked the morgue as a medical student. You get used to it. I'd rather be me. You do the dirty work but it is valuable. We are both helping the next potential victim and families of the ones already lost, even if it is after the fact. All the literature says not knowing is the worst part of the grief."

If this body truly was Rob Hanson's girlfriend, it changed the game again. That would be the same method the killer had used before so it would be at least theoretically the same killer and Hanson was already a suspect but so was Drew Fletcher. It didn't rule out Drysden either.

Not to mention Heaston.

He hadn't yet worked a case that went truly cold so far. Chris wasn't about to do it now. "I actually think we see the picture in the same light. The victim is a lost cause but their families deserve justice."

"Indeed they do. I'm going to tell them to bag the body and put it in the van and you know the rest of the drill — a uniformed officer will escort her to where they'll perform the autopsy. Unless I can help you in any other way right now, I'm going home."

Yes, he did know the drill all too well. He held out his hand. "Thanks."

Loren was a formal man, they knew each other well enough for that. He shook it.

That was over but for Chris his work had just begun in earnest. He went up to the deck and knocked on the French doors. The less people on a scene the better so he'd asked both Hanson and Lauren Mathews if they wouldn't mind going up to the house.

Neither one objected.

He didn't blame them.

They had both known the woman in the lake and she was now dead. Watching her body being examined and taken away would not be pleasant and he sympathized.

Unless Hanson had killed her.

If so, he felt absolutely no remorse for a relentless quest for the truth. The door opened and he wasn't precisely invited in with enthusiasm, but that wasn't unexpected. Hanson did say with reasonable calm, "I realize it is just afternoon, but I'm having a beer. Want one or are you on duty?"

Ms. Mathews was drinking iced tea and looked very pale.

He was on duty technically 24/7. Like a doctor, if he got a call, he went. "I'm always on the job. Thanks for the offer, a beer sounds good. It is that kind of day, I agree. We need to have yet another conversation and I wish Fletcher was here to explain a few things. Let's sit down and talk."

"I'll be right back. Let's get this over with."

That said it all.

The beer was tall and cold and had a Wisconsin label. Chris took a seat at the long dining-room table, wondered whoever entertained that many people at one time, rationalized it was people who lived in a house like this, and let it go. Hanson sat across from him, looking like too many people he'd seen before, suspended in disbelief.

The real question was whether it was due to the death of his houseguest or the fact that the body had washed up on his doorstep. That would make Chris pale and clammy too, either way. She'd been in the water — or so it seemed — for days now.

Hanson started it off somewhat unsteadily, "No, I didn't kill her and, no, Drew didn't either. She drove away in her car. It was the last I saw of her until today on that bank and I sincerely wish that never happened to me or to Lauren."

"I can understand that. I wish it had never happened to me either. Let's go over the timeline, can we?" Chris tried to stay impartial though he essentially liked Hanson so far, but the man could just be a good actor. The attempted break-in did exonerate him somewhat, but taking nothing at face value was the only way to handle an investigation.

"There is no timeline. Lauren and I were headed out to do some fishing after lunch, we saw someone floating in the water, recognized Karen's clothes, and I sent Lauren up to call for emergency services. I pulled her up out of the water and regret to say I quickly realized there was no emergency."

No, that ship had sailed.

Chris wasn't a medical examiner, but he believed Loren's assessment. If the victim was knocked unconscious and then dumped in the lake at least he really now had a pattern. Not a pleasant one, but a pattern. "You responded correctly."

"Whether I'm guilty or not, right?"

"I don't see you in custody. I see me sitting here drinking a beer with you and trying to do my job by finding out what it is you might know that you just don't realize might help me. The body was not here when I came by yesterday evening?"

"I don't know. I hadn't been down the steps to the lake and where she was isn't visible from here."

True enough. "The storm might have brought the body up." Chris said it as an observation. "Had Ms. Foxton been out on the water during her stay?"

"No." Hanson was emphatic. "The great outdoors was not her thing apparently. The deck was about it for the short time she was here. And we all witnessed her driving away."

That didn't precisely put Drysden off the table but didn't help point a finger at him either. "Nice view," he observed. "Don't blame her."

"Yes, but only without a dead person floating in the water." Rob Hanson was shaken, no doubt about it.

Chris said, "I have never gotten quite used to it either. What is happening with Fletcher? I sense there's something that no one is talking about but might be valuable to me."

"He's married but in the middle of a divorce." Lauren finally spoke. "I suspect he canceled that flight to talk to his wife. She's balking at the divorce. I doubt it has anything to do with your investigation."

"I asked him, and he says he has a solid alibi and a reason for switching out the flight." Hanson interjected that interesting piece of information. "I would say, under his circumstances, talking to his wife would be a good reason."

The convoluted equation was still escaping him, but Chris was fairly used to having to decipher complicated situations. There was some sort of romantic connection between the two people sitting at the table with him and he might have even considered Ms. Mathews a suspect except with her slim build she just plain didn't have the physical strength to do it in his opinion. She also had not been here last summer and his inner voice said it was the same killer.

He listened to that voice. All good detectives did — even Carter who was so fact-driven and pragmatic, paid attention to his instincts just as much as his brain, Chris knew it. His partner might not admit it, but it was true.

"Let's go ahead and talk about Ms. Foxton even though I realize it isn't comfortable at all at this moment. She left because of a disagreement over your sexual relationship. Can we go over that once again? It's a very different discussion than when she was just missing. We were treating her disappearance as a possible homicide then, but I think the possible has been taken out of the equation now, unless she parked her car after she left and decided to walk back about twenty miles or so, and go swimming in her clothes."

He wasn't discussing the investigation, but just stating the obvious. They were both intelligent people, he'd already come to that conclusion, so they understood the gravity of all this.

"I'll recap it for you." Hanson rubbed his forehead. "We didn't really disagree, because there was no agreement to begin with, but she got angry and broke it off and left. That was fine with me because I really wasn't all that into it in the first place. It's a short story."

"But you invited her here."

"No, she invited herself like I said before. I was relieved when she left in a fit of affront, and there was no broken heart on my side. I'm feeling pretty bad about the entire thing right now, as you can imagine, but I don't think her heart was broken either. A crime of passion would actually require some passion, on at least one side."

He definitely was sticking to his story. "She didn't get very far," Chris pointed out.

"She might have stopped off to see Heaston." Lauren Mathews explained with credible calm. "He came over and gave me a signed book. Karen had mentioned she wanted one for her sister."

Heaston again. That was exactly what he needed. A clue that might — or might not — mean something, but it really could. Karen Foxton had ended up right back at the place she left.

Heaston.

The usual problem was ferreting out a suspect. In this case it was having quite a few more than he wanted.

He said to Hanson, "I requested you stay so I could talk to you again, but now I am asking you to stay here in this county until we make an arrest. Ms. Mathews, you can leave at any time."

CHAPTER TWENTY-FIVE

He didn't even want to dial the number but he did it.

As expected, his reception was chilly.

"What the hell do you want?"

Ice cold. He admired that about her.

He tried for cordial but maybe he wasn't any better than her, and that was a hard pill to swallow. "I think we should talk about it, don't you?"

"No."

"The police are really on this."

"They better be. I'm going to come down to talk to them in person. I'm not really satisfied with how the investigation is going. After all, she's my sister."

"She's my wife."

Stony silence.

Then Felicity said, "Fuck off, Glenn."

He just hung up.

* * *

Well, this was one hell of an evening. That text from Rob had him off balance already and that had been a bumpy flight from New York to London.

Karen is dead.

Nothing more. What the hell?

Now this?

Drew didn't expect to find Cassandra in the lobby of the hotel. He stopped cold when he realized she was there, reminded himself that when she wanted a conversation, she really wanted one, and made a cautious approach. She was sitting at a tall table on a stool, long elegant legs crossed, a martini in front of her. Two olives, only a whisper of vermouth. He remembered well her preferences, in and out of bed.

He hoped she'd already had dinner if she was drinking. It was nine thirty in England, thanks to the time difference.

"Hello."

That inadequate greeting won him a twitch of her lips. "Hello? That's all you have to say to your wife when you find her unexpectedly in London?"

"I admit you always have the ability to take me off guard." That was the truth. "We just saw each other."

"Have a seat and I'll buy you a drink."

"How did you even know I was here?" He did take a chair because she'd come a damn long way to have another conversation. Still in uniform, he set down his overnight bag, the rest of his luggage still on the plane for an early-morning take-off tomorrow.

"A simple phone call. If there is one thing I know, it is all the right people in the business world. Tracking down your location and where you are staying wasn't too hard to do."

"Not for you obviously." He pointed at her glass as he obeyed. "I guess I'll just have the same."

"You don't drink gin."

"Maybe I need to give it a try. Tonight seems to be a wise choice to switch over to the hard stuff."

"And here I thought I'd be a happy surprise. Take off your tie and unwind."

He followed the suggestion about his tie and tugged it loose. As for unwinding, that depended on why she'd tracked him down. "You are not the problem but maybe tell me why you flew all this way when we just talked?"

"I wasn't completely honest because I was frankly nervous. I really felt we needed to talk face to face again."

Enough for her to fly all this way? It was an expensive hotel and his arrival had been duly noted. A waiter appeared and Cassandra indicated her glass in a silent request the man understood. "Okay. Tell me why."

"Let's wait until your drink arrives."

It did a few minutes later, presented with an understated British flourish. He nodded his thanks to the server. Perplexed, he just looked at her, wondering what the hell was going on now.

"When we split up, I was pregnant. I didn't know when we mutually made the decision."

What? He just stared at her, not able to find an immediate response.

"I never told you because I was trying to figure out how to handle it when I miscarried. Remember our last trip together? We weren't careful. Passionate and carried away, but not careful." Her voice was calm but there was a sudden shimmer in her eyes. "There it is. Not a phone conversation topic. I wanted to clarify my position on this by giving you all the facts."

He'd already not had the best day ever . . . *but this*?

The visceral reaction wasn't what he expected. He'd lost a child?

He took a much-needed drink. No, he didn't like gin usually, but it served the moment quite well. She was right, for this, maybe face to face was better.

"I'm sorry," he finally managed to say, "for both of us. You are certainly good at throwing me curve balls."

"The experience taught me something about myself I didn't know. First, that I wasn't aware how much our marriage mattered to me. And second, how much I wanted a family. I was stunned and I grieved. My grandmother was a rock. She's the only person besides you I've told about it."

"You flew all this way to tell me now? Why didn't you at least pick up the phone at the time?"

"Drew, what could you do? It was over and I'd lost the baby."

She was not a woman to cry, but a glassy tear rolled down her cheek.

He searched for words. "Figuratively, anyway, I'd have held your hand."

Her expression softened. "I appreciate that. I could have used it at the time. Feel free to hold my hand now. I could still use it."

He wasn't positive that was a good idea but it did seem like the right thing to do. He reached over and touched her fingers, then twined them with his. "I'm here. We were together at dinner just two nights ago, why didn't you tell me then?"

The event was done. She went through it alone. Her strength was never in question, but he hated that.

"I want to move forward, and I want us to make another baby or two. I want to not sell the house and maybe get a pet and I realize that isn't the woman you thought you married. I know that."

It wasn't, that was true enough. Straightforward, but he was starting to realize that maybe his attraction to Lauren was because she wasn't entrenched in the corporate lifestyle. The separation from his professional life had been relaxing, and maybe that's why his friendship with Rob worked so well too. There was rarely a cell phone pressed to Rob Hanson's ear and he liked to be outdoors and had a sense of humor and a clear view of the world.

God help him, he'd known it all along Rob and Lauren were meant to be together.

Drew asked, "Cats are pretty independent, let's go that way. Or a goat? How about that? Extremely easy to care for unless they decide to eat all the furniture on your back deck."

"You are so irreverent at times." Cassandra shook her head, but the gloss of tears was at least blinked away. "I'm afraid I'm going to decline the goat, but I do like cats."

"Cat it is—"

She interrupted. "I understand you need to process all of this, but I wanted to see you in person and that isn't as easy as it sounds. It isn't like you are in an office around the corner."

There was no argument to that. "No. That's true enough." He said quietly, "This comes with the territory. It isn't an ultimatum, it's an observation. I'm coming to the conclusion we had an affair, not a marriage. I've also achieved some clarity on what I want in life. A family would make the list, but I would still be gone most of the time. It would fall mostly on you. I admit with your schedule — and mine as well — I didn't think it would be possible for us."

"I may have stepped down but I negotiated to make very close to the same money. A nanny could help me out and you can hire someone to feed our cat."

"Sweetheart, if you can't manage that, God help our children."

He was joking. She could do anything. Details were her specialty. She knew it too and gave a small laugh. "I'll read up on the feline diet."

"You've thought this through, then."

"I have. Your turn. Where does it stand with your girlfriend?"

He was sure he'd lost Lauren. That didn't mean he should turn back to Cassandra just because she was there, but he couldn't help but wonder if she didn't understand him better. He smiled ruefully. "I think it is safe to say that's over. In a very strange way, I suppose I sort of played cupid."

To think he was pretty sure Rob had wondered how to handle being best man at *his* wedding given his feelings for Lauren. Now the tables were turned.

Life really had some interesting twists.

Cassandra was as ever upfront. "I'd say I was sorry, but I'm understandably not. I'd prefer if you'd consider my proposition and let us try again."

"Maybe we should make sure I'm not truly considered a prime suspect in a murder investigation first."

She wasn't the only one good at dropping bombshells. Cassandra sat back, her eyes widening. "*What?*"

"It's somewhat of a long story. I'd order another drink before I fill you in."

If there was one thing he could say for Cassandra, she was able to rally quickly. She said, "I think I will. Please explain."

"I can't explain. That's the problem."

* * *

"I picked one hell of a time to go on vacation," Carter said, unable apparently to distance himself even while walking in the sand with seagulls overhead and losing at golf to his wife. "Hanson and Fletcher are pretty obvious if the ME decides Karen Foxton's case is a homicide."

Chris argued, "They are both too smart for that. Drysden sounds the most promising to me now. Oh, he's smart too, but he's no angel. He also knew Foxton on a professional level."

"He knew her? Any indication he knew she'd be at the same lake?"

"No confirmation I can make yet. Just because he wasn't charged doesn't mean he didn't assault his girlfriend. He was arrested for it. Swore he accidentally knocked her with his elbow, but her story is entirely different. Both Hanson and Fletcher claim to have seen him and a dark-haired girl together, and before you point it out, I know they have a vested interest in deflecting our investigation away from them."

"But what if they are telling the truth?" It was a reflective comment from Carter. "We can put them there but that door swings both ways. We can float the idea that that opportunity is also a facet when it comes to Drysden."

"I agree. I think they are telling the truth. My gut says they are."

"You shoot from the hip a little too much, but in this case I agree. It is worth pursuing Drysden."

"He isn't likable. I hope it isn't swaying my judgment." Chris had to say it.

"Or maybe he's not a good guy and you sense it. Keep that in mind."

Wise words. "He isn't a good guy because he hit his girlfriend, but it doesn't make him a murderer. And all I had to show them was a morgue photo and neither one could say if it was our victim with him or not."

"There are plenty of women in this world with dark hair."

"What about Heaston? We've got his wife's car and, to me, there's some weird history to his relationship with his missing wife. I'm not the only one thinking that way either, Lauren Mathews is bothered by their neighbor."

"Then don't ignore that." Carter was emphatic.

"I don't disagree, but we just plain need evidence of some kind linked to one of our suspects. When Foxton left, Hanson was out swimming in the lake and Fletcher was in full view of Ms. Mathews. Once again though, suspects confirming alibis. However, she did also say it was possible Foxton stopped off to see Heaston."

"What does he say?"

"Well, first of all, you should be drinking something fruity by the pool and not thinking about this, and second of all, I've been a little busy and haven't pursued that yet. I also haven't told him about his wife's car. I want a full report from the crime lab first. It is all so circumstantial but it is possible Ms. Mathews gave us a good, if kind of macabre, lead."

Carter was the king of understated delivery. "A young student — a female — also died under suspicious circumstances when Angela Heaston, then Barrett, was a student up north in Vermont. The victim was found in a fountain on campus. Blow to the head, but she'd drowned."

Well, *shit*. That did make Chris take notice. "What? What college? I guess I'll look up that file. How did you find that piece of information?"

"Stumbled across it on the database looking at cold cases involving blunt force trauma and drowning. I get bored on vacation. That case is decades old but the name struck me since her sister calls us practically every day. Angela Barrett was interviewed because she belonged to the same sorority."

"Heaston's wife can be linked to an unsolved case? This is like wandering through a maze. Every time I think I might have a sense of direction I have to make a sharp turn."

"You aren't alone on that one."

"It's two victims if the unidentified woman was murdered, three if Angela Heaston washes up. I'm wondering where Drysden went to school."

"Why?"

"I've been looking too. I have a suspicious drowning of a student at Ohio State during the time Hanson and Fletcher were there. I'll work those angles and let you know."

First order of business was to call the investigators of the drowning victim in Ohio. Neither one was available on the weekend but the one who had inherited the case called him right back. "No suspects, Detective," he said when Chris stated why he was calling. "The case is seven years old. She just disappeared and her roommate finally got worried enough to call her parents. Our department, plus, of course, the campus police were all over it. No sign of her until she showed up weeks later in the river. How she got there? No one has any idea."

"Marks on the body? Head trauma?"

"The body was too decomposed and beat up by the current to tell. The report just said drowning as cause of death. Her lungs were still full of water. Undetermined as manner of death. Sound familiar, Detective?"

Yes, it did. "I think we might want to talk again after the medical examiner delivers his report."

"If you can help me put this case to rest, I'm all in."

That was good to know. "I will."

His next step was to go look into Drysden. That struck gold. Not in undergrad, but he did attend the Moritz College of Law at Ohio State University. Chris stared at the screen, not sure whether to be elated or not. Now he had three suspects he could put there at the time of the murder.

If even it was a murder.

The date of the drowning was about right. Drysden was older than Fletcher and Hanson, but then again, he would have been there in Columbus at the same time during graduate school. The choice of school made sense since he was from Kentucky, so it was close by and a reputable institution by any standard.

It didn't narrow the field, just kept it wide open.

He called the detective right back. "I think I might have a lead. You'll be hearing from me again soon. In the case notes, was the victim seeing anyone? Or had she *been* seeing anyone? I can get the basic facts from the database but not the personal notations."

"They did interviews but really didn't come up with anything solid. No finger-pointing. It just isn't there. I know these officers and they are seasoned and professional. One has retired and one was moved to an administrative position, but they handled it very well in my opinion. There was just nothing to work with."

"No mention of the name Drysden?"

"It doesn't ring a bell and I just went over the whole file."

It didn't mean the new information wasn't relevant. "I have a connection — tenuous but still a connection — between a drowning case here and yours. We were looking at two other suspects and found another person that could be a viable lead tied to your investigation."

The detective gave a low whistle. "That's interesting."

"It really has my attention."

"Drysden? I'm making a phone call tomorrow just to be sure his name isn't noted because he was considered but ruled out for some reason."

"That would be appreciated."

What wasn't appreciated was his necessary trip to see the medical examiner, a good sixty miles away. Dr. Kane was a talented doctor but his reports were so sparse that face to face was always worth the drive. He liked to talk, but not write reports. Getting him on the phone was nearly impossible since he served several counties, but if you were willing to pay him a visit during working hours, he remembered each autopsy with startling clarity.

Damn, Chris hated the morgue.

But he'd have to pay a visit tomorrow. The ME had agreed to step it up and do the autopsy first thing because there were multiple cases on the line.

Maybe, he could link them all together.

CHAPTER TWENTY-SIX

He listened to Chopin. Nocturne Opus 9. *One of his favorites.*

The book had stalled. It had swept him along in a maelstrom of poignant emotion and angst and erotic passion mixed with violent results. Then somehow, he'd gotten snagged in the middle of the rushing stream of inspiration, hung up in the water, not able to jerk free.

Poetic, that, and though he certainly might be able to turn a phrase that caught the attention of the average reader, he was not a true lyrical wordsmith.

This part always happened, a part of the process. He suspected that it was similar to childbirth, but while a woman wanted pregnancy over and done, writing was like releasing a part of yourself and then letting it go out in the world. The comfort was in the nurturing, in the life story you shared, and then control was gone in an instant.

Angela had made it clear she didn't want children.

He wondered about that as he gazed out over the black sheen of the water. Some people just didn't. Usually women did, but not all of them. Her selfish tendencies were well-hidden for the most part under a sophisticated and charming facade and they had that in common at least. Also a love of music was mutual, and a taste for luxury cars and expensive houses. He hadn't married her for her money — the allure was already there without the fortune at her fingertips — but it hadn't hurt.

She'd had secrets . . . but so had he.
An almost perfect marriage.
But not quite is just not quite.

* * *

Lauren stayed.

He'd more than offered to take her so she could rent a car and get away from the idyllic vacation from hell, but she said no.

Even worse, in the middle of the night, Rob was lying there sleepless — what were the odds of that — and she'd walked into his room, a slender silhouette in the moonlight, and quietly slipped into bed next to him again. "I can't sleep. Do you mind?"

Jesus.

"No."

He did mind, especially when her breathing softened into a rhythm that indicated she had drifted off, but he was acutely aware of her sharing his bed in the most platonic way possible. He could hardly blame her for not wanting to stay awake, conscious of every sound. It wasn't as if he wasn't doing the same thing.

Unfortunately, he was damned straight to hell now. The situation wasn't romantic in the least with a murderer roaming loose, but they weren't exactly indifferent to each other and ignoring the fact she was in the next bedroom would be hard enough, much less within touching distance. He was a healthy adult male and there was no doubt he wanted the full measure of a relationship with Lauren, both emotionally and sexually.

His unruly body certainly was on board with the latter, but for the moment, he was just going to have to ignore his physical reaction to having her close.

The consolation prize was that he could roll over and smell the fragrance of her hair and feel the warmth of her body.

Dawn couldn't come soon enough.

* * *

Ten in the morning. What a great way to start his day.

The morgue smelled like disinfectant, but of course it did, just like it was always bone-chillingly cold. But it was the faint metallic hint of blood hanging hung in the air that really bothered him. Or did Chris imagine it?

Hard to say. Every time he visited, he saw dead bodies, so maybe that was just a natural assumption. Maybe it didn't smell at all and was just an illusion. Whatever it was he didn't enjoy it.

"Doctor." They just nodded at each other since Kane had a scalpel in one hand and a subject on the table. "I was hoping we could discuss the drowning case. We appreciate you handling it so quickly."

"Oh yes. The young lady. Foxton? I ruled that one a homicide — she did not go into the water dead, but the drowning was because she was unconscious. Quite the blow to her head. It reminded me of a previous case of yours down there."

Pay dirt there anyway. "Anything else you can tell me?"

"Son, she was bludgeoned to an unconscious state and thrown in the water. How much clearer could I be?"

"Your report said your opinion was the cause was drowning, the manner was homicide. That was it, besides the technical stuff. Seven words."

"That sums it up." Kane was a stout man in his mid-sixties and as no-nonsense as they came. Bald head, neatly trimmed gray mustache, and always wore a bow tie. "Neatly done with no messy wounds. Karen Foxton had consumed some alcohol but not more than a glass or so since path didn't show her at impaired levels."

That followed the story he'd been told anyway. One glass of wine before she'd gotten angry and left. "No defensive wounds?"

"None."

"Any idea what she might have been hit with?"

Kane shook his head. "Something smooth and blunt. It left no debris. Caught her right here." He demonstrated on the subject he was currently engaged in examining, pointing to a portion of the skull just above the right ear. "It broke the skin and she was also probably bleeding from her nose and ear. If she was transported to the lake, I would guess there would be traces on the journey."

He refrained from asking about the man on the table. That was not his case. Multiple gunshot wounds that he could see . . . he could probably just watch the news. The ME's office served quite a portion of the state.

On the journey was no good. That was days ago, and torrential rains had happened since. Not to mention she hadn't been taken anywhere in her car.

One last stab in the dark. After all he drove over an hour one way for this information. "Anything else you can recall? Lacerations to both ears were noted. What does that mean?"

Kane frowned. "Her earrings had been ripped out from her earlobes. It was not a gentle act. Now we move into your realm of expertise. A trophy? That would be my guess. I can't say she was wearing earrings because they were gone, but I can't see those lacerations coming from another cause."

That was exactly the type of detail he needed. Chris had no idea what it meant, but it probably did mean something if he could just figure it out. "Anything else, Doc? A detail I wouldn't know except for you? I know you see it all here, but your memory makes you a legend down in our neck of the woods."

He shook his head. "No, just that they were both very pretty girls and they'd drowned in the same place in the same way. The only reason I didn't put in my report homicide on manner in the first case was that she had been hit solidly across the back of the skull, which could be consistent with a fall. She'd also been in the water much longer and that always makes the examination more difficult."

"I can imagine." And wished he couldn't.

"I hope you catch him, Detective."

"If nothing else, you can be assured I will try my best."

"I know you will. That actually makes me sleep better at night." Kane lifted the scalpel. "Now, unless you want to stay for this, I need to weigh his liver and it involves—"

"I'm long gone," Chris interrupted hastily and beat it toward the exit, happily discarding his mask, gown and gloves into the proper bins.

He'd gotten what he came for, he thought, as he went out into the parking lot, fishing for his keys in his pocket. Why take her earrings? It meant something.

Killers left signatures.

He hadn't handled a serial case before. Multiple murders at the same time in one terrible family case — there had been no mystery there — multiple homicide unfortunately, yes, but serial, no.

This qualified.

Same method, same location, and now what just might be a ritualistic part of the murders. He really wanted to get back to the office so he could search and see if it popped up anywhere else.

He was with Dr. Kane. He really wanted to catch this killer.

Carter was going to appreciate the information, but not like the implications. He didn't like them either. As distasteful as it was, he needed to talk to Drysden again. The level of cooperation would be zero, but he needed to do it anyway.

He needed to talk to Lauren Mathews and Rob Hanson again as well. He had a couple of pointed questions. Up front and center: was Karen Foxton wearing earrings the day she decamped?

He was very interested in that detail. Drysden could claim he'd never even met the dark-haired unknown victim. Hanson didn't have that option with his ex-girlfriend. He'd seen Foxton right before she packed up and left. It didn't mean he'd remember her earrings, but maybe he would. It was Lauren Mathews he was counting on more because women noticed details like that about each other. What they wore, a new hairstyle, the color of their lipstick . . . women supposedly dressed for other women, a fact which he'd determined in his lifetime was probably true.

Yes, Mathews was his best bet.

He had some other cases to deal with and paperwork to drop off at the courthouse, so it was late when he headed toward what seemed to be his daily destination.

But they weren't home at the posh lake house. It sat silent, no vehicle in sight. He walked around the back to what appeared to be used as the main entrance.

Good news, they hadn't just picked up and left because there was an open paperback on the table and a half-finished bottle of water. Out running errands maybe, and quite frankly, after two hours of driving and a visit to the morgue, plus a long day, he could sit for a minute and look at the view.

Think about the case.

CHAPTER TWENTY-SEVEN

Some patterns were predictable.

Of course his sister-in-law would turn up. He'd known it all along when he made the phone call and Felicity had even declared she was coming.

She'd surface like she always did, that was the irony of it. Willful, for lack of a better term, described her. She did as she pleased and God help you if you got in her way. Maybe it was the privileged upbringing, or maybe it was innate.

Angela had been the same way.

He was drinking his usual scotch and Felicity gave him a disdainful look because it wasn't quite cocktail hour, but then helped herself to the bar, opening a very nice bottle of French burgundy and pouring a generous glass without even letting it breathe. Her first words were combative, but they would be.

"So they found her car."

"That's what I hear." He was relaxed in a comfortable chair. "You didn't have to come all the way from Lexington to manage this. I don't know anything else."

She took a chair opposite and crossed her legs in a leisurely, elegant movement. Her smile was feline and her eyes cold. The sophisticated hairstyle she favored at the moment framed her features, a swing of deep-auburn hair following her jawline. "Like hell you don't. I hope you realize you married the wrong sister, Glenn."

He did. Now.

Before this moment, he'd never been sure. Fairly certain, but sure? No.

His fingers tightened around his glass. He drawled, "My mistake evidently."

"You have no idea."

* * *

They pulled in and drove around and Rob couldn't help but let a feeling of dark resignation settle over him as he parked his truck next to Bailey's vehicle. He muttered, "Welcome home. I think he's here as much as we are."

Lauren said dryly, "Well, surely he'll be on our doorstep with good news one day. To be fair, *we've* called *him* too."

Bailey was seemingly relaxed in a deck chair, legs extended, in his usual jeans and denim shirt, his badge pinned to the breast pocket, cowboy boots worn but polished. He looked like a young sheriff in a western movie, gun and all. "I have an important question and when I discovered you weren't home, I sat to enjoy the view for a minute hoping you'd return soon. I could look at that lake all day but don't worry, I don't have all day. Just one question. Well, make that two."

"We're buying food currently one day at a time with the high hopes to be able to leave sometime soon," Rob informed him, but he doubted Bailey expected an effusive welcome. "Let me take this stuff inside."

"No problem."

But no reassurance forthcoming on that optimistic comment, he noticed as he disarmed the security system and waited for Lauren to precede him into the house. That was never a hardship since he had quite a nice view of what he considered to be a very shapely body from the back, the fall of her hair shimmering in the light from the high windows.

As Drew had remarked once, she had a world-class ass. Rob agreed, even though he might word the compliment a bit differently within her hearing.

224

It was a nice distraction from whatever conversation he was about to have yet again with local law enforcement. They stowed away the perishables swiftly and went back outside.

Bailey waited, now leaning against the rail. He turned and lifted his brows. "Was Karen Foxton wearing earrings when she left so abruptly?"

That inquiry wasn't what he expected.

Rob couldn't remember. Talk about a bad moment to realize you were clueless, but here it was. He shook his head finally. "Karen? I don't know."

Lauren saved him. "Yes, she was wearing earrings. They were noticeable. Very pretty and unusual. I asked where she'd gotten them and she said at an artist colony in Indiana on a trip with her sister."

He hadn't paid attention, but maybe it had been the tension between them. "I obviously need to improve on my observational skills, but I focused more on how little I wanted the confrontation I knew was coming. I feel certain Lauren knows better than I do. How on earth can that be important?"

"It is," Bailey replied with equanimity. "Second question: did she go out on the lake at any time? You've answered this question before but think about it again."

"No."

"Did she mention she knew someone else with a house here?"

At least he could answer that one with honesty as well. "No, but Lauren is right, she wanted a signed book from Dr. Heaston next door."

Karen was bold and she had been really pissed off. The more he thought about it, and Heaston's behavior in general, the more he wondered if Lauren wasn't right and he was a little unhinged.

"And he knew she was here." Lauren pointed out. "He told me he watched her leave."

"I see." Bailey obviously assessed that information — it was there in his expression even though Rob was fairly sure he tried to keep it controlled. He wasn't as unreadable as his older partner. "Would you mind telling me the context of that conversation in more detail?"

More than two questions but they'd brought that on themselves. Lauren didn't seem to be deterred. She nodded decisively. "He watches us and that's not a secret, but doesn't seem worried about his wife's disappearance, just more interested in us. He brought me a book — which is nice — but seems more intent on what is going on here than his own life. I find Dr. Heaston very odd. I know that my opinion means nothing solid but here it is. That is a very strange man. If you discover he's murdered his wife, I won't faint in surprise."

Rob said, "If you do faint, I'll catch you."

"If that is your attempt at gallantry, you need to work on your technique." She gave him a look that would wither anyone who tried for that flippancy.

He was well aware this was serious, and for him, very serious. "I know you aren't the fainting type, don't worry. I'll keep the smelling salts in my pocket though, just in case."

Bailey seemed amused but was still his usual focused self. "I am interested in all angles, so go on. Tell me what about Heaston makes you uneasy."

She hesitated, but then said simply, "He's very interested in murder. Yes, he writes historical novels and is quite successful at it, but he always chooses female figures from the past that have killed successfully and ruthlessly. The fascination bothers me with all that has happened and I barely know the man. In person he seems very pleasant, but I don't think he is quite normal. He's written books about Lizzie Borden and Bonnie and Clyde, not to mention others."

Rob agreed. "In a logistic sense he's right here."

"Like I said, I'm looking at all the angles."

Heaston certainly should be as much a person of interest as either he or Drew, that was for sure. He didn't point it out though it was tempting, but Bailey already knew it. "I'm with Lauren in that normal doesn't really apply to our interesting neighbor."

Lauren said slowly, "He wrote a book called *Deadly Heiress*. It was based on his wife's grandmother. Her last name was Barrett. She was accused of murdering her husband's mistress and finally acquitted, but the victim was unconscious when she drowned in their pool. In short, in their backyard."

That revelation won her a keen-eyed look. "Really?"

She frowned. "I only looked into it because he keeps referring to me as a femme fatale. I am not a psychologist, but he seems to have a certain obsession. Novels about murder are hardly a new literary genre, but he seems focused in a very specific way on notorious women."

"Trust me, I listen to all information." Bailey just looked at Rob instead of giving an indication of whether he agreed or not. "You seem to know the specific area well and this lake in particular. Where would you put the body?"

That was hardly a welcome question.

His answer was in a tight voice. "Is this a test? No, thank you. What if I guessed correctly and you interpreted it as that I *knew*?"

Bailey shook his head and looked not exactly amused, but there was a hint of humor in his tone. "That would be an interesting turn in the case, I admit, but I just wondered if you might have an idea. I'd appreciate the cooperation."

This was like being handed a loaded gun and asked to play Russian roulette. Rob exhaled audibly. "I'd bet she's in the lake. If it is Heaston, that's where he'd put her. What Lauren saw that morning . . . he put something in his boat."

"I could bring in divers." Bailey sounded like he was thinking it over and not for the first time. "I've been wondering if there couldn't be more bodies out there. It isn't as simple as it sounds, and I'd really need a good cause to call in SAR."

That was a chilling thought, but it had occurred to him already. "Heaston doesn't live here all the time."

"Oh, I'm well aware. But that piece of property has been in his wife's family for quite a while. He's just the one that applied for the permits to build the house about six years or so ago."

That Rob did not know. "I knew it was a more recent structure but wasn't aware of exactly when. My uncle owns this place but is rarely here. My aunt did say vaguely the neighbors are people who've owned the property for a while."

Bailey stood. "I'm quite aware of that too. Thank you for talking to me and have a nice evening."

In the wake of his departure Rob said to Lauren, "Uh, I can't tell if that went well or not. Was he just baiting me?"

She wasn't sure either, he could tell. "He's not that easy to read."

"Which is fine unless he's examining you under his Sherlock Holmes magnifying glass. I don't want to understand him, just to never see him again if possible. Polite guy, but he seems to be under the impression I might be capable of murder."

"It seemed to me more as if you got a nod in the other direction." Lauren gave him a level look. "My impression is he was enlisting your help to maybe look closer at Heaston."

"I gave it." Rob looked back at her. "I didn't know what else to say because I believe it."

"The lake."

He nodded. "In the water."

* * *

They went in and Rob opened a bottle of wine, poured them each a glass and they went back out onto the deck in unspoken agreement.

Quiet evening, dusk sneaking in, the dimming illumination over the placid water, the surface liquid and obsidian, frogs in the trees . . . the growing dark was eerie, but it was probably just the mood and the circumstances.

Too much imagination.

Lauren didn't like to think about it, but who would. Drowning was just not the way she wanted to exit the world.

She wanted to be like her grandmother who had gone to sleep and just never woken up. Pretty much everyone felt that way at a guess. No one remotely rational wanted a violent end.

She murmured, "I'm still hoping Mrs. Heaston is fine."

"I am too." Her companion sipped his wine, long legs crossed at the ankle, his acceptance of the statement telling her he was thinking along the same lines.

She believed him. Rob was an intelligent, strikingly good-looking guy, but he was also a very decent human being. She was sure enough of that to be there alone with him despite the hint of suspicion from law enforcement. "Heaston is off-color somehow."

"I didn't disagree, did I?"

"No, you didn't." She considered him in the slanting light. "I have this policy. If it occurs to me once, I can dismiss it. If it occurs to me twice, I need to really take a look at the situation."

"Did you do that with me?" Hazel eyes were suddenly direct.

That was a switch in subject and it took her a little off guard. Then she admitted, "Yes."

"I'm glad I got a second consideration then." His voice was soft and the curve of his mouth rueful. "Guilty about Drew though and have been all along."

"I think we both are." Her return smile was probably strained. But she meant it. "I wondered all along if Drew and I stood on shifting sands and now I know why. I also felt guilty for being attracted to you but have come to the conclusion all three of us felt guilty in some way."

"That's true enough. I don't want him to try to make it work with his wife just because he thinks he lost you."

To me. He didn't say it.

"You and I both know Drew will make it work if he wants it to work and will walk away if he doesn't." She was confident in that statement. "There's a reason he never mentioned to me he was married. I feel like a fool in some ways. I think he was trying to put it behind him but couldn't entirely."

"I'm not, just for the record. Married, that is."

"Good to know. I appreciate the information." The breeze was warm and humid, but she didn't care. It felt good across her bare shoulders.

"I mean, not yet anyway."

She wasn't sure what to say but luckily he changed the subject.

"The earring thing. Where did that come from? It seems like a very off-the-wall question to me."

Back to Bailey.

"I don't know," she responded truthfully, puzzled also. "They caught my eye because they were truly unique and I was trying to be friendly. I was sincere, they were pretty. But as to how it might apply to her death, I really have no idea."

Rob looked suddenly remote, the same breeze ruffling his dark hair. "Apply to her death? I feel so responsible somehow but had nothing to do with it. I don't even have any idea how to respond to what questions her family might have. She's from Illinois originally. I've never even met them. We were just casually dating, as you know full well. I assume since the police have her car and phone, law enforcement has contacted them. I wouldn't even know how to go about it."

"I'm sure they have. The moment they found her car."

"It's a question I should have asked Bailey but if you haven't noticed, he isn't big on giving information."

"I've noticed."

Had they not been outside on the deck, they would never have heard the shots. Rapid fire retorts, just moments apart.

Had they been anywhere else it could have been a car backfiring, but not here.

Lauren stared at Rob, seeing her own startled reaction in his expression.

He said, "I don't suppose there is any way we can both pretend we didn't hear that, is there?"

CHAPTER TWENTY-EIGHT

He pulled himself out of the house on his stomach, leaving a swath of blood like a garden slug with a slimy trail on a sidewalk.

He couldn't stand but at least he could crawl. It was something anyway even if he was bleeding, maybe to death. He'd left his phone on the back deck and he needed it.

She'd shot him. He hadn't seen it coming.

What a fool.

He'd known what he was dealing with, just maybe not who exactly.

If he was feeling more prophetic, he might compare himself to a lion tamer who understood the score walking into the arena. The potentially deadly beast could turn on you at any time, but that decision to taunt it had been yours.

All those pictures of Lauren Mathews.

He'd uploaded them to his computer, printed them out, and they were on the desk in his study. Felicity had gone in there.

The book wasn't finished. He was only part of the way through the story.

Maybe it didn't have the ending he imagined.

* * *

Chris answered his phone with alacrity because of the name that came up. "This is Bailey."

"You . . . are . . . talking to a dead man."

What the hell?

The tone was raspy, barely audible, and it didn't sound remotely normal. "Care to clarify? Dr. Heaston?"

"She's killed me."

It sounded like it was close to the truth from the ragged weak breathing on the other end of the call. He asked urgently, "Did you call 911?"

"I . . . I called *you*."

"Help is on its way."

"You can try, but I really don't think it will matter. She . . . shot me at least twice. Maybe more . . . God, I'm bleeding . . . everywhere."

"Who?"

"Lauren."

"Ms. Mathews shot you?"

Silence.

"Dr. Heaston?"

Not good. Disbelief flooded through him and he swung into action, pulling into the next visible driveway to turn around. He was almost back to town. It had only been about twenty minutes since he'd left the lake.

The accusation seemed implausible, but then again, Lauren more than made clear she found him suspicious and Heaston by all accounts had displayed an unsettling level of interest in his lovely neighbor. She was also the closest thing to a witness if he'd done something to his wife, since she'd seen him put something in his boat and he knew it.

He pushed the right buttons and it took a few moments before he got an answer which meant they were either understaffed this evening, or the phones were busy. "We have a victim of a shooting on a nearby lake — let me give you the address. I'm on my way to the scene but I'm not a paramedic. I just talked to him and it sounded bad. Multiple gunshot wounds."

He knew the dispatcher. Rachel said, "Whoa, okay, Detective, the victim called you first? You ask and you shall receive. The responders will be on their way pronto."

It sounded like they might not be in time but, for all he knew, the man was playing him.

That was a sobering possibility. His wife's car found, the net closing in . . .

Maybe Chris was walking into a trap. Though he couldn't see the point in killing a police officer who was pursuing the case but not actually ready to arrest anyone. Of course, Heaston didn't know exactly where the case stood, because Chris didn't even know himself.

His phone pinged. *It sounds like maybe there was gunfire next door.*

Lauren Mathews' number for the text.

Next door? It seemed unlikely she'd contact him to say she'd heard shots if she'd fired them . . . what the hell was going on?

He couldn't text back because he was truly driving like a bat flying out of hell.

Or was it, in this situation, into hell?

* * *

"He didn't answer. It's been fifteen minutes."

Rob was well aware. "He's probably as sick of us as we are of him at this point. Besides, we can't tell if it means a thing. This is Tennessee and not even close to a town. People fire guns here. This is the country."

"I am not an expert, but it sounded close."

It had.

But — and that was the applicable word — he would go over and check it out except he wasn't about to take Lauren into possible harm's way, nor did he want to leave her behind alone.

"For all we know Heaston is a gun aficionado and likes to take them out and target shoot now and then. It is not against the law on your own property and he owns a lot of it."

"Just two shots for target practice?"

He had to agree. "Not worth it, is the probable answer for that theory, but on the other hand we can hardly go

233

tramping through the woods searching for someone with a discharged firearm."

"No, I suppose not." Lauren looked unsettled. "If it was one shot . . ."

When she trailed off, he said, "Suicide? No, Heaston isn't the type, not that *I'm* an expert on that, but I somehow doubt it."

"I doubt it too because two shots are unlikely for that."

"True enough."

The shadows were thickening, lending amber lights to her hair. Rob abstractly admired the view and wondered just how they'd gotten into this situation. "Bailey will get back to you eventually. Let's give him a break, maybe he'd like to eat dinner or something. I know we are on edge, but it really might be nothing."

As if to contradict him, suddenly there was a faint wail of sirens in the background.

Lauren's eyes widened. "Okay, maybe he did get my message."

It had to be more than that, Rob thought with a frisson of foreboding. Getting disturbing news was a phenomenon he'd prefer would go away.

There weren't sirens for a mere text like that.

He muttered, "Well, *shit*."

* * *

It was gothic with the lowering sun lending a lurid reddish hue to the sky, the windows of the huge house unlit, no sign of life anywhere, but Heaston's pricey SUV sat in the driveway.

If the man was home, there was no indication of it besides the car.

Chris got out and registered the quiet with caution, drawing his weapon, which he had done only a few times in his career as a law enforcement officer. That call had been unsettling and he was leery, but when he went up the steps to knock, he noticed that the beautiful front door, heavy polished wood obviously custom-made, was not quite closed.

"Dr. Heaston?" He rapped once, but pushed it open and called out, "Police. This is Detective Bailey. I'm coming in."

Silence.

Ominous, and the place was dark inside as he heard the rescue unit roll up the driveway. The turn-off was easy to miss but they had evidently found it, the flashing red-and-blue lights giving a macabre illumination to the interior of the house.

He hit the lights after using his phone as a flashlight.

No Heaston. He extended his Glock in defensive mode, sweeping the large foyer with an assessing glance, moving toward the main living space and finding the expansive room empty. Expensive furniture, stone fireplace, but no one in sight.

"Where's the victim?"

First responder at the door right behind him.

"Give me a minute. Stay back. I just got here. For all I know, there's a gunman inside."

"Let us know."

"You'll be the first."

He found the crime scene easily enough, the floor of the family room at the back of the house showing a smeared trail of blood toward the open French doors, still no evidence of movement or sound, but by now he had adrenalin pumping pretty high and Chris went out onto the deck, gun still out.

Heaston was sprawled on his stomach in a welter of blood, the pool alarming, his face turned away. His cell phone lay right next to his right hand, but Chris knew he'd lost consciousness during their phone call, or at least the ability to still hold the phone and speak.

"I've got a victim out here," he shouted. "Back deck."

More vehicles were arriving, he could hear them, doors slamming and voices as he tried to find a pulse. Then, as it should be because he'd told the truth, that while he knew the basics, he was not a paramedic, it was all out of his hands and he stepped back for the team to do their work. All he said was, "Two wounds, or that's what he told me on the phone. I haven't moved him."

It took a moment, but one of the paramedics said, "Okay, we have respiration, but man, it's shallow."

"Detective? What do we have here?"

Chris turned and saw two deputies had come out and was glad for the help. "Well, we have a gunshot victim and I want to start by searching the house first to make sure whoever did this isn't sticking around. It's a big place. If you'll check out the upper floor, I will take a look at where the shooting took place." He pulled out gloves again for the second time in just a short period of time. "We don't have a warrant, so just take a look around for a possible intruder and don't touch anything."

He didn't have to be a forensics crime scene tech to figure out exactly what had happened. Heaston had been sitting in a chair and there was a broken tumbler on the floor, the liquid surrounding the debris of shattered glass smelling like it came from a bottle of bourbon sitting on a small table nearby. The trail of blood led directly from right in front of the chair like he'd collapsed forward, and, from the amount of blood, had lain there for a short while anyway, then managed to crawl to the deck.

There was an uncorked bottle of wine on the polished bar at the end of the room, but no wineglass in sight.

She's killed me . . .

No weapon in sight either and the likelihood of the wounds being self-inflicted were low since Heaston didn't seem in good enough shape to have disposed of the gun, plus he made the call. No, not an aborted suicide, and it did look like maybe he had a visitor.

Lauren?

Chris stood there, thinking hard, only abstractedly registering all the frantic activity around him, the stretcher coming in and the terse conversations of the rescue personnel. He came to the conclusion that while his next stop was inevitably next door yet again, it seemed just too unlikely to him Ms. Mathews would ever agree to a glass of wine with Glenn Heaston. It was even more unlikely Rob Hanson would let her near him alone.

If not her, why did Heaston mention her name?

And who was his visitor, because that was — not that he was a judge but from his surroundings could guess — an expensive bottle of wine to leave sitting opened with what looked like only a glass or maybe two, poured? It didn't look like Heaston had been drinking it.

Maybe, he thought grimly, he finally had something to work with. He couldn't help but wish Carter was there to help him think this out, but so it went.

Mrs. Heaston was still missing.

But was she dead?

Standing there, he had to ask himself that question.

That would be an ironic twist.

There was no question about it, shuffling the queue of suspects was getting tedious. He needed a break in this case that did not involve more victims. It seemed like with all the evidence they had, they could figure out a pattern that didn't point them all in different directions.

Maybe Heaston would do him a favor and live.

CHAPTER TWENTY-NINE

Fading in and out.

He tried to find a middle space where he really couldn't feel any-thing but was still aware.

It eluded him.

Pain, yes, certainly that, and a hazy recollection of an event he could now only vaguely assimilate.

Had it been an illusion? He drifted in a foggy world . . .

He didn't know.

* * *

Lauren had absolutely no idea what to say. "Excuse me?"

"Is that your first glass of wine of the evening?" Bailey repeated the question and looked bland as usual, dark-blond brows raised and his tone moderate.

She and Rob had sat there on the deck and listened to the commotion next door, the house too far away for them to hear anything and the line of vision blocked by trees from where they sat, so all they were aware of was the activity and the sirens, both for arrival and ominously, departure.

Then Bailey had pulled in and come up to join them.

"Why?" she asked cautiously.

Bailey was not the type to ask frivolous questions. Due to unfortunate circumstances, she knew that much about him.

He sat down, put his elbows on his knees and looked at her. "Because it looks like someone had one next door with Heaston right before they shot him."

"If I may interject here," Rob said in obvious disbelief. "I've been present when Lauren has told you directly she believes the man murdered his wife. Please give her — and me, because I would never let her — credit enough to know she wouldn't risk being alone with him for two seconds, much less to sip a glass of wine."

"I don't actually think she would, but I had to ask." He leaned back and rubbed his jaw. "Look, after he was shot, Heaston called me. His exact words were 'she's killed me', and then he said your name, Ms. Mathews. If you can come up with an explanation, I'm all ears."

She couldn't. She just stared at him, the background noise of insects and water rippling under the slight breeze quiet and peaceful compared to the discussion. It was Rob who said, "We were sitting right here when we heard two shots. We haven't left, either one of us, since you were here not that long ago."

Bailey's faint smile was ironic. "Why is it I seem to only have suspects who can supply alibis for other suspects? Let's move forward on the assumption he said your name for another reason." There was a slight hesitation and then he told her. "I found a photograph of you on the floor of what apparently is his study, or home office. It looks like it fell off while someone gathered up his laptop and from the gaps in the otherwise fairly cluttered surface of his desk, maybe they also took some of his notes."

Lauren wasn't sure she even wanted an answer. "What kind of picture, and don't even bother to ask, no, I never posed for any or knew he'd taken one."

"It's evidence, so I took a picture of it with my phone." He took it out and pulled it up and handed it over.

She was on the dock in her bathing suit, but though there was nothing risqué about it, it made her self-conscious anyway because it was one thing to pose for a picture like that with lots of bare skin, and another to have someone taking it without your knowledge.

Her voice was brittle as she handed back the phone. "Why am I not surprised? I knew he was watching us."

"Tell me what else you learned about Angela Heaston when you were looking up her background. I have literally not had time to go back to my desk and check for myself, but she's still a missing person, not a homicide at this point."

Lauren caught the direction of his question easily enough. "You think *she* could have shot him?"

He didn't answer directly because that was not how he operated. "I think a spouse is always a consideration in a crime like this."

Because this was clearly a crime. Angela Heaston might be voluntarily absent, but someone tried to kill her husband. Lauren regrouped. "Okay, let me get my laptop. It isn't against the law for me to have another glass of wine either, is it?"

"No."

"Good, I was starting to wonder." She got up. "I'll be right back."

She retrieved her computer, saw Rob had thoughtfully refilled her glass, thanked him with a smile, and sat back down to boot up. "I made a file just by saving bits and parts I found interesting. I'll pull it up and feel free to help yourself. You can copy and send it to yourself if you wish."

"That'll save me time, thank you."

She rose and went to sit by Rob, sipping from her glass, very aware of him silent next to her. Communication without words worked, since she was sure neither one of them knew what to say. He reached over and touched her hand, and then took it, lacing their fingers together. Rather nice. If there wasn't a detective going through her computer to try to catch a killer, it would even be a romantic gesture she could appreciate.

"Angela Heaston's sister went to the same school in Vermont as she did?" Bailey was looking at her, but abstractly as if he were more thinking out loud than asking a question.

She hadn't paid a lot of attention to that detail — as far as she knew, there wasn't much of a reason to note it but she had. "I think she's only one year younger, yes. Same school, same sorority even."

"That's interesting." Bailey shut her computer and stood. "I'm going to assume we aren't going to see each other again tonight, but it goes without saying, if something happens, call me."

"What else could happen?" Rob's question was ironic at best.

Bailey responded in kind. "I'm asking myself the same thing."

They listened to his car start and pull away. Rob turned to her. "That's interesting? That she and her sister went to the same school? Why?"

"I don't know." She didn't.

* * *

Chris had seen better evenings. No dinner, a possible murder on his watch, and there was going to be a lot of paperwork.

He wanted a Carter vacation. Golf — okay he was even worse at golf than Carter, probably since he never played it except a few times in college — but a beach sounded good right now.

Carter would be back tomorrow and he had some theories to run by his conservative partner that might push the edge, but this whole case — cases, he wasn't sure what applied — fit that criteria. Was it all tied together? He thought so, but Carter was old-school and would disagree without solid proof.

So that's what he needed.

Sara was at the kitchen table when he walked in, an empty plate in front of her, her expression distracted as she looked at her phone. "I went ahead and ate. Sorry, but it's getting a little on the late side and you didn't call with your plans."

"True. I'm sorry too." He went over and dropped a kiss on the top of her head. "Tough case."

"What did you expect?"

He moved to the refrigerator and took out a beer. "Tonight? Not finding a gunshot victim who was a suspect."

"No." She finally glanced up. "I meant when you became a detective."

He stopped in the act of taking a drink because of the tone of her voice. "I don't know."

"You know what *I* don't know?"

Oh, shit. He had an idea by the look in her dark eyes. "Not unless you tell me. If I could read minds I would be very, very good at my job."

"You already are." She smiled, but it wasn't genuine. "I'm focused but not like you. It was fun, but you don't have time for a relationship and it is just as much my fault since I thought I was good with that. Maybe I'm not, though, in retrospect from a current point of view. I'm moving into an apartment, so I hope you don't mind if I leave the moppet? I've already signed the lease and no pets."

It took a minute as he digested this new development. Did he mind about the dog? He needed to answer the question. "No. I might actually need someone who loves me."

"I still love you, Chris," Sara said firmly. "But it isn't meant to be."

He didn't have a choice. If she wanted to leave, she could, of course. Would he be devastated? He didn't think so, but time would tell.

She went upstairs and he thought about making a sandwich or something but decided against it. He called Carter instead. It was better than waiting for tomorrow and he needed something to do right now. "So someone shot Heaston," he began the conversation, no preamble, no greeting.

He *really* needed something else to think about.

"Is that so? Enlighten me."

"There's the rub, I can't. The tired saying 'I don't have a clue' doesn't apply either. I've got all kinds of them. Whoever put two bullets in our resident author was someone he knew, because he was sipping bourbon and sitting in a chair when it happened. He's in surgery now. We'll see how it goes."

"I picked one hell of a time to take a few days off. What clues?"

"His unfriendly visitor had a glass of wine, wiped the bottle and the corkscrew clean, which means they were the one to open it, and took the wineglass."

"I'd say he knew them well if he didn't even bother to play host." Carter sounded like he was thinking along the same lines. "The visitor felt comfortable doing it for themselves."

"*She* felt comfortable. He called me after it happened." Chris repeated the short conversation, including Lauren's name being the last thing Heaston managed to say.

Carter was silent for a moment. "If we didn't have his wife's car, I might think it was her."

"That occurred to me too, but here's another consideration. What about his sister-in-law? You also spoke to her on the phone about her sister's absence, correct? Did she suspect Heaston?"

"Actually, no, my impression during a very brief conversation was that she thought like he did, that her sister might be voluntarily absent and too inconsiderate to let them know her whereabouts, but that was early on, right after he reported his wife missing."

"She's been remarkably unemotional about her absent sister, I agree. But she is keeping tabs on the investigation." Chris paused, wondering if he was just deflecting from his personal situation and if that was a problem, he had with emotional intimacy that maybe someday he should address.

One issue at a time. When Sara had gone upstairs the moppet had stayed at his feet, as if she also knew it was over and there was nothing to be done. He said slowly, "Felicity Barrett was at the same private college as her sister when that girl was found drowned in the fountain. I wonder if she could have been here when the first victim was found in the lake. It's a family property, so surely she uses it too."

"Revenge being her motive for shooting Heaston because she suspects him in her sister's disappearance? Why kill Karen Foxton?"

"I'm feeling there's something in the equation that's starting to come together but is still hanging out there. Whoever shot Heaston took his computer, and from the way his desk was in disarray, I would guess his notes. He had a picture of Lauren Mathews — at least one. It was on the floor, so . . . dropped? I have a hunch there were more, and if so, maybe the shooter took those too."

"Whoa, cowboy. You always fly ahead so fast I'm surprised you can stay in the saddle. I'm not following."

"He wrote a book based on an old crime his wife's family was involved in. I think my question is — what is he working on now?"

"How could that be pertinent?"

Good question.

He didn't have the answer. "I just think maybe it is."

Carter said in surprising support, "I trust your instincts. I'll see you tomorrow."

He ended the call and sat there contemplating his beer bottle on the table in front of him, weary but still strung-up.

"I'll see you tomorrow."

The echo of Carter's words made him glance up. Sara had a duffle bag in one hand, her purse over one shoulder. She added, "I have some boxes in the garage to pick up. I'll text you my new address."

Then she was gone.

He hadn't ever felt Sara was *the* one, but he'd been attracted to her and they got along well for the most part. It had worked for a while, but this wasn't exactly what he needed on this particular evening.

"Damn," he mused out loud.

The moppet shifted position, so her head rested on his foot and when he reached down to scratch behind her ears, she licked his hand.

He wasn't entirely alone, he thought philosophically.

Things could be worse. He could be Heaston with two bullets in him and wondered if the man would make it or not.

CHAPTER THIRTY

Drew had an unexpected and unwelcome surprise at the Ft Lauderdale airport. A man he recognized all too well was sitting at a table as he walked in to get a cup of much-needed coffee. Long night and long flight. Time zones were always an issue.

Why would Detective Carter be there waiting for him? *Shit.*

Only one reason he could think of was to arrest him on suspicion of murder and he was trying to currently get his life in better order so the timing was really, really bad — though the timing for that would always be bad.

He squared his shoulders and took the initiative. "Detective, fancy seeing you here."

"The same." Carter looked convincingly surprised.

Drew wasn't instantly reassured. "You aren't here looking for me?"

"I'm just returning from a not-so-very relaxing vacation."

"I see."

He did look tanned, but not all that relaxed. "I played golf, swam in the ocean, and while I was gone nothing good happened in your neck of the woods."

That hardly sounded promising. "I've heard some of it. What are you referring to? Are Lauren and Rob okay?"

"Let me see your passport, please."

Drew showed it so often it was hardly a chore and he had nothing to hide. He pulled it from his bag and gave it up. "Here you go. I always have it handy, as you can imagine. But please answer my question. Are they okay?"

"As far as I know, they are."

"Who isn't?"

Carter handed back the passport after he examined it. "Since it seems like you've been out of the country this entire time, I will tell you that you are off the hot list. I think they are calling my flight so please excuse me. My wife just went to the restroom, so I need to find her. You know how this all works. I don't want to miss my plane."

Off the hot list?

Drew ordered his coffee and sat down at a table to call Rob immediately. Thankfully he answered. "Drew?"

"I'm back in the States. Care to tell me what the hell is going on?"

"Wish I knew."

"I really can't make this up, I just ran into Detective Carter by accident in Florida. My absence apparently exonerated me from something that was not explained before he went off to catch a plane."

"Well, you didn't try to kill Heaston last night if you were flying over the deep blue sea, so you get a free pass on that possible murder anyway. I don't have any idea if he lived through the night or not. I am grateful to say law enforcement hasn't been by yet this morning to give us an update."

Us. Lauren was still there with him then. There was a pang, but he needed to let it go. Cassandra was going to meet him in Columbus at the airport.

Drew took a sip from his coffee and muttered, "What the hell?"

"My thoughts exactly."

"You said someone tried to kill him."

"Shot him twice. We heard it."

"Jesus, Hanson, I'm never going on vacation with you again."

Rob answered with cynical emphasis, "Join the club. I doubt I'm ever going on vacation with me again either."

* * *

Chris went into the meeting at one o'clock. He'd known it was going to happen, so he put on the blue shirt his mother had given him for Christmas that he'd never wear otherwise, dark slacks, and even showed up with a tie.

He hated ties, but this was his job. If the occasion warranted it, he could look like a detective.

If he'd learned nothing else from this experience, he knew now how much he valued what he did for a living, but not just that. What he *did*.

The sheriff pointed at a chair at his entrance. "Bailey, this is Agent Wright with the FBI. Fill us in."

He acknowledged the introduction with a simple, "Ma'am."

Wright was middle-aged, with stylishly cut, ash-blonde hair, a tailored jacket and sensible skirt, and a businesslike demeanor. Light-blue eyes gave him an assessing study as he took a seat in the sheriff's department's small conference room, probably slotted him as a homegrown boy with a badge — which would be accurate — and nodded.

It wasn't like he didn't know the sheriff was a man of few words, so he responded in kind because he could relate to it and that's why they got along very well. "I'll do my best."

He wasn't sure why the FBI was interested, but then again, wasn't all that surprised either. The department had been using their resources in more than one case now, including ViCAP. It was a valuable database, and he'd certainly been accessing it.

"Carter and I have currently one drowning that is labeled undetermined for manner of death, a missing person case, a drowning that is considered a homicide, and now a possible fatal shooting victim, all linked to the same general area, which is a lake in this county. More than that, we are not convinced that there might not be some unsolved murders in other jurisdictions connected to our case."

Agent Wright said, "We are wondering the same thing. There are some similarities that the Violent Criminal Apprehension Program flagged on cold cases in different states but with some disturbing ties. Your probing questions, Detective Bailey, prompted some digging in other places."

"If I can help with the other investigations, I'll be more than happy to share, and both Carter and I will also be appreciative if anyone has information for us."

"I have some questions. Enough that I decided to come in person from our field office in Nashville after I was contacted by a cold case investigator from Vermont because one of your follow-up questions rang a bell with him." She folded her hands on the table and looked him in the eye. "Tell me about the earrings."

Of all the things he thought she'd ask, that was not particularly expected, but he answered readily enough. "Our only confirmed homicide, unless Glenn Heaston dies, is Karen Foxton, an attorney from Ohio here on vacation with friends. I went to interview the ME. He's notorious for his succinct reports but remembers everything. Taking the time to go see him face to face is worth it, so I hoofed it over there to talk to him in person to see if there was something not in the report that might help. There were lacerations that indicated to him maybe she was wearing earrings and they were torn from her in a violent way. I confirmed later with a witness that saw the victim on the day she disappeared that, indeed, she was wearing earrings."

Agent Wright shook her head. "Small bits and pieces can make cases, so well done. There's a link to the Vermont case. Two links actually. Angela Heaston, who was then Ms. Barrett, your current missing person, was interviewed in relation to that homicide at the college. The victim in that case also had her earrings removed quite viciously. Ms.

Heaston was not considered a serious suspect at the time, but was a sorority sister to the victim. All the young women living in the house were interviewed. Now we have a solid connection."

More than one, Chris thought grimly. "So Angela can be linked to a similar murder to Foxton's, and maybe one last summer tied to the same lake, she has disappeared, and her husband — who is obsessed with female serial killers — has been shot. I'm not a federal agent, but there's a clear pattern to me."

"Clear as mud, son." Sheriff Lawrence was old-school and he wanted definitive investigations with concise answers. "Who? Heaston didn't shoot himself, we are operating on the angle his wife is a possible homicide, and Foxton is more tied to the witness who supplied you the information about the earrings than anyone else, and her friends are suspects."

So Lawrence was paying attention to the reports. Chris was never sure, since the man had other problems looming constantly. Drug crime in the county was growing at an alarming rate. "All true. Why do you think I was tapping into whatever resources are available to make sense of it all?"

Carter, who so far had let him do the talking, looking irritatingly like he had been out in the sun, interjected, "Fletcher didn't shoot Heaston because he clearly wasn't in the country, it is unlikely any of them harmed Foxton, and there's only speculation over last summer, *if* she's a victim of anything besides an unfortunate accident."

"But then why has she not been reported missing?" Chris had to point to that argument.

"We always do come back to that."

"I think I can help you there." Agent Wright reached down and pulled a file from a leather case by her chair, set it on the table and opened it. She extracted a picture and extended it. "Until we have DNA confirmation we won't be sure, but I believe we've managed to ID your drowning victim. Once again, if you hadn't been poking the system from this location, the dots would not have connected."

Long dark hair, a much different reflection of the young woman retrieved from the lake, her smile engaging, her arm around an older woman who had to be her mother, the resemblance was so striking. Chris handed it to Carter. He said tightly, "It looks like her to me, but alive and happy and dead in the water for days are pretty different. What's the story?"

"Foreign exchange student from Italy. She was attending a college in Kentucky when she disappeared. Her parents didn't know for weeks she was missing because the girls she was staying with in a small house off campus didn't report it right away. According to them, she was seeing someone, but was secretive about it. The Italian family isn't affluent but did contact the embassy eventually when they were having trouble communicating with the local authorities. The father eventually flew over, but couldn't find any trace of her, so the case was left with the special agent in charge of the closest Kentucky office."

"So, a foreign national reported missing after some time in a different state . . . I'm getting it. What about the college?" Chris was working it out, tying in Kentucky to the equation. "Let me guess, Heaston is connected to it somehow."

Wright's smile was thin. "Adjunct professor of history and literature. Yes, Gabriella Marino took his class the semester before she disappeared."

"Hell's bells," Lawrence said with a shake of his head. "Now we're talking. This is starting to unravel."

It was. Chris felt a flicker of triumph that was tempered by other undeniable concerns. "What now? Surely law enforcement state by state is drawn into this as we overlap, so I take it this might be a federal case and no longer a local investigation."

"Actually, Detectives Bailey and Carter, we will be coordinating the ongoing progress on an overall basis especially since the Italian government is now involved, but by all means continue on with the good work. You seem to be the catalyst for a possible serial apprehension." She paused and lifted a brow, looking at Chris. "I know, for instance, you stayed up as far as I can tell all last night looking into dozens of cases that had any similarities to the ones you are currently working. Any luck? I am here to collect all the information I can so we can assist."

He'd stayed up all night because his girlfriend had decamped and he was at a loose end, calling the hospital every couple of hours to check in on Heaston's condition, ready to go if he was stable enough for a few words, if he even regained consciousness.

It was, he was told by a patient but tired nurse staffing the phone, still very much touch and go. One of the bullets had gone through the fleshy part of his right arm and that was not the problem. The other one had lodged itself in the patient's spine and that was, he'd been informed, a very tricky surgery.

"Some luck." He refrained from revealing just why he'd been sleepless — it was no one else's business that Sara had walked out — and explained, "I did a measured search by location and date based on where Angela Heaston has lived for the past twenty years and drownings that happened nearby during that time. Then I did another search with a different suspect in mind. I found a match that might eliminate Mrs. Heaston, which probably means she's dead, but narrows it down to someone who might have committed all the murders and shot her husband."

"Felicity Barrett?" Carter's inquiring gaze was razor sharp. "You were right?"

"I don't know but there's a similar case that fits. A young woman found in a pond in a subdivision years after the college incident in Vermont. The only way I narrowed it down to Felicity Barrett was that I went through her employment records. They worked together at an advertising firm according to the files. The victim was unconscious when she went into the water. It's thin, I admit, but it waved a flag at me."

"So it should." Wright had her laptop out and was making notes. "What else?"

"Quite frankly, Lauren Mathews, who seems to be Heaston's latest focus, is the one who connected the books he writes with his relationship to his wife. It isn't a secret what subject matter he chooses for his books, but she connected that first title to his wife's family, and did draw what I feel is some decent psychological conclusions about the man. I'm hardly an expert either, but his interest in Ms. Mathews would bother me as well, and if she hadn't told me the circumstances, I wouldn't have seen it."

"An amateur profiler?" Wright's tone was dry. "Maybe we should offer her a job with AUB if she's correct. What conclusions?"

"He calls her the 'femme fatale' and I think maybe he's writing a book inspired by her complicated relationship with both Andrew Fletcher and Rob Hanson, who are no longer in my headlights as suspects, but at one time were at the top of the list."

Carter never accepted an unsupported theory. "You have evidence of this?"

"Nope, but whoever shot Heaston does. They took his computer and whatever notes he might have had lying around. His desk was a mess and obviously had been rifled. I *do* have proof he's been taking pictures of Lauren Mathews without her knowledge, much less her permission."

He'd brought an envelope with the picture in it and took it out.

"Hmm." Wright studied it. "Pretty young woman. If she was my daughter and some man was taking clandestine pictures of her like this, I would not be a happy parent. Define complicated relationship. Why do you think Heaston would be interested?"

Surprisingly enough, it was Carter who supplied the answer. "It's rather clear both men have a romantic or at least sexual interest in Ms. Mathews. I have to admit I realized it almost immediately, and really have only been around all three of them a couple of times. It isn't a new story by any means, but I suppose I can see how it might evoke a premise of upcoming conflict. Fletcher and Hanson are lifelong friends. I wondered about it and I am not half as imaginative as a bestselling author."

That was very wordy for his usually stoic partner, but Chris didn't disagree.

"It doesn't fit the killer's profile to try to kill Dr. Heaston. The way she, if it is a she, went about it, is quite dissimilar." Wright didn't look convinced.

Chris had thought of that too. "Different kind of killing and a far different motive. He's male, he's aware of what she's capable of and, you have to admit, it is farsighted to take him by surprise by using a gun, instead of knocking him unconscious. I doubt he's unaware enough to let the latter happen."

She handed back the photo. "I'm going to trust you on this one, and if you'll keep me up to date and we can solve multiple cases, you'll make my life a lot easier."

"I have Heaston's phone and I took it this morning to the local service center and produced my badge. They accessed it for me without having to jump through hoops, and Felicity Barrett's number was listed in his contacts. When she uses her phone again, we should be able to trace her location. I'm going to guess she isn't too worried she's a suspect. She's been getting away with it for a long time. Maybe she didn't know where his phone was, or even where to look for it. Whoever it was certainly looked through his office."

Everyone filed out except for the sheriff who came over and lifted his bushy brows and clapped Chris on the shoulder.

Not for a job well done necessarily.

"Son, you are such a Tennessee cowboy. You 'hoofed' it to see the ME?"

Chris gave a rueful laugh. Maybe that hadn't been very sophisticated. "I meant—"

"I know exactly what you meant because I'm an old Tennessee boy myself. That said, you're obviously doing a good job on this case."

High praise from a tough old lawman who rarely said more than a brusque hello on a good morning.

"I'm trying. So is Carter."

"I know he isn't the easiest to work with but I had a hunch that you'd impress him. Why do you think you're the youngest man I've ever promoted to detective?"

"I wasn't aware of that." He wasn't.

"Be aware. And dammit, solve these cases because we're talkin' the FBI here, Bailey."

Of that he *was* aware.

CHAPTER THIRTY-ONE

He'd been a scholar, a student intent on learning the philosophy of conscious evil, if he wanted to put it in lofty terms.

Such fascinating subject matter, no situation quite the same, but the underlying theme repeated itself over and over until it stumbled over an obstacle that could not be overcome, or was simply a mistake to try to vanquish.

If one learned from such mistakes the lessons could be very harsh.

Machines beeping were the background music of his world. Mozart and Albinoni were silent notes played by an orchestra in his memory.

* * *

Lauren glanced at her cell and then up at Rob. "Bailey probably won't like this."

He stowed the second suitcase in the back seat of his truck and shut the door. "Bailey and Carter's objections to us leaving are immaterial unless they want to arrest me. Quite frankly, I can't spend another night here. I'm available to answer any questions I can, but not in Tennessee."

Not to stay and lie in bed with you and not able to do more besides listen to you breathe in the dark . . .

He agreed on principle that making love to the woman of his inappropriate dreams would be much more enjoyable if the situation was much less unfettered by recent events, so he was willing to wait. Several murders and an attempted homicide were a bit off-putting in the romance department, so was constant visits by the police. He agreed that together was no doubt safer, but this wasn't summer camp and the platonic arrangement was definitely not his preference.

"I agree." Lauren looked lovely as ever with her fall of chestnut hair but there was a hint of shadow under her eyes, so he doubted he was the only sleepless one, and she was subdued. "Home sounds like a good idea."

"The situation is undeniably dangerous. Ask Heaston. Oh wait, you can't because for all we know the man is dead. We should have left days ago."

She lifted a brow. "I have the same caustic view, but I do think if he didn't make it, Bailey would tell us. We stayed because when detectives ask you to do so, law-abiding citizens comply."

He gave a humorless smile. "Caustic? How about we qualify it as realistic instead? I'm going to go do a final walk-through to make sure we have everything, set the alarm, grab the cooler on the deck, and then we are out of here."

"I'll wait here." The tailgate was open, his fishing gear the last thing he symbolically packed each time, pole and tackle box ready to be stowed. She leaned against the truck as she waited for him.

Late-afternoon sun sifted through the leaves and the breeze was warm and clean. He didn't blame her. He went up the steps and into the quiet house, wondering if he'd ever feel the same about the place. Making a swift sweep to be certain all the lights were off and no belongings left behind, he went back down the stairs. Earlier he'd put the boat on the lift and dealt with the motor, so all that was left was to finish putting the cooler in the back of truck and the drive back to Ohio.

He went outside and closed the door, pushed the right buttons on the alarm, grabbed the cooler and turned only to stop abruptly, aware of voices. His first thought was he hadn't heard a car pull up, but then again he'd been inside.

Two female voices.

Lauren was still by the truck and he didn't recognize the woman standing a few feet from her — auburn hair, dressed in shorts and sandals, sunglasses hiding her face . . .

Or *did* he recognize her?

Whatever conversation they were having stopped when he reached the edge of the deck and started down the steps and he realized two things at once.

Lauren was pale as death and the visitor had a gun.

The unknown woman said pleasantly, "You must be Rob."

Then she pointed the gun at him and the next thing he knew he stumbled as if he'd been pushed violently, the impact spinning him backward.

* * *

The sound of the shot rang in her ears.

The minute Lauren had noticed the woman who walked out of the woods, she'd been at first startled, and then as a dawning awareness of just who it might be settled over her, a sense of uncertainty as to what to do.

Now, that feeling turned to pure horror as Rob reached out at the railing in a failed attempt to keep his feet as he went down with a sickening thud, sliding downward several steps.

Paralyzed with shock, Lauren couldn't move, even when the woman swung around and walked slowly toward her.

Rob. Maybe she screamed his name, she wasn't sure.

"You're fatal, that's for certain, Ms. Fatale. Glenn's obsessed with you. Well, that's over, isn't it?"

Close enough Lauren could clearly see her face now. She had a chilling conviction of the identity of the uninvited guest because she resembled pictures of her sister.

When Felicity Barrett reversed the gun and jumped for her, she wasn't exactly ready, but her muscles unlocked enough that she reacted, reflexively throwing up her arm and the blow meant for her head instead hit her shoulder with such excruciating force she was slammed into the tailgate.

Pain shot through her and she rolled sideways, another blow coming that managed to miss her but clanged viciously into the metal of the truck. One flailing hand found something and Lauren grabbed it and swung it in self-defense, hearing a satisfying thud as she evidently made contact.

Her assailant staggered, but it wasn't far enough away and it was like a nightmare as the woman came at her again, blood now gushing down one cheek.

Lauren held on to whatever it was and hit again, panting and desperate, not even aware of what she had in her hand except it was thin and flexible and evidently was effective since one end was heavy.

She lost that round to a glancing blow to her already damaged arm, crying out in pain but lashed out in turn, blindly trying to stop the relentless assault, at least exacting equal contact if the resulting echo was an answer to a prayer.

Then . . . silence.

She managed to shake the hair out of her eyes, battered but alive, half-sprawled across the tailgate. Rob, looking like he might collapse at any moment, stood a few feet away, one bloodied hand pressed to his side. A river of crimson ran down his leg.

"Looks like we've been on vacation after all. Who says you don't know how to use a fishing pole? And I just hit her with a beer cooler."

What did that mean? Then she realized she was still clutching the object she used to fend off the attack in her right hand, the flexible feel of it explained, the heavy metal reel at the end no doubt making it an effective weapon. She began to laugh weakly, which proved to be a mistake of the painful variety.

"Lauren, you're hurt."

"Says the man bleeding all over the place." She certainly was, but not like him.

Felicity, if it was her, lay on her side, her eyes closed, but she was making low noises and moving a little, as if just stunned and not really unconscious. The cooler hadn't been empty and now there were scattered cans all over the ground, along with a decent amount of ice.

"We need to call 911." Lauren didn't mean for their attacker, she meant for Rob.

"Probably."

She thought she could, but there was no doubt her left arm was broken and her phone was in her purse on the front seat of the truck. "I'll try."

Luckily there was the sound of a car and a few moments later a familiar vehicle pulled in, doors flying open as two men scrambled out, the passengers emerging with drawn weapons.

Rob said weakly, "No need. Better late than never. Why am I not surprised. This might be the first time I've been happy to see them. Tell Bailey to help himself to a beer."

Then he swayed and sank down.

* * *

The cell phone had finally activated at a very well-known location and he and Carter had been on their way when dispatch had directed them next door.

A dream come true and a nightmare rolled into one.

"Three injured," Chris said into the radio. "I'm not sure about the severity of the other two but at least one gunshot wound that needs immediate attention. It looks like a possible concussion for another one, and multiple fractures on the third one." It didn't hurt to do amateur triage in his experience, so the responders had an idea what they might be walking into upon arrival.

Hanson was bleeding pretty profusely but it looked to him like the bullet had gone clear through his side, hopefully missing any vital organs. Lauren Mathews' left arm was clearly broken in at least two places, the bruising already vivid and alarming, and she was in pain and visibly pale, but he thought the pallor was more due to Hanson's condition than hers.

As for Barrett, she was also pale and bruised, but had come to consciousness on her own and Carter had her in cuffs and in the back of the car, the gun already bagged as evidence, and he would bet everything he owned — except the moppet — that ballistics would show that gun was used in Heaston's assault. Attempted murder was a serious charge.

Serial murder even more so.

He was still working it out but the stars were coming into alignment.

"They are on their way," he told Lauren, sympathetic to her stricken expression. She was on her knees next to Hanson, her eyes glassy with tears.

The sound of sirens was very welcome and about three minutes later, help arrived in the form of several of the paramedics who greeted him by name and went right to work. Hanson was given priority, treated and put into the ambulance first, Ms. Mathews next.

Barrett accepted first aid but refused the hospital. Chris let Carter be the one to inform her she was being detained and had no choice and she immediately asked for a lawyer.

Hard-eyed and unfazed, she looked cool and every inch the privileged impervious type he suspected she thought herself to be. If she was afraid, it did not show. Chin lifted, she didn't say a word.

Fine with him.

If that was the gun used previously now in their possession, they had her cold. Even without the gun matching Heaston's attack, they had her on shooting Rob Hanson and attacking Lauren Mathews. Chris said evenly, "You should definitely have a lawyer. I advise to retain a really good one, Ms. Barrett. We can hold you for twenty-four hours before we charge you for a crime, and we *will* charge you on multiple counts." He looked at Carter. "Let's go."

* * *

His phone rang.

"Who?"

Drew recognized the number and glanced at Cassandra, feeling unsure about how to respond. He and Rob were okay. He and Lauren were on much more shaky ground, so he was surprised she'd ever call him. "It's Lauren."

"Answer it."

"Executive permission?" He was going to answer anyway. "I don't need it."

"Drew, I meant she would only contact you if she needed to, so answer it." Cassandra's tone was exasperated. "I'm not in competition with her. Our relationship is between the two of us."

He agreed with that sentiment and took the call. "Lauren?"

"Rob has been shot . . . I'm at the hospital with him. Actually, I've been admitted too."

Shock held him immobile for a second. "Shot? And you're hurt?"

What the hell?

Before she could respond, he said swiftly, "I can come down."

Cassandra said in the background, "I'm with you."

"It's okay." But Lauren's voice broke and he cared about both of them. He cared a *lot* about both of them.

"Lauren, I'm on my way."

"Thanks." There was a definite sob in there. "Just a second."

A familiar male voice came on the call, so she'd obviously handed off her phone. "Drew, let me give you the name and location of the hospital. I think that your presence will be helpful and I'd prefer it if you would let the Hanson family know what's going on. I can do it, but I know from experience they'd much rather not get a call from a police officer. Rob is in surgery now, and Lauren might possibly need to have a pin put in her fractured arm. The doctors are going to decide in the morning. Either way, having someone here will be helpful for everyone involved."

Drew, Rob and Lauren? They certainly were brothers in arms as such by now, so apparently Bailey felt comfortable dropping his always polite professional approach, at least at the moment, in favor of first names.

"I'll call both of their families. What the hell happened?"

Bailey was still Bailey. All he said was: "We have someone in custody. Drive safely."

Drew pressed a button and glanced at his wife, his mouth tight. "If you mean it, let's go. I think the sooner I get there the better."

To her credit Cassandra said decisively, "I don't know exactly what's going on, but I'll drive while you make your phone calls and maybe sleep a little. You flew all night, Drew. I've never been to Tennessee. Who knew it was such a dangerous place."

He agreed grimly, "Who knew. It will be a new experience. Picture trees."

"I've seen trees."

"I'll be interested in your opinion of rural America, which by your own admission, you have not really experienced."

"Real backwoods, huh?" She was already headed toward the stairs. "I can pack in about five minutes flat."

"Let me grab my keys."

His bag, still unpacked, sat by the front door. Backwoods? He thought about that beautiful house that overlooked a gorgeous — deadly — lake. He didn't think that term quite qualified, but it was dangerous territory, that was inarguable.

CHAPTER THIRTY-TWO

So, she was already in custody.

"History is relentless and it demonstrates a house of cards must fall eventually." He knew it was an innocuous remark.

The blond detective was definitely dangerous, a born hunter with an interesting edge that indicated a perception of the darkness he entered now and then.

Monsters hid in those shadows. They were alike in that way. They sought out those wicked creatures.

"You didn't exactly answer my question, Dr. Heaston. Do you know why your sister-in-law shot you? Do you have any idea why she'd target Lauren Mathews and Rob Hanson in such a violent fashion?"

He certainly had a theory but now was not the time to make a crucial mistake — he was medicated and, he had to admit, weak and disoriented. "Felicity has always been unpredictable . . . maybe I could say unstable. She has constantly accused me of infidelity to my wife, which is partially why, when Angela disappeared so suddenly, I wasn't alarmed. I thought she'd just finally believed it and left me." He paused and added, "Felicity is very jealous of Angela. Just before she took out the gun, she told me I'd married the wrong sister."

That was true.

He left out the details of why.

He said with as much gravity as he could summon, considering he was most certainly not at his best, "I will say, Detective, after our almost deadly conversation, I am concerned now Felicity might have killed my wife. She also caused me to spill a glass of Blanton's. I don't think I can forgive her for either one. That bourbon is a favorite of mine and hard to find."

* * *

When the blood pressure cuff inflated it woke him up, and the first person Rob saw was Drew, sitting in a chair by the side of the bed. He reflexively went to sit up, winced and thought better of it, and said, "Lauren?"

"She's sleeping."

"What time is it?"

"Not dawn yet. Five maybe." There was a pause. "You look like shit, Hanson."

"Actually, so do you. I have a decent excuse, what's yours?"

He did. A faint beard, his hair was rumpled, he wore a T-shirt and faded jeans, and if Drew had slept at all in the past thirty-six hours, Rob would be surprised. This was not the professional pilot persona, but the lifelong friend, tired and worried, stubble on his chin and an atypical serious expression.

Drew laughed ruefully and shook his head. "My best friend got shot. What can I say? How are you feeling?"

"Like a deranged woman I've never even met tried to kill me. You swear to me Lauren is okay?"

"I swear."

He relaxed because Drew was straightforward and, especially if asked a direct question, he would never sugarcoat the truth. "Thanks. I'm feeling a little helpless here. I assume she called you, or was it Bailey?"

"Both of them. She called, but I also talked to him. Cassandra and I were out the door in less than ten minutes. That wasn't a fun drive. I had no details. I still don't really."

Rob didn't either. The remnants of what happened were hazy at best. He'd walked out to the steps of the deck, seen

265

Lauren's face, known something was very wrong, and some woman he'd never seen before pointed a gun at him and then it was a blur. Coming back in snippets, but unclear, so he wasn't sure what was real and might be embellished by anesthetic dreams.

"She came for Lauren." He said it slowly. "I happened to walk out —she barely looked at me but she did know my name. That was all she said. 'You must be Rob', before she shot me. It was very out of hand." The recollection was chilling. "Like an afterthought. Swatting an annoying fly. She wasn't there for me."

Drew had never been slow on the uptake. "All the victims so far have been women, so I suppose maybe you just got in the way. What does Bailey have to say?"

All were women except for Heaston.

"Fletcher, he isn't exactly here holding my hand. How the hell would I know what is going on?"

But it was a good question.

He conceded, "Lauren did some research Bailey seemed to find interesting. He even copied the file. It seems that Heaston wrote a book based on a sensational murder case where his wife's grandmother was the prime suspect. It involved a drowning."

Drew's brows went up. "No shit?"

"Bailey had the same reaction."

* * *

Nine o'clock morning meeting after another long night.

Very long night.

Most of it Chris had spent thinking over the case, partly at the hospital because he had waited to hear how Hanson came through surgery, some of it at home at the table later, elbow propped and chin on fist, a glass of Tennessee's finest nearby but not touched much as he weighed the facts all measure by measure.

Felicity Barrett was under arrest for three separate counts of assault with a deadly weapon and attempted murder.

So another shirt and tie deal. This time the district attorney and Agent Wright were already at the table and he was not the last arrival, Carter was right behind him.

"Detectives."

The DA was a stickler, always skeptical of taking a chance on a higher charge, which was why he and Carter were old friends and saw eye to eye on almost every prosecution.

Edward Hanover was not going to like the various jurisdictions' issue with multiple crimes possibly connected to each other, especially since some of the cases were over a decade old. He was not an edgy lawyer — that could be good because you always knew what to expect — but then again, even if you knew you had a perpetrator on your hands, there had to be a case without a single crack in it for him to really go after it.

There were fissures all over this one.

"Counselor. Agent Wright." Chris sat down and wished he'd had a third cup of coffee.

Taking notes by hand was a signature old-school habit Hanover hung on to also, and he sat, gray-haired and distinguished — so he looked the part, pen in hand. "You gentlemen have had a busy few days. Outline it for me."

"Bailey has handled a lot of this on his own, so I'll let him sketch it out." Carter didn't look like he'd gotten much sleep either.

Chris had brought all his notes, but he didn't need them really, he'd read them over so many times. "Okay, we can start at several points, but I think I'll begin where we entered into the picture. Last summer we had a suspicious death with a drowning victim that, thanks to Agent Wright, has possibly been identified now. There is a direct connection to Professor Heaston. The crime — unless it was an accident — happened in this county. The victim is a foreign national with a visa address in another state, hence the delay in identifying her."

Hanover's pen was busy. "Go on. Connect her to Heaston how?"

"She was a student at a college in Kentucky who took his class and she drowned in a lake where he has a vacation home here in Tennessee."

"That is certainly solid, especially damning in that I take it he did not report her missing and the assumption is she was his guest."

"No, he didn't, nor did his wife."

"Who is now missing as well." A statement, not a question.

"Yes," Carter confirmed. "Everyone who had a place on the lake was questioned when the body was reported. No one could provide her identity or give an explanation of why she might be there."

"Or didn't want to provide it," Chris added. "There's more. Heaston told me in my brief window to interview him in the hospital, that his sister-in-law, who is the one we arrested last night for multiple charges of assault and, he has confirmed shot him, constantly accused him of being unfaithful. He said in his statement when his wife disappeared he thought she'd finally believed it and left him."

Agent Wright interjected, "Gabriella Marino was seeing someone but was secretive about it according to her few friends at school. I realize that is hearsay, but why was she in Tennessee at the lake house of a professor she knows? An older married man. It does make for an argument Felicity Barrett could be right and he was cheating on his wife."

"And his wife is linked back to a murder that happened in Vermont when she was in college. Very similar circumstances with a blow to the head and then a drowning." Chris paused. "But Felicity has a connection as well. And to an unsolved homicide in Kentucky, which as far as I can tell, she's the only one of the three who could have a motive and opportunity, not to mention we certainly now know she has a propensity for violence."

"And jealousy perhaps?" Carter said the words slowly. "Heaston has a thing for pretty young women and becomes obsessed with Lauren Mathews, taking pictures of her, and Felicity sees them and steals his computer, then attacks her . . . it fits. Heaston said to Bailey he's worried now maybe his sister-in-law had something to do with his wife's disappearance. I'm starting to wonder as well."

"The only death we have as a confirmed homicide that we're investigating is Karen Foxton." Hanover was succinct and to the point. "I agree it all looks like it is tied together, but if you could put Ms. Barrett in Tennessee when Foxton vanished and then turned up dead, I would want to move forward with an indictment on some level of murder charges to put before a grand jury, though I doubt in any of these cases we could get premeditation. These seem like crimes of passion and opportunity to me, with impulse involved."

Chris agreed, at the moment they had no proof except for the two shootings and the attack on Lauren.

Except one long shot once he could talk to Lauren.

He said quietly, "I might be able to help there, but I also think this is more complicated than it might seem."

"Possible serial murder undetected for this length of time complicated?" Wright's tone was ironic. "Imagine that. However, you've caught a thread no one else seems to have picked up, Detective Bailey. So, please if there's another lead, follow it and let us know what happens since our office is definitely looking into how to prosecute Felicity Barrett."

He and Carter walked out to their cars, not speaking until Carter asked, "What's the angle?"

Chris turned, hands in his pockets, thinking hard. "Heaston is a smart man. Is he smarter than us?"

"What the hell does that mean?"

"I'm wondering." He stopped in the parking lot. "Look, he might be playing us. He knows female serial killers inside and out. That's really not an arguable fact. He studies them. He writes books based on their stories. We can certainly prove that. But, where's his wife? Can we keep in mind Lauren Mathews first noticed him dumping something heavy into his boat?"

"We can. Is that the ace up your sleeve?"

Chris dug out his car keys. "No. The ace up my sleeve might send Felicity Barrett straight to a murder charge. I'll let you know."

Carter muttered, "I can't wait. God, I need another vacation."

* * *

A second set of pictures reviewed and the orthopedic doctor decided to Lauren's relief that putting in a pin wasn't necessary.

But it was rather awkward once she signed the hospital paperwork and was released — her only option was Drew.

And his wife as it turned out.

Of course, the woman was attractive and self-assured, and Lauren had her arm in a cast and a sling, and her only clothes were blood-stained. She had retrieved her purse, thanks to Bailey, so she had her phone at the hospital. Lauren had done some one-handed repair to her hair and had been provided with a toothbrush and was able to wash her face to achieve some resemblance to normal, but she still looked like someone who'd had a rough night.

No exaggeration there.

"I'm Cassandra."

Lauren managed a hello from the wheelchair the hospital insisted be used so she could actually leave.

Drew was thankfully not blind to her discomfort, both physically and emotionally as he walked beside her. "Cassandra drove most of the way since I'd just gotten off a long flight when you called. Rob is probably going to be released later today. I can drive his truck back to Ohio and Cassandra can drive my car. In the meantime, Bailey wants to talk to you. Is back at the house okay? Your suitcase is there in the truck according to Rob and he gave me the code for the alarm and his keys. You can change while we wait for the call Rob is discharged."

That would most certainly be welcome, although she had absolutely no idea what more she could tell Bailey. "Did Heaston make it?"

"He did." Drew's gaze was steady. "Somehow, I think that's why Bailey needs a word."

* * *

They waited on the deck. Chris would miss this, if nothing else. A lake house would be nice, but he might decline one next to Heaston's address. Next to him, Agent Wright said, "Oh, I could get used to this view."

"Right." He agreed wholeheartedly.

Lauren came out of the doors and looked a bit fragile when she sat down, but resolute, her expression reflecting his attitude. No longer battered and disheveled but back to smooth shining hair and a hint of gloss on her lips, a cast up past her elbow, the sling for her broken collarbone. "I'm not sure why we need to have another conversation, but here I am."

It was Wright who said in her businesslike way, "Ms. Mathews, describe Karen Foxton's earrings."

She gazed at Chris in understandable question. "What? I think I told you she was wearing earrings . . . I don't understand how this is important."

"It is."

She didn't hesitate, which was good. "They were butterflies. They looked like stained glass maybe, I don't know, but certainly handmade, very pretty as I told her at the time. She even told me where she got them, so her sister could possibly verify it."

Chris took out a photograph and handed it to her. "These?"

"Yes, exactly." She glanced up. "Why?"

He accepted the picture back. "I think you just helped us solve Ms. Foxton's murder. As a matter of fact, you have helped law enforcement a great deal on your eventful vacation."

"It has been interesting," she agreed with a small ironic smile, probably for his non-answer. "Rob is supposed to be released later this afternoon and we are going home."

"Have a safe trip." He hesitated, but then again, she'd probably already figured it out, so he added, "You'll have to testify in a trial, I imagine, down the road. Indictments take a while and this is a complicated case with multiple charges. If you have any questions or think of anything else that might help us, call me please."

"I have your number. By the way, we have the attack by Felicity Barrett on us recorded by a field camera. As you know, Rob put up two of them after the night of the break-in and once we decided to leave, we forgot about them because we were understandably anxious to just leave this all behind us."

No shit? He almost said it out loud.

"I had Drew take the camera down and get out the SD card. It's inside. Let me go get it."

He eyed her cast and visible pallor. "I'll go," he suggested gently. "I've been in that house a time or two. Tell me where."

"Kitchen counter."

Sure enough, he saw it and picked it up. When he went back out, he promised an evidence receipt and Wright said in evident satisfaction as they walked back to the car, "*That* was worth a trip. We need to call Hanover and let him know we have direct evidence linking Felicity Barrett to the Foxton murder and the attack on tape."

"We do." It was an acknowledgment but not necessarily an agreement that the case was solved. "I don't want us to underestimate Heaston."

She swung around, frowning. "Wait a minute. When Barrett was taken into custody those earrings were in her purse. You, Detective, were the one who made that connection to the Vermont murder."

"I know." His response was measured, his gaze steady. "She said in the one statement she made without her attorney yet present that she'd never seen them before."

"What else would you expect her to say, Detective? They tie her to a crime."

"I'd expect her to say nothing." He'd been really thinking about it. "Stony silence on everything else, but she denies that. I'm thinking I believe her. Why would she say anything at all? Because she was surprised and didn't know what significance they had."

"She's a killer. We have her." Agent Wright looked thoughtful though.

Out of habit, he politely opened the passenger door for her. "At any time Heaston could have put those earrings in her purse. When she was opening that bottle of wine and turned her back, if she went to the bathroom . . . anytime."

"Right before she shot him? Jesus." Wright sighed. "Two killers?"

"Let's assume, given his research into murder was how he met Angela and Felicity Barrett, he knew about the murder of one of their sorority sisters." Chris had been seriously giving it all some consideration. "If Felicity killed that young woman, she'd know about the earrings. But I bet so would Heaston. Lauren Mathews said Karen Foxton wanted a signed book for her sister, who is a fan of Heaston's novels. What if when she left, all ticked off at Hanson, she decided to stop next door and ask him for one? She supposedly declared she wasn't too shy to do just that."

"Why would he then kill her? His wife, I get — we've certainly seen that before — but why some woman he doesn't know simply asking for a signed book?"

He stood there and lifted his brows. "We aren't supposed to draw conclusions. I'm not a psychologist, or a profiler, but I have an idea."

"I'm all ears."

"The fascination with his neighbors. I think it is as simple as Karen Foxton did not fit into the dynamic of the relationship between Hanson and Fletcher both being involved with Lauren Mathews, his own femme fatale as he started

273

calling her. So if Foxton really showed up on his doorstep, he eliminated her from the equation."

She didn't get in the car but instead folded her arms. "And then incriminated his sister-in-law?"

"If we really started to look at him, he could steer us at her instead. I don't think there's much doubt she's probably involved in at least two other murders and he capitalized on it. How easy is it to shift the blame for a murder to another murderer?"

Wright slid into the car. "If you're right, give us proof and we'll go for it."

Yeah, he thought darkly, easier said than done.

The opponent was farsighted and played by no rules he quite understood.

However, he'd always thought he was pretty quick on his feet.

CHAPTER THIRTY-THREE

He was paralyzed.

They wouldn't say it directly, but it was there in the background humming like the proverbial fly in the window, a refrain in his brain.

He asked directly and the physician hedged. Give it time. Sometimes we are surprised.

Ominous. No soft violins played with precise virtuosity, but instead the dissonant melody of bittersweet resignation over costly ambition and secret desire.

The only thing he could do was recalculate.

Luckily, that bitch would pay.

However, it wasn't like he would walk free.

He would never walk again.

* * *

Long drive home.

Quiet freeway without much traffic after full dark.

Lauren sat in the front seat of the truck because Rob could then lie down and sleep in the back seat, which he certainly needed, and she dozed on and off.

Drew drove in sympathetic silence, even the radio was very subdued on volume, just to keep him company since his two companions were not very talkative. Cassandra's headlights were in his rear-view mirror.

It was more than a little difficult to assimilate how he'd gotten into this particular situation.

My own damn fault. Sort of.

"Hmm." Lauren stirred and opened her eyes. "Sorry . . . I—"

"You're fine," he interrupted quietly. "Don't apologize, Lauren."

She sat up to straighten her position and openly winced. "I'm not apologizing really, I just appreciate you coming back to help and, while your job is to get people from here to there, this was not what you signed on for as far as I know."

"I invited you on this vacation. I hardly think it was what you signed on for either."

Darkness except for passing headlights until she gave a mirthless laugh. "Okay, we agree."

"You and Rob . . . I'm the most reluctant matchmaker ever."

She was silent for a moment, before she said, "Look at it this way, the way things worked out is probably for the best. All three of us were going to have to make a choice eventually. I take it, since she came with you, you and Cassandra are both willing to give the marriage a second try."

His smile was wry. "It's more appropriate to say that we are going to give it a first try. We had a love affair between two people who lived separate lives and somehow thought it would work. She has made some major changes in her life to try for us to have time together as a husband and wife." He wasn't sure if he needed to tell the whole story, but maybe he did. "After we decided to separate and divorce, she found out she was pregnant. She lost the baby and it shook her world to discover how much she wanted it. To be honest with you, and I am being very honest for the record because I do owe you that, it shook me up to realize I had lost a child I never even knew existed."

Lauren was as perceptive as ever. "So she wants a family. I could never tell if you were in favor of it or would just go along with it."

He shot her a sidelong look. "I wasn't sure either. It seems I do. I know for a fact the all-American boy with the gunshot wound in the backseat does."

"Fletcher, I'm not asleep. So, any personal observations you make about me, keep in mind I have a lot of dirt on you."

Drew gave a muffled laugh. "Duly warned, and hey, I didn't say anything bad, like how you can only catch a fish if you happen to snag one."

It was impossible to tell if the noise Rob made as he sat up was a snort of derision or a groan of pain. "Yeah, right. Neither one of us, since you brought it up, are as good with a fishing pole as Lauren."

Drew raised his brows. "Is that so?"

The woman in question just shook her head. "I don't suppose I'll ever live it down, but I grabbed the closest thing I could get my hands on when Felicity Barrett shot Rob and came after me. It happened to be a fishing pole. I caught her with the reel right in the face luckily, but Rob finished her off with a small cooler filled with beer."

"Let's hope that story never gets around. Not how I want to be remembered," Rob muttered with cynical emphasis.

No one had given him any details before now. All he knew was whoever had shot Heaston had then come after them.

He really had no idea what to say to that bizarre rendition of what had happened. He finally settled for: "My lips are sealed, but I guess I want to know one important thing. Hanson, what happened to the beer?"

From the back seat, Rob said on a strangled sound, "Dammit, Fletcher, don't make me laugh. It hurts like hell. I—"

"You know, the dinner we had with Heaston?" Lauren interrupted, her profile averted as she stared out the side window, obviously struck by something because she frowned, her expression distracted. Slowly, she said, "Do you both remember what he said about the lake? I wonder if it meant something. I thought it was really strange at the time, and he was just trying to emphasize his literary knowledge when he quoted Milton."

From the back seat Rob muttered, "Yeah, I do. That whole thing was weird all the way around, but I didn't recognize the quote though I think in my dissolute college days I did read *Paradise Lost*. Why did this suddenly occur to you? Pain meds? Mine could be working better for the record."

"He was telling me about the TVA and all of that, but more importantly he mentioned the outlet pipe to prevent flooding that led to a small river. 'The slow and silent stream, Lethe the river of oblivion rolls'. I swear to you, I think, because he's not exactly your average man, he might have been referencing where he put his wife's body."

Drew felt a chill of conviction she could just be right.

It was Rob who said grimly, "He's the type that it might get him off to obliquely tell us in just that way. I think even though it's pretty late and maybe a long shot, Bailey wouldn't mind a call."

* * *

Chris's feelings weren't hurt that he wasn't her favorite person from the disdainful look on her face, but then again, fair was fair, she wasn't his either. He took the chair across from Felicity Barrett and a distinguished man in a very expensive suit at the table and lifted his brows. "You wanted to talk to me?"

Her lawyer was the one who spoke. "Our understanding is that you've been the lead investigator on this case as well as being the arresting officer."

"My partner and I, yes, but he was on vacation for part of it, so I suppose that is true."

"Glenn Heaston called your personal phone to report his injury?"

"Injury? Being shot twice by your client? I guess you can define that as being injured. We think of it as attempted murder. I usually ask the questions, so let me go ahead. Why am I here and what is it you wish to discuss?"

The lawyer was unfazed, but then again, no doubt whoever he was, he knew exactly how to handle whatever situation this might be and was paid accordingly. "My client can help your investigation."

"I am not the one who can make a plea arrangement and you know it."

"Indeed I do. But hear her out."

Felicity had made bail without any difficulty at all, which didn't surprise him a bit, and was composed and dressed in a flattering summer dress that no doubt had an expensive designer label, her perfectly cut hair in place, only the tell-tale bruises from the altercation marring her otherwise well-groomed appearance. "Detective, suppose I tell you I read my brother-in-law's latest work in progress, and it is very interesting."

"I hope so, since he seems to sell quite a lot of books . . . but they are fiction, Ms. Barrett. I'm aware his computer is missing. No doubt if he had been capable of stopping the person who stole it, he would have, so it follows it happened after he was shot. Are we supposed to add theft of personal property to the list of complaints against you?"

"His books are fiction based on real stories as he studies and interprets them." She leaned forward, her gaze intent, a faint smile on her mouth. "I've been sleeping with him for over a decade because he was never sure if *I* was the one who inherited the murderous gene in our family. He married Angela but fucked me on the side, just to have the full experience. I know who I'm dealing with."

The frank revelation and matching language took him a little off guard but he'd seen and heard quite a bit in the course of his career already, so Chris regrouped easily enough. "Okay. Explain to me how this helps our investigations."

"He killed my sister and that Foxton woman, and he'd love to pin both of them on me. In his quest to experience the thrill of the kill himself, he crossed the wrong person. Lesson one and my advice for him would be don't leave a literary footprint of your crimes within reach of someone who knows exactly what you've done."

It was telling her lawyer suddenly looked uneasy. "Felicity, maybe we should pause this conversation."

Whatever his client was going to say, a declaration resembling a confession wasn't it evidently. Chris merely said, "I'm certainly listening."

Her eyes narrowed and her expression was intense. "My brother-in-law was working on a different book but he set that aside apparently and outlined a new one recently. I doubt he ever intended this one for his publisher. It is a personal indulgence, if you will. A fantasy fulfilled on paper."

"Go on, Ms. Barrett."

"Let me give you a synopsis, Detective. It's about two friends who want the same woman and their changing relationship as they struggle to not fight over her, and her struggle, of course, to choose one over the other. Not a new story by any means, but in Glenn's version there is another slant. An older man in the shadows who also desires her and who watches and waits for his chance to seduce her. This character is referred to as an homme fatal, a man who successfully and insidiously preys on beautiful women and when his jealous wife discovers his infidelities, she is his assassin, his weapon, if you will, and she eliminates the competition."

He digested that, though he wasn't all that surprised because basically Lauren Mathews had mentioned his unusual interest and as for her relationship with Fletcher and Hanson, the storyline seemed to follow, though it looked to him like it had been settled between the three of them without any bloodthirsty fallout.

Except for two men shot and the injuries to Lauren, not to mention Foxton's murder and the missing Mrs. Heaston, but none of that had been done by them.

"A serial killer by proxy?"

"That sums it up pretty well. Charles Manson certainly used that method, didn't he." Her smile was just a thinning of her lips. "And I didn't steal the computer, just borrowed it. Glenn can have it back at any time."

"Were there more pictures of Ms. Mathews?"

"Don't answer that," her attorney interjected. "We are not talking about the alleged shooting incident."

"Let me ask something else then," Chris said swiftly. "In this book, does the homme fatal kill his wife?"

"He strangles her. He finally feels he can do it himself, so he doesn't need her any longer and he wants to try the thrill firsthand. That passage, where he decides to take that course, is very descriptive and even eloquent, if you will, about the pleasure of killing."

A poised, well-dressed, educated woman speaking about murder with a faint smile on her mouth? He tried to not let his revulsion show and stay professional. "Does it say where he puts her body?"

She looked at him without flinching and said with chilling softness, "Oh yes, it does."

Her lawyer chimed in, "Now is the point where we want to talk to the district attorney."

Four words explained that request. "I erased the file," she said without any repentance at all. "Unless Glenn tells you, I'm the only one who knows."

* * *

Carter looked at him, and finally shook his head. "So we are between a rock and a hard place, or better said, between one possible criminal and another. If we want to find the body, we have to make a devil's bargain and reduce the charges?"

That was true enough. "I haven't called Hanover or Lawrence yet for a very good reason."

There was no doubt if nothing else had happened, Chris and Carter had a different working relationship due to this case — these cases, because his partner asked him, "How do you want to play it?"

"She's a killer. What she wants is to blame it on her sister, and legally she could win because it could be argued either Angela or Felicity could have committed those early murders so that would be damned hard to prove, but I also think she and Heaston have screwed each other in more ways than one."

They weren't at their desks, but instead getting a cup of decent coffee at a small local bakery, where they could sit at a table and not be disturbed and *think* about it.

"She's playing us because we really do need to find the body."

Chris stirred cream into his cup. "She sure as hell is and capable of it too. What makes me think it's not Angela is the case of her co-worker. Angela had no connection to that victim but Felicity, her not-so-nice little sister, did. Heaston, in turn, I believe killed his wife. Hanson and Fletcher heard a woman scream the night they arrived. The next morning Lauren saw him put something heavy in his boat. That evening he makes an impromptu stop, a friendly neighborly gesture Hanson has never known him to do before. Maybe his sister-in-law is correct and he just has an interest in beautiful young women and wanted a closer look at Ms. Mathews, or maybe he wanted to ascertain whether or not she saw him put whatever it might have been in his boat."

"There's no way to tell if Felicity is telling us the truth about Heaston putting it in the draft of this supposed novel even if we find the body. She could have easily killed her sister and is trying to frame him." Carter was as straightforward in this thinking as usual. "If we find his wife where Ms. Barrett says the body is, he's going to say she's lying about the book and put the body there herself."

"If we find the body and the cause of death is strangulation, she could be telling the truth. It's an interesting dilemma."

"I agree. I'm on the cautious side so I say tell Hanover and let him decide."

And of course, Hanover would agree to a plea, because he always went for the sure conviction. Chris was pretty invested in this. He sat back and then shook his head decisively. "I'm going to call on the great powers of the Federal Bureau of Investigation and see how quickly they can get divers in that lake. I wasn't inclined to start an operation like that until we found Angela Heaston's car to prove it was worth the time and resources, and since then, it has all been happening so fast we really haven't had the time."

"If we found the body without her assistance, I agree, it would be better."

"I think we can. At least I have a pretty good idea where to look thanks to our witness that has so far done quite a lot of the investigation for us."

"Lauren Mathews?"

"She called me after she remembered something that might be a lead. If it works out, we can thank Heaston's lofty arrogance too, because he handed her the location. I'm not inclined to bargain on this case. Look, Gabriella Marino was killed for a reason and it has to be Heaston, whether he did it or not, he was cheating on his wife if Felicity Barrett can be believed, and by her own admission, in essence cheating on her. And I do believe her, because he was so quickly obsessed with Lauren Mathews. As far as Barrett goes, Heaston wasn't responsible for that murder at her college or that of her co-worker, so I think they are both cold-blooded sociopaths and at this point if she goes down for Foxton's murder because he set her up, I think that's justice well-served if we can get him as well for his wife. I'm not taking their word, either way, for anything, much less letting them manipulate this investigation. Let's wait to go to Hanover and see what Wright can do."

Calmly, Carter took a sip of coffee. Then he said, "Okay, let's play this your way."

CHAPTER THIRTY-FOUR

A cornered beast will bare its teeth and fight with hooked claws, drawing blood and shredding flesh in desperation.

I am well aware of what the police are doing, putting us in the same cage to watch us circle each other.

Felicity's problem is I am not animal in the same sense she is. Cunning is not her forte. She is governed by emotion, and I am guilty of that as well, but my demons are very different to hers, and jealousy and envy just don't exist for me. Even for my unfeeling father I never felt hatred, just repugnance for his lack of depth and his shallow motivations.

Felicity and I were never lovers as she has claimed to the police, though I welcomed the chance to confirm her story, laughing inwardly at how she was drawing the net around her, gathering it like a doomsday cloak over her shoulders, intent on doing to herself what she had done so clumsily to others.

I was informed they've found Angela's body.

The tightrope begins.

I wonder if she realizes even a crippled man can walk it better than she can manage.

* * *

The trip to the house of horrors was done and over. Autopsy results were in hand, the medical examiner's opinion noted and the interview in person.

The body had been lodged in the pipe for over a week, decomposing in the warm weather, but the clothing had gotten caught on a rough part of the outlet, snagged there rather than poetically drifting away down the stream into oblivion.

Angela Heaston had not been strangled.

Felicity lost that round of leverage.

In a familiar scenario, she'd been knocked unconscious according to her fractured skull, and drowned, but there was one difference and Chris wasn't sure it was to Felicity's advantage either.

"So, the traces of chlorine in her lungs mean she probably was put in their pool. Sounds a lot like the grandmother's crime, or that is how I view it." Carter was driving as usual. "Full circle. He met his wife because of that crime and he got rid of her the same way."

Beautiful day, blue summer skies with a few wispy clouds here and there, and the morgue behind them, but the subject of death still lingered.

As far as Chris was concerned, that was exactly what happened. "Heaston did it on purpose. The lake was right there but he is a student of calculated murder and impulsive murder. If Felicity Barrett killed before, the cases against her are thin with no physical evidence besides the earrings but, she did have opportunity and the earrings are pretty damning."

The question was, did Heaston know about that murder in Vermont? Did he know about the earrings?

The answer was, probably.

Chris went on, thinking out loud. "In his case, one quote from Milton — I've looked at the book by the way and it is a tome, I can't believe any one person could recognize a couple of lines — is going to get laughed at in court. We have the scream that wasn't reported because they thought it was a bird, and a witness to him putting something in his boat, but she doesn't know what it was. Hanover won't go for it."

"No, he won't." Carter sounded for once less like the voice of reason, but on the same unhappy page.

"But that quote led us to the body because of the context of the conversation. They were talking about that outlet pipe when he said it."

"It did. Maybe we would have found it anyway, but maybe not as the water rose and fell. Time would have not worked in our favor."

It was so true. As gruesome as it sounded, as the body deteriorated and the flow of the water changed, she would have floated away in bits and pieces, making her body very difficult to find and identify.

Chris leaned back in his seat and tried to come to terms with it. It wasn't easy. "He might get away with this."

"Look at it this way, I doubt Felicity Barrett will. We have a preponderant mountain of circumstantial evidence to argue that she committed those murders in addition to attacking both Lauren Mathews and Rob Hanson. Then there is her shooting Heaston. Attempted murder. The weapon matched the crime. We have her dead on with motive, opportunity and intent."

They did, but the point was not being addressed. Heaston.

"So you agree, he's going to get away with it."

"Not really." Carter's voice held conviction. "We caught him, we know he did it, and he knows we know. But he operates without rules, and we can't. Not smarter, just without a conscience. I think that for both of them, it is ironic justice that he framed her for two murders she didn't commit because she is indeed a serial offender, and she almost killed him and has certainly left him in the chains of a wheelchair."

"True enough, I don't think he'll be seducing any young women except maybe in his imagination." It was a sardonic comment. "What's ironic is that we'll probably get her on the murder charge for Foxton since she can't pin that one on her already dead sister like she is going to try for with the three other cases. I wish we could help them with the drowning in Ohio, but I don't think it's connected. I looked at it because of Hanson, Fletcher and Drysden and they are clearly not our killer."

They pulled into the lot outside the sheriff's office building a half an hour later and got out, walking toward the building. Carter said conversationally, "Agent Wright told me she talked to you about the FBI."

She had approached him and asked if he ever considered federal law enforcement, but Carter had asked him that question before already. Chris shrugged. "Do you have any idea how many people apply, most of them law enforcement or military, and how few are actually accepted? No matter how qualified you are the odds are not good."

"It seems to me she's recruiting you because you've impressed her."

"Hiring agents isn't up to her alone. It's fairly arduous from what I understand."

"I wasn't all that excited when you were assigned as my partner, but you've kind of grown on me, Bailey."

Chris gave a muffled laugh. "Like a rash or something, huh?"

"You're good. I'd hate to see you go."

That was quite a compliment from Carter.

He was a Tennessee boy through and through as the sheriff had pointed out, but maybe he should expand his horizons. He murmured, "Thanks."

* * *

It was an interesting adjustment.

For both of them.

A natural move though, neither of them were able to really just go back to their normal life, so with a little persuasion on his part Lauren agreed maybe she should just stay at his house which Rob applauded wholeheartedly.

Mutual convalescence. What a storybook take on a relationship, he thought in wry acknowledgment.

Sleeping together just meant sleeping, but they'd done that before and if he wasn't able to make love to her just yet thanks to their injuries, the intimacy was satisfying. Her warmth and respiration in the dark . . . he wasn't precisely satisfied, but he was happy she was there more than he could say.

He settled into bed next to her. "What did Bailey have to say?"

Her lashes settled lower, her silky hair spilled over the pillowslip. It was a very nice view. She hesitated a moment. "Felicity Barrett is going down for Karen's murder in his opinion. You know him, no details."

It was impossible to not say in a dry tone, "Yes, I do."

"Can I point out he insisted on staying at the hospital during your surgery?"

"I never said for a moment I didn't think he wasn't anything but a decent, intelligent man doing a very good job in a difficult profession. I just said I do know him, and no details doesn't surprise me." He couldn't resist but threaded his fingers through her hair, smoothing it back from her face.

Her lips were warm and inviting.

She summed it all up in a few words, her good arm sliding around his neck. "I think, if it's possible for this whole thing to turn out the way it was supposed to, it really works for me."

It did for him too.

He kissed her again.

EPILOGUE

Late autumn now, the holidays looming, the air crisp and evenings usually included a nice blaze in the fireplace in the living room, which she really enjoyed.

Good decision to move in. Rob had a nice house and certainly had chosen to buy one much too large for a bachelor. He'd admitted with his devastating boyish smile, that somehow managed to be sexy at the same time, that he bought a family home because that was quite simply part of his plans.

Lauren answered the expected knock on the door, admittedly curious why Bailey would travel all the way to Ohio just to have a word, as he put it. "Hello, Detective."

Bailey looked better rested than when she'd seen him several months ago, dressed casually in jeans and a leather jacket, not the shirt and tie ensemble when she'd seen him last, which was in a courtroom. It had been decided that even with the video they wanted the court to hear her testify. So much of the investigation only had wide-reaching circumstantial evidence, and they needed her to detail her conversations with Heaston and what exactly the verbal exchange was before Felicity Barrett shot Rob and attacked her.

She hadn't looked forward to it, but she and Rob had gone back to Tennessee and even if the trial was far from over, at least her part was done.

"Hello." He pointed at his companion. "Sorry, I had to bring my dog along. I hope you don't mind. It's a long trip and I'm not really able to give her enough attention as it is."

"No, not at all. Come in."

The breed seemed an unusual choice for a man who carried a gun at all times and pursued serious criminals. A petite and long-haired miniature something, with big soulful eyes, more suitable for lounging on a canopied bed than the companion of a tall police officer who Lauren knew full well was very serious about his job. "She's really sweet." Lauren accepted a very enthusiastic hello, and petted the dog's silky head.

"I call her Moppet, but I think my girlfriend named her Alexa." His eyes held a hint of resigned humor. "Girlfriend is gone, her dog remains. I have a feeling I'm going to have to find her a home soon. I've applied for a job with federal law enforcement. Let's see how it goes. The review process is moving along pretty well. I can't spend months at Quantico and board her all that time."

They had never discussed anything about his personal life, so she was surprised, but he knew a lot about hers, so fair enough now that she wasn't involved in the investigation any longer.

Or was she? He'd come for a reason.

She asked neutrally, "So FBI?"

"Maybe, it isn't exactly a given to get in." His gaze was as usual, keen and focused. "Don't you want to know why I came all this way?"

She did. "Let's sit down. The kitchen works for me if it does for you. I can get you — and me — something to drink? Why is it I feel this has something to do with Dr. Heaston and it makes me want a glass of wine?"

"Because it does." He followed her through the arched doorway, his tone without inflection, hands carelessly in his pockets. "Are you surprised?"

"Obviously not." She went to the refrigerator to take out two beers since Rob was heading toward the house from the backyard with the lab puppy right behind him. She had to give due credit, he was doing his best to train that rambunctious addition to their household. She'd have preferred something a little smaller.

But no argument, she was . . . happy. He seemed to be as well.

Hopefully Bailey's arrival wasn't going to change that in any way.

Rob came through the sliding glass doors from the back deck, and the puppy took one look at the guest dog and of course fell in love, dashing across the floor in an awkward display of instant affection and friendship.

To her credit, Bailey's little dog stood firm and accepted the effusive welcome with a wagging tail.

Rob, whom she hadn't told about Bailey's message, in turn, stiffened and paused, before he slowly turned and closed the door, then shrugged out of his coat. "Detective."

Bailey could read people, she'd give him that. "Lauren didn't tell you I was coming?"

In her defense, Lauren said to Rob mildly, "If you asked me why, I would not have had an answer. We'll discover together I suspect in a minute."

Bailey accepted the beer and took a seat at the counter on one of the stools. "Heaston asked to see me. I went because I was curious, I admit it, and he's not able to drive. He gave me an envelope he wanted me to give to you, no one else. Wise man. If he had given it to anyone else, they probably would have opened it, since you were a witness for the prosecution and it could be a threat. I rather doubt it is, but who knows."

"And you brought it in person in the hope she'll tell you what it says." Rob leaned on the counter, but his casual stance was belied by the sharpness of his gaze.

Bailey took an envelope from the pocket of his jacket and set it down. His tone was mild as he admitted, "That's pretty accurate. It gets to me we couldn't charge him."

Felicity Barrett on the other hand, hadn't fared quite so well. The tape of the assault had made that charge indefensible and her attorneys' attempt to plea down had not worked. The murder charges were still pending since so many cases were involved.

Heaston had definitely won, all the way around, though the truth was, he hadn't escaped unscathed.

What on earth could he possibly have to say that she'd be remotely interested in hearing?

She pointed. "I think I need that glass of wine before I open that."

Rob lifted his brows. "I'll pour you one. I'm certainly as curious as Bailey."

So was she. Heaston had given her pause from the very first encounter.

She sat down next to Bailey and picked up the envelope, tearing it open.

The irony of it all does not escape me. The water, the beautiful woman, the two lovers at war with each other in a combat fraught with sexual longing and conflicted loyalty . . .

The inspiration struck like a bolt of jagged lightning.

What single woman has caused more death than Helen of Troy? A different sort of murderess for certain, but not without secret desires, so not an innocent one. The ultimate femme fatale, after all. A thousand ships is not a small war.

I thought you might wonder why I chose you.

Angela was much more efficient than Felicity, so her death probably saved your life.

It was my obsession, after all, that could have made you pay the ultimate price. If it is any consolation, I will not walk away from this unscathed.

Literally.

I know you know your Milton, but how is your Hemingway? Think of a more obscure one.

Winner Take Nothing, *written in 1933.*

She wondered if it was necessary to let Bailey see it. Both he and Rob were looking at her in open inquiry.

After a moment, she simply handed it over. "Go ahead, but while there's a veiled confession, there's also an interesting implication."

His expression reflected a conflicted reaction as Bailey read it. Then he frowned. "Is he saying his wife really was the one who committed the earlier murders?"

"I think he's obliquely not saying anything." How it was worded required interpretation.

"I don't know if this changes anything." The words were said slowly. "The woman who was murdered in Kentucky was tied to Felicity but not her sister. I suppose it could have been either one of them in Vermont." He ran his fingers through his hair and then shook his head. "It has occurred to me more than once that both of them might be involved."

Lauren took a sip of wine, thinking it over.

Rob cleared his throat. "Anyone care to let *me* see it? I'm in the dark here."

Bailey handed it over and Rob scanned it quickly. When he looked up, he said succinctly, "If my two cents count for anything, it could be he's just being cryptic because he enjoys the game, but if it is the truth, he was involved with both of them in about every way possible, so maybe they were the ultimate draw for him. What if he couldn't decide which one was the dangerous one."

"An interesting theory that I think I agree could be the truth, but then again, Carter tells me I spend far too much time trying to figure out how people like Heaston think."

Lauren said with prosaic reflection, "He's right about one thing, I did wonder why he'd take an interest in me since I have never killed anyone."

Rob said dryly, "I understand. You certainly interest me, and the reason is fairly flattering even if the attention unwanted."

"Your interest is fine." Lauren did not look flattered. "And apparently part of the problem. However, his was a nightmare, flattering or not."

Bailey finished his beer and contemplated the two dogs, at the moment tussling over a twisted rope in a tug of war, neither one winning, but enjoying the game. "Well, I didn't expect a signed confession, but I didn't come up here for nothing. The moppet could use a friend other than me now and then."

It was on the impulsive side, but Lauren was guilty of that now and then. Look at her relationship with Rob and so far, that had been a very good one. She offered, "We'll take Moppet if you need us to. She's welcome and I think her new friend would agree."

To give him credit, Rob didn't blink an eye. "Sure, she's welcome. I want another dog anyway."

"Leave my best friend with the femme fatale and the previous suspect in a murder case?" Bailey took a sip from his beer and smiled. "If you are serious, I will take you up on that when I have a date if it all works out. Thanks."

After he left, Rob gazed at her in open inquiry. She supplied, "He's applied to the FBI so he's going to have to find a home for her. We have the room and you have to admit, she's pretty cute."

"Not exactly my style, but I doubt she's Bailey's style either. If you want her, that's absolutely fine with me. However, that's not what I'm asking."

She'd half finished her glass of wine already, but it seemed like whenever she was around Bailey, she needed some. "What *are* you asking?"

"I think you challenged Dr. Heaston. Do you know the Hemingway reference?"

"I might. I did a paper on that particular work and one quote is pretty memorable. I recall it so easily because it struck me and I used it in the assignment."

"And?"

Her voice was quiet. "'*If he wrote it, he could get rid of it. He had gotten rid of many things by writing them*.'"

He was silent for a moment. Then he asked, and it was easy to hear the reluctance in his question, "Do you think he meant to indicate you were slated to be his next victim?"

She took a sip of wine and looked out the window. Autumn leaves were falling, drifting slowly to the ground in colorful piles. "It makes you wonder, doesn't it?"

THE END

Thank you for reading this book.

If you enjoyed it please leave feedback on Amazon or Goodreads, and if there is anything we missed or you have a question about, then please get in touch. We appreciate you choosing our book.

Founded in 2014 in Shoreditch, London, we at Joffe Books pride ourselves on our history of innovative publishing. We were thrilled to be shortlisted for Independent Publisher of the Year at the British Book Awards.

www.joffebooks.com

We're very grateful to eagle-eyed readers who take the time to contact us. Please send any errors you find to corrections@joffebooks.com. We'll get them fixed ASAP.